This collection of 16 science fiction and fantasy stories is the work of **Jon Platz**. He was born in London in 1948. He studied in York, London and Sussex, and with the Open University. He is trained in chemistry and publishing, has degrees in psychology and artificial intelligence, and has worked in a variety of jobs, including chemical factory worker, political campaign organiser, intelligent systems builder, and university lecturer. He lives in Motspur Park, in South West London.

The measure of all things

Jon Platz

Copyright © John Platts, 2014

This is a work of fiction. Names, characters, places and incidents either are the product of the author's imagination, or are used fictitiously. Any resemblance to actual persons, living or dead, is entirely coincidental.

All rights reserved.

Without limiting the rights under copyright reserved above, no part of this publication may be reproduced, stored in or introduced into a retrieval system, or transmitted, in any form or by any means, (electronic, mechanical, photocopying, recording or otherwise), without the prior written permission of the copyright owner.

Our website: jonplatz.com

Available from Amazon.com and other retail outlets.

Printed by CreateSpace, Charleston SC, USA.
An Amazon.com Company.

ISBN: 978-1502532343

To my beloved Liz

Acknowledgements

This is my first published collection of short stories. It comprises pieces that I wrote while I was a member of the New Malden Writing Group, between 2011 and 2014. I would like to express my thanks to my fellow members of the group, who heard all of these stories first, and who provided valuable criticism and support. Particular thanks are due to Elizabeth Kay, leader of the group, and a respected novelist in her own right.

Re-reading these stories, I realise that I also owe a debt to the various science fiction short story authors of the 1950s, 60s and 70s whom I read when I was young. They wrote some terrific stuff. If my stories have something of the same style, it's no coincidence.

Contents

à Capella ... 9

The girl from Salisbury Road ... 21

The Mackenzie River in flood ... 27

Sanctuario omnia secreta ... 38

My song can't bind a human heart ... 46

This machine reads your mind ... 50

At the centre of the labyrinth ... 59

A pocketful of space ... 68

The Star-Traveller's Rest, Aragona ... 77

Be careful what you prove ... 84

The ghost in the machine ... 89

The ambassador's tale ... 99

The Maid of Orleans I'm not ... 110

The trial ... 116

Army of the dawn ... 125

To talk of many things ... 135

A trace of glue in the sands of time ... 141

In some strange power's employ ... 155

Le crime a ses degrés ... 165

Snow upon the desert's dusty face ... 172

Legionnaire's disease ... 179

The nourris fee ... 188

I learned my lesson well ... 197

What we did on our holidays ... 202
A handful of dust ... 218
The measure of all things ... 228
Two gentlemen of Tushkek ... 237
Witch in the closet ... 246
The make-believe planet ... 257
Exeat ... 261
The Sylvani ... 273
Surprise ingredient ... 282
Riding on a smile and a shoeshine ... 287
Exploring history ... 293
Taking the train up to London ... 303
Hark the herald angels sing ... 311
Bounty of the soil ... 320
They that take the sword ... 323
Last man standing ... 334
A masque ... 341

à Capella

I've been to a lot of spaceports, and every one of them had a vivarium. Somewhere, there must be a college where they teach you to design spaceports, and you don't pass the course unless your graduation exam design has a vivarium in it. Right in the middle of the concourse, where the incoming travellers can't miss it: a big glass box, open to the sky, with the most winsome of the planet's living things in it. Flowering shrubs, if the local flora runs to flowers; pretty foliage if it doesn't. Cuddly, furry creatures if there are any on the planet; otherwise, any local animals that aren't too gross or too microscopic. I once went to a planet – Gamma Pavonis-4 – where the life hadn't evolved beyond moss, and even *they* had a vivarium. Full of garishly-coloured pseudo-bryophytes, clothing large concrete boulders, and swathed in artificial mist.

The vivarium very effectively separates the tourists from the business people. The tourists make straight for it, like tacks attracted to a magnet. The business people can't be bothered, and walk straight past. Naturally, I headed for the big glass tank, and ogled the pretty little creatures on their pretty little plants. I didn't particularly want the security men, who were certainly watching us on CCTV, to know what my business was.

There were quite a few tourists. Rich boys and girls making the grand tour. Elderly matrons, hoping to find love on an exotic new world. By far the largest

The measure of all things

group was the Tau Ceti 4 football team, here for a qualifying match for the inter-world cup. OK, they weren't strictly speaking tourists, but they behaved as if they were. There were fifteen of them: eleven players, two substitutes, a coach and a trainer. The coach doubled as the manager. Tau Ceti 4 isn't a particularly rich world – it's not part of the Federacy – and interstellar flight doesn't come cheap: fifteen tickets were all that the TC4FA could afford.

After a few minutes, a loudspeaker-voice invited us all to move on to the Immigration Service desks. I found myself sitting opposite a polite young man, in a restrained grey uniform, with a crossed-key-and-sword emblem on his cap.

"Is this your first visit to our planet?"

"Yes it is."

"You're from Gamma Serpentis-6. Is this your first trip between stars?"

"Yes it is."

"And you're here purely as a tourist?"

"Yes, that's right."

"Fine. I hope you enjoy your trip." He gave me a perfunctory smile, which I returned.

Of course, the questions were largely irrelevant. The real purpose of the interview was for them to scan my irises and sample my DNA. Most people wouldn't have noticed the tiny camera behind and above the officer's left shoulder. Nor felt the lightest of touches, as the chair arm licked their wrist. Naturally, I did. As I got up and walked towards the area labelled 'baggage reclaim', I assumed they were searching their

à Capella

files for known terrorists, spies, criminals and so forth. They wouldn't find anything.

During the previous ten minutes, several floors below, they had been X-raying and chemically analysing my and everyone else's baggage. The Capellan authorities weren't much interested in drugs or illicit documents, but they took particular interest in anything large enough to be a bomb, a hand gun, or any other large piece of weaponry. When they examined my case, they'd find a change of clothes, a toilet bag, a pair of slippers and a pair of pyjamas.

With my case, I walked out of the big glass doors at the front of the terminal building and hailed a cab.

"Where to, buddy?" The cab driver certainly looked the part – middle-aged, low-to-medium income, bored with his job – but I assumed, routinely, that he was working for the security services.

"Hotel Intergalactica." I smiled to myself. One of the stupidest hotel names I'd ever heard. It was an up-market hotel, but, with a name like that, it didn't deserve to be.

The cabs on this planet drove themselves, and there wasn't much for the cabbie to do but chat.

"You an off-worlder?"

"Yup. From Gamma Serpentis-6."

"What do you think about the crisis? Are we going to have an interstellar war?"

"Doubt it. This isn't the twenty-first century. People have given up on wars."

He laughed. "I like you, buddy. You're an optimist."

The measure of all things

At the hotel, I paid him and gave him the standard tip. No sense in being remembered as a stingy or a generous tipper. I booked into the hotel, handed over my passport, had my irises scanned again, found my room and unpacked. I had a shower and changed. I sent a text message to my aunt, telling her that I'd touched down, and that I'd drop in on her the following morning. (I don't, in fact, have an aunt on this or any other world. The message was a risk, but, given the speed with which the crisis was developing, it was justified.) I had another hour to kill, so I spent a little time memorising the city subway map. Then I watched the news.

The Prime Minister, who was a fat man with a ruddy complexion, had just made a speech in which he declared that the people had nothing to fear from their adversaries. The armed forces were quite capable of repelling any attack and, if there were such an attack, they would take the fight to their enemies. And, he added (with a pronounced glower), those same enemies would learn a lesson they'd never forget.

Depressing, very depressing. The worst of it was that he appeared to believe it, and the people appeared to have vested their trust in him.

Of course, he hadn't had the briefings that I had had. The art of warfare prediction had progressed slowly over the centuries, but it *had* progressed. The Federacy's military experts knew a lot about weaponry and who had it; they knew a lot about the psychology of all the generals and admirals on all the inhabited worlds, including our own. They were able to say, with a high degree of certainty, how this particular war would proceed, if it ever got started.

à Capella

And this is how it would go: there would be a few inconsequential space battles, and then it would get deadly serious. Diffident, cautious military leaders would be replaced by ruthless attack dogs. Political leaders, on both sides, would decide that it wasn't good politics to interfere with military decisions. The fate of a planet like Capella-5 was quite clear. A salvo of missiles would drop out of hyperspace, a few hundred miles above the planet's surface. Too many, and travelling too fast, for the planetary defences to intercept them all, and each one tipped with a planet-wrecker bomb. In a very few minutes, the planet would become a graveyard: uninhabited and uninhabitable. Then the war would move on to other worlds, which would each receive the same treatment. Both sides could easily muster the technology, and, once this phase had started, they wouldn't hold back. Eventually, there would be just a handful of inhabited worlds left. Or maybe just one. Or maybe not even that.

We in the Federacy could see the future pretty clearly. Our diplomats had tried to convey this vision to all the other inhabited worlds. They hadn't succeeded. The spirit of gung-ho nationalism was enjoying one of its periodic revivals. A lot of planetary leaders had convinced themselves that, provided they could imbue their people with iron-willed defiance, they could stand secure against any threat.

I left the hotel via the side entrance, and walked to the local subway station. As I turned a corner, I dropped the newspaper I was carrying, and bent down to pick it up. As my gaze met the paving stones, I slipped a couple of contact lenses into my eyes. Then I straightened up and strode into the station. The cameras pointing at the entrance would scan my

The measure of all things

irises, but they'd find a different pattern to the one at the spaceport. The irises of a local man, who might perhaps have business in this part of town. Eventually, alarm bells would ring somewhere, but I reckoned I had at least an hour before someone started fretting about the off-worlder who'd gone for a walk and disappeared.

In a cheaper hotel – the New Skyline – in the southern suburbs, a group of outworlders suddenly stopped what they were doing and went into what seemed to be a practiced routine. An observer might have felt that there was something robotic about the way in which they went about their work: each man had a detached, almost absent-minded air. They didn't talk. They each dismantled their luggage, peeling back the covering from their cases, and extracting several small blocks from the framework inside. They slotted them together, and, by the time they had finished, they had assembled quite a large, sophisticated machine. One of them dragged it outside, to the hotel's rubbish bin area, and put a tarpaulin over it. Then, just as methodically, they reassembled the luggage so that it seemed nothing had changed. Finally, they gradually lost their detached, dream-like air.

"What did we just do?" said one.

"Damned if I know," said another. "Space travel, eh? Plays tricks on your mind."

That seemed to satisfy them.

I took the subway to one of the north-western suburbs. By the time I arrived, my hair was a different colour, my face was a subtly different shape, and, of course, my iris patterns were different again.

The Scarlet Dolphin café wasn't up to much. The front hadn't been painted in years. Their speciality, a home-made beverage containing home-formulated opiates, tasted vinegary, and didn't provide much of a drug-induced high. The café had a tea-garden, but it was too cold and noisy to attract many customers. Just right for me. I sat in the corner of the shabby little garden, affecting to sip my scarlet-dolphin tea (though none of it passed my lips), and the only other customer barely glanced at me.

After a while, he finished his beer and got up to go. He was a small man, with thinning hair, dressed like an unsuccessful businessman. Passing my table, he smiled and pointed at my newspaper, open at the racing page, and said, "Who do you fancy for the big race?"

I smiled back and said "Aphrodite". Aphrodite is the name of an ancient goddess, from planet Earth, and such names are never used for racing animals on Capella-5.

The man pulled back a chair at my table and sat down.

"I got the aunt message", he said. "Am I glad to see you." He handed me a memory stick. "Cabinet minutes for the last week. The Government will declare war in the next forty-eight hours, unless something scares them pretty badly."

I smiled, sunnily. "Thank you, my friend. We're really grateful."

Inside, I was seething. Handing me the stick in the open, and telling me what was on it? When there might be a camera focussed on us, from across the street? This man's fieldcraft was rubbish. But he was

The measure of all things

the last spy we had left on this world, so I wasn't in a position to complain. I slipped the stick into an inner pocket.

"What will you do? I mean, what will the Federacy do?" he asked.

"You don't need to know that."

Worse and worse. If a camera **was** focussed on us, it would certainly pick up the lip movements corresponding to the word 'Federacy', and start to record our conversation.

"What you need to do," I continued, "is lie low. We'll pay you through the usual channels. We'll contact you when it's necessary."

I smiled again, and got up and left, before he had time to say anything else.

Capella-5 was the sort of world that had public libraries. I found one, went in, and found a vacant booth with an information screen. I ignored it, and used my own secure portable reader to examine the contents of the memory stick.

My spy was absolutely right. The government of Capella-5 had made up its mind. I pressed a concealed button on my key-ring, which sent a message across the city to the southern suburbs, where the fancy machine behind the dustbins responded by coming to life. A clock started ticking.

Time to get off-planet, as fast as possible. Another subway trip, another cab ride, and I was back at the spaceport. By then I had a different appearance and different papers. No sign of increased security activity.

à Capella

I had some time to kill before departure. I watched the news broadcasts on the public screens. The story about the rising tension between the Federacy and its enemies was delivered with bland reassurance – clearly, the Government didn't want the public to know how dangerous things really were. The news bulletin devoted more space to the forthcoming match between the world team and the visitors from Tau Ceti 4.

There were shops in the concourse – there always are. I popped into a bookshop and bought a popular history of the 20th and 21st century wars, in case I needed distraction on the flight home. Then I popped into the shop next door and bought a telephone.

There was a kiosk outside another shop, adorned with a life-size picture of some renaissance artist, holding a palette and a paintbrush, and looking at the passers-by with an appraising eye. The sign explained that, for a modest fee, the kiosk would paint your portrait, in oils, and deliver the finished painting, in a gilt frame, one minute later. Gratefully, I slipped inside and sat down. I didn't bother with the camera – in fact, I hung my coat over the lens. Instead, I opened up the back of the telephone and inserted a chip, designed to wait an hour, then make a phone call to a certain number and deliver a certain message. Then I went into a shop selling socks, dropped the phone into a litterbin, and made my way to the emigration desk.

The polite young man in the grey uniform wasn't that different to the one I'd seen three hours earlier. Idly, I wondered whether they were all clones. Coming out of some vat, already wearing the uniform.

"Is this your first trip off Capella-5?"

The measure of all things

"Yes it is. Frankly, I wish I wasn't going. I don't hold with a man leaving his home planet. But the lawyers say, if I don't go to Sigma Draconis-5 in person, I can't claim my inheritance."

The young man nodded sympathetically.

"Will you be gone long?"

"A very few days, I hope. If there's going to be a war, I don't want to be in the Federacy when it breaks out."

He stamped my papers, I boarded the SS Charles the Twenty-third, and we blasted off.

And that was it. I was safe.

* * * * *

Capella-5 became a tiny spot in the sky behind us, and we prepared for the hyperspace jump. The passengers, myself included, remained strapped into our seats. The others read, or chatted, or listened to music. I considered reading my new book, but decided I couldn't be bothered. Instead, I sat and brooded about the Tau Ceti 4 football team.

Poor bastards. They were mercenaries, fighting in someone else's war, without even realising it. And, if things went wrong, they'd get fried. Not me; them. Together with my friend at the Scarlet Dolphin café.

The TC4FA hadn't been able to scrape up enough money to send a team to the qualifier. So we – the agency I work for – had stepped in and supplied the missing cash. All in strictest confidence, of course. The TC4FA realised, too late, that they couldn't object when our psychologists subjected the entire squad to deep hypnotic conditioning. And replaced all *à Capella*

their luggage. Afterwards, neither the players, the coach, the trainer, nor the general public on Tau Ceti 4 had a clue as to what had happened.

I also brooded about nuclear weapons. They're easy enough to make, of course – hell, people have been making them for centuries. But, because of the immutable laws of physics, you can't miniaturise them very much. There *has* to be a certain minimum amount of fissile material, and fusile material, and other things. But the craftsmen we have working for the agency are exceedingly good at breaking them up into bits which, when slotted together, make an effective weapon. Forty-five midget guns, each firing a tiny bullet of trans-uranic matter. And doing it simultaneously, with such precision that the bullets collide in the very centre of the bomb at precisely the same instant. The centre being the middle of a large sphere of polymer, consisting mostly of lithium deuteride. The reaction of the critical mass of fissile material in the centre, and the thermonuclear fusion that follows a moment later, provides the basis for quite a sizeable nuclear explosion.

Forty-five midget guns, slotted into the framework of fifteen different suitcases, and cloaked so that they wouldn't show up when the suitcases were X-rayed. Together with sixteen segments of the special polymer eggshell, and sundry other bits and pieces. All designed to slot together like a child's puzzle. Outstanding craftsmanship.

Back in the spaceport, in the rubbish bin in the shop selling socks, my phone came to life and made its call.

"Hello, this is the Prime Minister's office?"

"I left a package behind the New Skyline Hotel."

The measure of all things

"Who is this? You've obviously got the wrong number …"

"It's a twelve bomb."

"Oh … my God …"

"Provided you find it and defuse it in the next ten hours, you won't lose your capital city. But the point is this: we didn't need to send a battle fleet to your star system. One tourist was enough. And we could send more, if we wanted. You can't cut yourself off from interstellar trade, because that's what keeps your planet going. And the Universal Trade Treaty says that trade has to include tourists. So let's have no more nonsense about declaring war on the Federacy. If you stay neutral, we won't send any more bombs."

* * * * *

Back on Sigma Draconis-5, the Immigration Officer was a pretty young woman in a turquoise uniform.

"You were on Capella-5 for how long?" she asked.

"Between three and four hours."

"Oh… And the purpose of the visit?"

"I'm a terrorist. I had to stop a war."

It was just about the only truthful thing I'd said all day. The young woman gave me a 'please be serious' look.

The girl from Salisbury Road

Jack McBraddon strides out of the Midnight Express club, and stands in front of the entrance. He gazes first one way along Salisbury Road, then the other. He's young; good looking; fit. He's wearing a blue denim shirt, which leaves his forearms exposed, a bracelet of black beads on one wrist, and a military-style wristwatch on the other. He has mid-brown hair, swept up, and blue eyes. No beard or moustache, but a hint of designer stubble.

PC Ann Watson is the only other person in the street, and she is on the other side of the road. She is in uniform and on foot, making a routine patrol of an area where there have been complaints about noise and disorder – from the nightclub, obviously. Really, she's showing the flag. He sees her, and looks directly at her, with a steady gaze, and what might be a half-smile. She smiles at him, and crosses the street.

"Good evening, Mr McBraddon. All quiet?"

"All quiet so far, officer. But you wouldn't expect trouble this early in the evening."

"Right. But if anything big crops up – any disruptions – you'll call us straight away, understood?"

"Understood, officer. You can be sure that we will." She smiles again, and goes on her way. She is eager to

The measure of all things

become a CID officer, and is glad that she has contacts with people like Jack McBraddon. Looked at one way, nightclub bouncers are part of society's first line of defence against lawlessness; in the same business as the police. But then again, the profession tends to attract violent men, and violent gangsters often use a bouncer's job as cover for their real work. PC Watson wants to learn all she can about this world.

Idly, she recalls McBraddon's expression. That steady, penetrating stare – what exactly was going on in his mind? Aggression? Hatred for the police? She would very much like to know.

Inside the *Midnight Express*, not much is happening. A student from the local music college is earning a few quid playing smooth jazz on a keyboard, but it's just background music. Some executives from a local printing firm are entertaining clients to an early evening drink. The rest of the tables are empty. Two waitresses are quietly chatting behind the bar. The real show will start in half an hour: in the dressing room, tonight's featured singer is putting her make-up on. In the meantime, Jack can afford to stand outside, on the pavement, looking out for Kiera.

And, after a while, Kiera walks down the street.

She's young and attractive, slender but shapely, with long slim legs. She is wearing a grey top, a short grey skirt and light grey tights, but no visible jewellery. She has long, sleek, black hair, flowing over her shoulders, with a centre parting. She has smooth skin and good teeth. She has a wide smile, which suggests she's enjoying whatever she's experiencing, but she doesn't seem to be looking at anyone in particular. She is wearing a pair of dark glasses. Two small red boxes,

The girl from Salisbury Road

each with a rather tiny hole in its centre, are mounted on the frame: one above her right eye, the other above her left.

Jack catches sight of her and, for a moment, it seems as though he is going to call out, call her name. But he doesn't. He watches her as she saunters along the road, looking at no one, and occasionally chuckling quietly.

PC Watson is back. She has prevailed upon DC Javid to take her on a tour of her beat, pointing out the things that she should have noticed, that she would have noticed if she'd been an experienced detective. He has known this manor for a long time. They are cruising down Salisbury Road, when they spot Jack and Keira. DC Javid – Anil to his friends – quietly parks the car, a little way away, across the street. Jack doesn't notice. All his attention is on Keira.

"What do you see when you look at her?" asks Anil.

"She's wearing sunglasses, even though it's early evening?" suggests Ann.

"Good. But they're not sunglasses," says Anil. He turns the engine off and opens the car window a little.

Keira is about to walk past Jack without noticing him. He calls out to her, softly.

"Keira."

She stops, turns towards him.

"Jack? Is that you?"

He steps forward and hugs her. She rests her head on his shoulder, and puts her arms round him. They sway slightly. For a moment, they are just two young lovers, happy in each others' company.

The measure of all things

"Jack" she murmurs, "I wish that things were … were …"

"Like they used to be?" He completes the thought for her.

She nods. Then she extracts herself from his arms, and takes a few steps away from him.

"Hey, I've got to go," she says.

"Yeah," he says.

"Come round later."

"You know I will."

He looks after her, as she wanders off. The big smile is back on her face. It's as if she's forgotten him. From where they're sitting, they can't see his expression.

Anil closes the window. They've heard some of the conversation – caught the gist.

"Is she blind?" asks Ann.

"No, not really. She's got no white cane, and she's not walking into lamp-posts or wandering into the road."

"But there's something wrong with her."

Anil nods. "What's wrong with her is extremely rare. Not unique, but almost." He sighs. "I knew them, a few years ago. They were teenage lovers. But they couldn't set up house together because they had no money. So Jack signed up for the army. Served a term in Afghanistan. Normally you can tell ex-squaddies by their tattoos, but Jack didn't get any. But maybe there's something of the soldier in the way he holds himself."

"And what happened to Kiera?"

The girl from Salisbury Road

"Bad things. She didn't cope well. She became a crack addict."

"Oh. And she still is?"

"No. You'd be able to tell if she was, from her skin. From the state of her hair, probably. And her clothes. They cured her."

"How would they do that?"

"They put her into a special research programme at the University. A crack addict gets a big high, a few seconds after smoking a rock. Eight seconds, they say. Lasts for about ten minutes. At the Uni, they said, 'If we can give her an intense sensory experience instead, the hit from the coke will be drowned out. She'll just stop taking crack because she won't want it anymore.' So they fixed her brain, somehow, so that she's very sensitive to bright, flashing, colourful pictures – they go straight into her pleasure centres. Then they gave her a pair of data glasses. Those dark glasses you noticed – she wears them all the time. They have two little projectors built-in, and they feed those bright, flashing, pictures straight into her eyes. It worked like a charm. She never takes crack anymore." He fumbles in his pocket for a packet of cigarettes, then remembers that he's in the process of giving them up. No point in looking – they're locked in his desk, back at the station. He continues: "Except now she's addicted to the data glasses. Lots of exciting stuff gets projected onto the inside of the lenses, all the time. If she takes them off for more than a few minutes, she starts screaming. I've seen it happen."

"Not much of a bargain, then. Not much of a cure," says Ann.

25

The measure of all things

"No. When they heard about the details, the Government weren't interested. It wasn't the cure they'd been promised." Absent-mindedly, Anil is still fumbling in his pockets. He sighs, again. "Looked at one way, she's better. She's healthier. She doesn't give all her money to crack peddlers any more. All she needs to feed her habit is triple-A batteries."

He starts the engine. "She lives with her sister, in a flat at the far end of the road. Doesn't go out much. But every night, round about now, her sister sends her out for a walk. To get some fresh air and sun." He puts the car into gear. "Jack supports the family, on what he earns at the nightclub. If you were wondering what that expression of his means, when he stares at you, it's a deep, deep feeling of regret."

Across the street, the door to the club is open, and Jack is checking the membership cards of the clients as they turn up. Inside, the featured singer has started her first song – *the Girl from Ipanema*. The words drift across the road:

> *Oh, but he watches so sadly -*
> *How can he tell her he loves her?*
> *Yes, he would give his heart gladly,*
> *But each day when she walks to the sea,*
> *She looks straight ahead – not at he…*

Anil nods and says "Yes, that seems about right."

The song continues:

> *Tall and tan and young and lovely,*
> *The girl from Ipanema goes walking*
> *And when she passes, he smiles, but she doesn't see…*

The Mackenzie River in flood

Friday
A dispiriting day. Went to the job interview at Golden Plum films and got nowhere. Had I had any experience shooting motor racing? No, I hadn't. Thanks and goodbye. They could have found out I hadn't, if they'd bothered to read my resumé. Maybe they just assumed I didn't keep my resumé up to date.

I rang Sheila at the agency, trying not to sound desperate. Anything coming up, in my line of work? Cameraman, Shooting PD, something like that? Yes, there is, but it's a bit weird, she says. A bunch of geologists need a cameraman, the smaller the better. I'll give them your name if you're interested. Now I've got an interview tomorrow. Saturday! Who interviews people on a Saturday?

Saturday
Well, I got the job, but Sheila was right about it being weird. The interview was in a poky little office in Dollis Hill. Three people on the panel – Professor Buckley, who's a small, middle-aged, blonde woman, Professor Adamenko, a white-haired man in his sixties, and Doctor Lewis, a nervous little man in his forties. Dr Lewis does all the talking. He shakes hands, and says "Mr Lockyer, we urgently need a

The measure of all things

replacement cameraman – the person we had broke her leg." He looks at my resumé. He says, "So, you're an experienced cameraman?" I nod, and agree that I am. "You're used to location work?" I nod. "Are you good at getting camera equipment up and running, when it malfunctions?" I say something about how it's not a good idea to keep the Director and crew waiting on a location shoot – you get fired if you do. So far, the two professors haven't said a word, and Lewis hasn't found out anything that wasn't on the paper in front of him. Then he says, "Mr Lockyer, I hope you don't mind – it's not on your C.V. – may I ask how much you weigh?" I manage not to do a comic double-take and say, "About ten stones". (You could call me slightly built, I guess). Dr Lewis beams and says "Good – I think you're the man we need." He seems to have given me the job. He says, "It will be up to a week's work. We can offer you four thousand pounds. Will that be acceptable?" It's way over the going rate. I think about my mortgage arrears and make up my mind to say yes, there and then. But before I do, I say, "What's the job? What do you want me to film?" Lewis says "It's a geological event. You could call it a ... torrent." Professor Buckley laughs, and says "Yes, a torrent is about right".

I sign the contract, and promise to be on site, Monday morning.

So I've been hired because I'm a lightweight. What <u>is</u> this all about?

Sunday

I read through the contract. It's awfully vague. I'll be taken to a certain location – they don't say where – and I'll remain there for up to seven days. I'll set up

The Mackenzie River in flood

the cameras, and make sure they keep working. I'll take my orders from the Project Manager. However long it takes, I get paid a lump sum of four grand. I indemnify them for any accidental harm that befalls me. There's a secrecy clause – I'm not allowed to say where I've been or what I've done.

It really could say more, couldn't it?

The location: it can't be anywhere that requires a visa, but I'd better take my passport.

Ah well, I've been promised a complete briefing tomorrow morning.

Monday
So much for the complete briefing. I turned up at 9:30 sharp, as instructed. The same place as for the interview: a disused factory in Dollis Hill. This time, I'm sent upstairs, to a big room, full of jury-rigged electrical machinery. The two professors, and Lewis, were there, plus a large bunch of technicians. Everyone was in a fair old panic. When she saw me, Buckley said "Thank Christ you're here. See that changing room? Get in there, put a coverall on, leave your clothes in the locker, then get back here. We're leaving in ten minutes."

While she was speaking, Lewis was ripping the packaging off a light-blue coverall, which he handed to me.

"Umm" I said, "...the briefing?"

"No time for that", Buckley barked, "Adamenko got his sums wrong".

The measure of all things

Professor Adamenko looked miserable. "That's unfair," he said. "No one's ever done this before. I had to invent the mathematics ..."

She cut him off. "I said, we haven't time. Lockyer, get changed. Be back here in eight minutes."

I was. Dressed like a garage mechanic. I got ushered into what looked like an aircraft hanger, and then into what could have been a military transport aircraft – except that it hadn't any wings. They weighed me, on the sort of scale you find in a clinic. Buckley was wearing a coverall too, with a rucksack on her back, and they weighed her as well. Weirder and weirder.

"How long have we got?" asked Buckley.

"Two minutes thirty eight seconds," said a technician.

"Right, follow me."

I followed her into what could have been the cargo-hold of the plane. Some heavy machinery had started up: the floor was throbbing. Buckley had to shout to make herself heard.

"That end of the room –" she pointed "– will turn blue. Think of it as a sort of curtain. I'll run through it. Follow me. If you stumble on the other side, get up and get clear. They'll be pushing pallets through after us."

"Ten seconds," shouted a technician.

Then the end of the room, which had been plain metal, *did* turn into a glowing blue surface. Buckley got up, ran at it, and dived through. I looked around wildly. "Get going!" shouted the technician. So I ran at the blue wall. Jumped through it ...

The Mackenzie River in flood

... and found myself on a grassy hillside, overlooking a big valley, with a small river below us. Buckley was crouched a little way in front of me. A cold wind was blowing.

There was a large thump behind me, then another. I turned. Two shrink-wrapped pallets had appeared, buried a little way into the soft ground. But there was no sign of the blue curtain. Or the aircraft. Or London. And it was a lot colder than London had been.

"Where the hell are we?" I asked in a loud voice. Then I realised I didn't have to shout: there was no throbbing noise either.

"The Mackenzie River valley," said Buckley.

"You'd better explain," I said.

"Can't. Sorry. No time. Or rather, I don't know how much time we've got. Look, one of those pallets has twenty video cameras on it. Plus monopod stakes to mount them on. It's the one with '1' written on the side. Unpack them, please. Set them up. The batteries have been charged – the sooner they're rolling, the better."

"Is it just the two of us here?" I asked, weakly.

She smiled. "Yeah."

"Why?"

"Every gram we send through the barrier costs an enormous amount of energy. You're here because you don't weigh much. I'm here because I pulled rank. Plus, I'm small too."

"What's the barrier?"

The measure of all things

"Look, I'd be much happier if those cameras were rolling. It's that pallet, I think. Here's a packing knife."

Dutifully, I cut open the shrink-wrapping. The cameras were ENG Camcorders.

"Expensive," I said.

"And light-weight," said Buckley. She'd found the stakes, and a mallet, and was already hammering the first one into the ground.

I started to check the cameras over. Each one had a fully charged battery, and a fresh data card. No obvious malfunctions.

"Why stakes, rather than tripods?" I asked.

"There'll be some earth tremors."

"Look," I said, "About the barrier ... you people have got some way to move from one part of the world to another, haven't you? Instantly? Like a Star Trek Transporter?"

"Something like that," she said. "Here –" she handed me a pair of binoculars "– have a look at the glacier." She was using a second pair.

Through the binoculars, I could see that half the valley was filled by an enormous wall of ice. Behind it, the frozen mass stretched away, to a point where the valley twisted. Beyond that, you couldn't see what was in it. But the ice wall wasn't all that far away, and it was clear that melting ice at the foot of it was feeding the sluggish river that flowed past us.

"I want six cameras focussed on the ice wall," she said. "Close-ups of different points across it. Six pointing at the top of the glacier. Six ranged along the

The Mackenzie River in flood

river valley. Use one for a wide-angle shot of the whole valley, and one for you to point at whatever looks interesting."

"What's going to happen?"

She paused. She said "That glacier's not as solid as it looks. If a glacier's going to melt, it melts from the bottom up. Very soon, the whole ice wall will crack. As soon as you've positioned a camera, start it running. We have to be ready."

I did as I was told. Afterwards, I said, "How do you know?"

"An event like this produces an enormous number of positive ions in the atmosphere. We detected them. Plus those tremors I told you about."

There was a thunderclap. But there were no thunder clouds in the sky. We both turned our binoculars on the ice wall. It was visibly collapsing: enormous chunks of ice breaking free, and crashing into the pool below; vast spouts of foaming water pouring from the gaps in the ice.

She touched my shoulder. "Use your camera," she said.

I dropped the glasses and grabbed the last of the cameras. I got a nice wide shot of the ice wall as it collapsed in several places. I moved the viewpoint to the top of the glacier – holes had appeared, and they grew larger as I shot them.

"Get some shots of the river," she said.

I turned to the valley below the disintegrating ice wall. The shallow, sluggish river had become a wild torrent. Maybe twice as deep as before, and growing deeper

The measure of all things

by the minute. Ice chunks, carried along by the flow, were smashing down small trees that had been growing on the banks. The river was growing steadily wider.

"That's what several million cubic metres of meltwater look like when you release them," she murmured.

"I suppose there's a lake, somewhere upstream?" I said.

She laughed. "You could say: Lake Agassiz is the largest lake in the world. About 440,000 square kilometres. This flood isn't going to stop any time soon."

She gazed at the roaring flood, then said "The effects will be enormous. This is one of the greatest cataclysms of the last twenty thousand years."

I turned my camera back to the ice wall. It was now a vast cavity, with a colossal amount of water gushing out of it. Then I felt the earth shaking beneath my feet. Several of the camera stakes collapsed.

"Take this," I said, handing my camera to Buckley, as I scurried off to get the others upright again.

"Umm ... those river banks are eroding faster than I expected," she said.

The hillside below us now ended, about ten yards away, in an abrupt cliff, with the furious river water raging below it. The edge was crumbling fast.

"We'll have to relocate the cameras," she said.

We tried to wrench the stakes out of the ground. We managed a few, before it became apparent that the erosion was going to overtake us.

The Mackenzie River in flood

"Leave the stakes. Save the cameras," she shouted.

I detached half a dozen of the cameras, and scrambled to some high ground about twenty yards behind our vantage point, where I dropped them in a heap. She did the same. We ran back and rescued the others. I looked back at where we'd been standing, and saw the two pallets tip over the edge into the torrent. They tumbled off downstream, smashing against floating tree trunks.

"Damn" said Buckley.

"What was on the second pallet?" I asked.

"Our campsite. Tents, food, stoves, sleeping bags, spare clothes, water purification tablets." She sighed. "Time to go home, I think."

I looked at the river bank, creeping ever closer, and I had to agree with her.

She took a circular copper mesh out of her rucksack, and laid it on the ground. She put a small cape on the mesh, and we both piled the cameras onto it. "Stand on the mesh – as close to the middle as you can manage," she said. I did, and so did she. She pressed buttons on some sort of control box. Suddenly, we were surrounded by a glowing blue cylinder. She said "Follow me," and picked up one edge of the cape. She backed out, through the opaque blue glow, dragging the cape, with the pile of cameras, behind her. I swallowed hard, and stepped through myself.

And found myself in the cargo bay, in the hanger in London.

"We're back," said Buckley.

"So I see. That was quick," said Dr Lewis.

The measure of all things

Tuesday

I realise I didn't finish yesterday's entry. There's not much more to tell. Everyone seemed pleased with the way it had gone. Lewis handed me a cheque for four thousand, with no quibbling about it being a few hours' work rather than seven days. They were much more interested in what Professor Buckley had to report than anything I might say. Though she did have the good grace to shake me by the hand, and say she couldn't have done it without me. Someone took a photo of the two of us: explorers returned from the farthest reaches of the world. Which couldn't possibly be true. Lewis murmured that if they needed my help again, they'd get in touch, and reminded me that I was sworn to secrecy about what had happened.

One of the technicians drove me home. I questioned him, but he wouldn't say a thing.

I spent this morning in bed, exhausted.

Wednesday

I keep asking myself, what the hell was that all about? Possibly the most dramatic incident in my entire life, and I'm not even sure where it happened.

The Internet tells me that Professor Buckley is a distinguished geologist. Professor Adamenko is an even more distinguished physicist. But Lake Agassiz is *not* the world's largest lake – that would be Lake Superior. However, it *was*, 12,800 years ago. Then the ice dam that confined it to the middle of North America broke, and it drained, down the Mackenzie River valley, into the Arctic Ocean. All that ice-cold fresh water flowed into the north Atlantic, switched off the Gulf Stream, and wrecked Europe's climate for about 1300 years. Truly, a cataclysm.

The Mackenzie River in flood

Lake Agassiz doesn't exist anymore.

I'm feeling very confused. Time travel? That's impossible, isn't it?

If it wasn't time travel, was it some sort of elaborate con? It didn't seem like a con – it seemed extremely real. And why bother to con *me*? And pay me for the privilege?

I keep hoping that Buckley, Lewis, or someone, will contact me and give me some answers. Or publish something about their scientific triumph.

But, for reasons of their own, I suspect they never will.

Sanctuario omnia secreta

At five in the morning her alarm clock chimed softly, and Mother Clare awoke. She got up, yawned and stretched, then knelt in front of the crucifix to say a brief, silent, prayer. Thank you Lord, for protecting me through the night. Make me ready for the work I must do today, and let me take joy in it. Amen. Then she washed, shed her night-dress, and donned fresh underwear, a fresh habit, and the same sensible shoes that she'd worn for many a month.

She sat at her desk for a while, reading Teilhard de Chardin's "Writings in Time of War." She'd read it before, but she wanted to be very familiar with the nuances of Teilhard de Chardin's arguments. She had launched a scheme whereby the Abbey would publish his writings as audio-books, to be purchased online. Privately, she was convinced that she had the best reading voice of any of the sisters, and had therefore arranged that she would be reading out this work herself.

At ten to six, she set aside the book and reviewed the morning ahead. At six it would be Vigils. Then more reading time. At seven fifteen it would be Lauds. Then breakfast. Afterwards, she would discuss housekeeping with Sister Josephine – fifteen nuns was a large family to feed and, although they grew much

Sanctuario omnia secreta

of their food, there were always items that had to be bought in from outside. Then some paperwork. At eleven, Mass. Father Jerome would arrive in his little car at five minutes before the hour: she would meet him at the gates, and take him to the chapel. Afterwards, they'd talk about diocesan matters, then there'd be time for a little more paperwork, then at twelve thirty it would be midday prayers. Then ... her brow furrowed; she'd forgotten something. Oh yes, some policeman wanted to talk to her. At nine thirty. She could hardly refuse but, really, it was an intrusion she could do without.

She sighed, got up, and walked to the chapel. Sisters Amelia and Marilyn were arranging flowers in the hall, and they bowed to her as she passed. She smiled, and bowed back wordlessly. It was a rule of the Abbey that there was a Great Silence between the end of Compline (at 9:15 the previous night) and Lauds (at 8:15 this morning). In other words, no one spoke, or made more noise than they had to. Except for the service they were about to hold.

In the chapel she took her place as Abbess, behind the choir on the right hand side. She knelt and uttered a brief silent prayer – Lord, let this service be acceptable to you – then sat and waited as the rest of the sisters assembled. It was November, and dawn wouldn't be for another hour and a half. At this time of year, the Chapel seemed rather cold and dark, and too large and empty for their little congregation. She much preferred summer, when the rising sun shone through the stained glass gloriously. Still, God in his wisdom had made all the seasons – bright and dark, dry and wet, warm and chilly – and he deserved praise for all his works.

The measure of all things

She thought about what had happened just now, in the hall. A couple of generations ago, the sisters would have given her a full curtsey rather than a bow. But she'd changed that – simplified things – in keeping with the spirit of modern times. As to the Great Silence, there'd been no question of changing *that*: women would chatter incessantly, if you let them. There was no place for chatter in the contemplative life.

The choir struck up the seventeenth psalm, and the congregation joined in. Sister Anne read a lesson from the second book of Maccabees. Sister Claudette read one from St Luke's gospel. Mother Clare led the prayers. Then the service was over.

And so the day went on. Services, meals, administrative duties. Time to read, time to pray, but not as much as she'd like. Problems to be solved. Nuns needing advice, or encouragement, or mild admonishing. And then, at nine thirty, the policeman arrived. A certain Inspector Tyndall. And, it turned out that he had a companion, called Mr Blandford. She showed them into the lounge.

Inspector Tyndall seemed puzzled. "Is this a common room?"

"It's our lounge. We always meet visitors here. The rest of the Abbey is private."

"Don't you have an office?"

"Oh … yes, I do. Let's go there."

He sat by her filing cabinet. He was a rather overweight, balding, man in a grey suit, his white shirt open at the collar. Blandford sat beside him. He was fit and burly, with short greying hair. He also wore a

Sanctuario omnia secreta

grey suit, and a white shirt, but had a tie. Sitting behind her desk, she glanced at his tie, without making it too obvious. She didn't know much about such things, but she noticed it had rows of crossed swords and crowns on it. An army tie, perhaps? She turned to the policeman.

"What can I do for you, Inspector?" She smiled.

"It's about one of your nuns. We know her as Marion Bradford. To you, she's Sister Marion."

"Ah ... yes ... Sister Marion. She was with us for, I think, five months. As a postulant. Then she relinquished her vows and left. We were very sad. We thought she had a firm calling, and would be with us ... well, forever. Till she went to her true home."

"Oh. What's a postulant?"

"If a woman is called to become a nun, she takes temporary vows and joins us as a postulant for six months. Then she becomes a novice, for two years. Then she becomes a junior, for three years. Then she takes her eternal vows, and becomes a full member of our community."

"I see. I didn't understand that bit about 'going to her true home'".

"Why, going to Heaven, of course."

"Oh. Well, I might as well tell you, Marion was a fugitive from justice."

"A fugitive from justice?" She dwelt on the words, making them sound faintly ridiculous. Blandford clenched his jaw muscles slightly.

"Do you suppose," asked the Inspector. "That she regarded the Abbey as a refuge?"

The measure of all things

"Well, many of our nuns see the Abbey as a sanctuary. The outside world can be a cruel place. Part of our mission is to protect our sisters from that cruelty." She paused. "The abbey looks a bit like a medieval castle, doesn't it? That's just some foolish nineteenth century architect's idea of what a church building should look like. But, in a way, we *are* a fortress."

"Uh huh. We need to find out where she went, after she left here."

"Well, I'm sorry but I can't help you, Inspector. She left a forwarding address, of course, but, quite soon – after a couple of weeks, I think – the letters started coming back with 'not known at this address' written on them." She paused. "She may get in touch, though. When she came here, she donated her dowry, and it was deposited in the Abbey's bank account. She has a right to ask for it back." She smiled. "If she gets in touch with us, I'll ask her to get in touch with you."

Blandford leaned forward. "I don't think you understand. A serious crime has been committed. We intend to find her, and question her. She seems to have gone to ground. Asking her to get in touch isn't going to work."

She frowned. "A serious crime? And you think she did it? Mr Blandford, I must say, I find that highly unlikely. What could it be? Prostitution? Drug peddling? She wasn't the type. Robbery? Embezzlement? I don't think she cared about money at all. Most of us don't."

"You know what she did before she came here?"

"She was in the army, wasn't she?"

Sanctuario omnia secreta

"She was. She was a major in military intelligence. She had access to a large body of secret material. That material has since been released to the world, via the Internet."

"Oh. ... I suppose if her conscience ..." She left the sentence unfinished.

"Quite. No doubt she felt she was driven to do it by her conscience. Abbess, we all know that you Catholics confess your sins. Did she ..."

"Not to me," she said firmly. "To her confessor, perhaps. But anything she might have said to *him* is covered by the seal of the confessional, and he would never, ever break that."

"Pity. Ah well. I'll need that address, and we'll need to search her room."

"You can have the address. But searching her room, as you call it, is out of the question. I do not allow men to poke around in the private areas of our Abbey."

Tyndall looked worried. "I could get female officers to do it."

"No, Inspector. If you get a search warrant, I'll have to accede. Otherwise, definitely not. Anyway, I don't know what you expect to find. A nun doesn't have piles of possessions in her cell. A few devotional books ... a change of clothes ..."

"Look," Blandford interrupted, "She's released the first batch of material already, but we know there's a second batch. The seriously damaging stuff. The crown jewels, if you like. It could be on something as small as a memory stick. She's probably got it with her, but she knows that when we catch her, we'll take

The measure of all things

it off her. So she's probably made a duplicate and left it somewhere. If I were her, I'd leave it here."

"So," said the Inspector, "If you'd just let my female officers look at her ... cell ... And anything she left behind. A make-up bag, for instance."

"Nuns don't have make-up bags. No, Inspector, Mr Blandford, you do *not* have my co-operation. You'll need a search warrant."

"Right. A search warrant it is," said the Inspector.

"And," added Blandford, smoothly, "If we suspect that you're holding out on us, we could always invoke the special provisions of the Defence of the Realm Act, as amended last year. We'd declare the Abbey a designated area. Specially trained officers would turn it over, inch by inch. And no, they wouldn't be female officers."

"Good *day*, gentlemen," she said, in her severest voice. "This interview is over."

After they'd left, she mused silently for a while.

Then she opened a drawer in her desk and took out a copy of Teilhard de Chardin's "The Phenomenon of Man." She opened it. There was a rather handsome title page, bearing an omega symbol, then a long introduction by Sir Julian Huxley. She was struck by the quality of the paper, and the printing. Finally, on page 39, chapter one started. And there, someone had cut a cavity into the pages with a razor blade, just large enough for a thirtytwo-gigabyte memory stick. Sister Marion had entrusted the book to her, and she hadn't been too surprised to discover what was inside it.

Sanctuario omnia secreta

Of course, the memory stick wasn't there any more. She'd destroyed it, immediately after uploading the material to the Abbey's computer, and encrypting it. All the British Defence Ministry's grubby little secrets, and quite a few of the Pentagon's, too.

By God, she thought, if they defile my Abbey in any way, that'll find its way onto the Internet faster than you can say *'ex tenebras'*. And no, they won't ever be able to trace the source back to here. Not since Sister Marion taught us about Onion Router Uploads.

She picked up the book. It would have to be burned; a pity, but no help for it.

She made a detour to the kitchen and dropped it into the Aga. Then she set out for the instruction rooms. She'd managed to squeeze in an hour of bible study with the novices, and it was due to start now. As she walked through the cloister, she found herself humming a piece of music that Sister Marion had introduced to the Abbey. A hymn, by Christina Rosetti. How did it go? "Oh, hush your noise, ye men of strife, and hear the angels sing."

My song can't bind a human heart

She was wearing a tasteful blouse in sea-green silk, a pendant in the form of a tiny gold-framed mirror, some silver bangles, and nothing else. I was a little shaken, though not by her semi-nakedness. She was draped, full length, over a deep-brown leather sofa and, to be honest, I didn't know what to ask. She smiled that dazzling smile, which we've all seen on the television screen, and I heard myself saying "Is it your own couch?" She laughed, and said "Yes. Mine. I got it from 'World of Leather' and had it delivered here. The TV company tends to have cotton or wool covered sofas, which I can't really use. My ... um ... the bottom half of my body tends to be rather moist. Leather's fine, though."

The interview had only just started, and already I felt it slipping out of my grasp. Silently, I cursed Melissa's PA. She could have told me about Melissa's peculiar features when I first set the interview up, rather than five minutes before I met her. I said, "Forgive me, but ... do you have difficulty accessing the studio?" Melissa smiled again and said "Not really. My driver – Charles – is marvellous. He gets me out of the car, wheels me into the lift, and it brings me straight up here. But I must admit, if he has a day off, the props men tend to grumble. A hip-bath full of water is quite a lot heavier than a wheel-chair."

My song can't bind a human heart

I searched around for another question, my eyes straying to that astonishing expanse of gleaming scales. I said, "Did you always want to be a newsgirl?" Immediately I regretted the question – it was banal, and the answer was too obvious. But she didn't seem to notice. She said "No. When I was a little girl, I wanted to join the Royal Navy. I'd read a lot of war stories, and I could see myself leading a team of divers through an underwater minefield. All very stirring, very heroic. But it never came to anything. Good job too. I'd have been rubbish on a parade ground." The tips of her tail flicked reflexively.

"How did you get the job?"

"Well, we all know it's hard to break into television. All those arts graduates wanting a TV career, and practically no openings. You have to have some sort of edge. I sent them some tapes, and pointed out that, looked at one way, I was disabled. A fish out of water, so to speak. Looked at another way, I belonged to a minority culture. It seemed to do the trick. Ticked a couple of boxes on their corporate strategy."

"But they don't … er … how can I put it …"

"They don't let on that I'm a mermaid? No, they don't. I'm always sitting behind a desk, and you only see my top half. That's OK, I don't mind. I'm sorry to blow my own trumpet, but I think I do a pretty good job. Perhaps one day they will, but at the moment they don't think the nation's ready." She curled her lower half, slightly. I looked for any trace of knees, under the scales, but of course there wasn't any.

"Does it worry you that the viewers only see you as a glamorous young lady, rather than a professional journalist?"

The measure of all things

"No, honestly it doesn't. Well … just occasionally, I suppose. The other week, there was a story about marine pollution, and I thought 'I know more about this than any of you lot'. There are places I've been where the water tastes really horrible. I had a pet catfish, and she couldn't take it. The poor little thing just curled up and died. But I just delivered the script, straight off the autocue. Looking suitably concerned. That's what I'm paid to do."

"If you weren't doing this job, what would you like to do?"

"I'll tell you what I do when I'm on holiday. Any spare time I can grab, in fact. I'm a pot-holer."

"A pot-holer?"

"Mm, I love it. That's what I'd do if this job fell through – assuming money wasn't a problem, of course." She sounded a little wistful. "Let me loose in a Derbyshire cave system, I'll crawl around for hours. And I'm never happier than when I'm swimming in some underground river. It's a sort of home from home. Do you know that poem, 'Xanadu'?"

"*Where Alph the sacred river ran, through caverns measureless to man, down to a sunless sea*.'"

"Love that poem". Her face seemed to glow, and it might have been my imagination, but her scales seemed more iridescent than before. But I had the feeling that it was just that stanza she loved, not the whole poem. So I tried quoting the ending.

" '*A maiden with a dulcimer, in a vision once it saw. It was an Abyssinian maid, and on her dulcimer she played, singing of Mount Abora. Could I revive within me, her symphony and song* …*"*

My song can't bind a human heart

"Ooh, don't ask me to sing," she interrupted.

"Because you might lure me onto the rocks?"

She laughed, again. "No, because my singing's awful. I can't hold a note. Never could. My boyfriend says I'm tone-deaf."

"Tell me about your boyfriend."

"We go caving together. He's got lovely, strong arms. You know, I sometimes worry about getting lost underground. But it doesn't bother him in the least – he says he grew up with labyrinths, and this is no different."

"Do you think you'll get married? Have children?"

A shadow seemed to pass across her face. "No, we couldn't have children. He's a minotaur. We can't ... you know ... breed." That lovely smile returned, and she curled her tail playfully. "Look, I'm terribly sorry, but time's up. I've got to talk to the producer, about the script for tonight's news. Publish anything you like of what we've talked about. But I don't think anyone will believe you."

"Melissa, thank you very very much. It's been a revelation."

This machine reads your mind

Jack Knapp sat impassively in front of the desk. He was a well-built man, tanned and short-haired, wearing a lumberjack shirt and levis, with rugged brown leather boots. In fact, everything about him was rugged. It's a pretty good act, thought Harry Meacher. Knapp's shoulder bag was slung over the back of his chair, and the latest copy of *Farm and Ranch Life* was protruding from it. A nice touch.

The only jarring features were the blood-pressure cuff on Knapp's upper right arm, the skin monitors enveloping his finger tips, and the rubber straps round his torso, to measure his breathing, all with wires coiling away to the monitor unit on the desk. The standard accessories of a polygraph.

"Right, Mr Knapp," said Harry. "Here's a deck of cards. I'm going to ask you to pick a card – any card. Don't show it to me, but make a careful mental note of what it is. Then put it back in the deck." With a practised hand, he fanned the deck in front of Knapp. Knapp smiled an uncertain smile, and took a card from the middle of the fan. He pursed his brows slightly as he looked at it and put it back. Smoothly, Harry scooped the cards into a neat pack, and dropped them into a drawer in the desk, which he closed.

This machine reads your mind

"Now," said Harry. "I want you to answer 'no' to all of these questions, whatever the right answer is."

"Why would I do that?"

Harry sighed. "Just do it. Say 'no' to every question. Otherwise we'll have to start over." He was now gazing at the polygraph screen, his fingers resting lightly on the control knobs.

"Was it a red card?"

"No".

"Uh huh. Untrue, I think." Harry tweaked one of the knobs. "Was it a diamond?"

"No."

"Yes … yes, I think that was true." More tweaking. "Was it a picture card?"

"No".

"Yes … I think that was true, too. Was it ten, nine, eight, seven or six?"

"No".

"Uh huh. Don't think you're telling the truth. Was it six?"

"No".

"OK. Was it seven?"

"No".

"Bingo. The card was the seven of hearts. Am I right?"

"Dat's amazin."

"Yeah, this is a pretty clever machine; reads your mind. Really, though, *your* mind's fairly easy to read.

The measure of all things

"Now, some real questions. Answer them all yes or no, and I want you to be completely honest. OK?"

"OK."

"Is your name Jack Knapp?"

"Yeah."

"Do you know Jackson Point, Wisconsin?"

"Sure – dat's where I live."

"Have you ever got so drunk that you weren't fit to drive a car, but you drove it anyway?"

"No ... no."

"Is Paris the capital of France?"

"I guess so."

"Were you ever a member of the Nechayev Group?"

"Don't know what it is. So I guess da answer's no."

"Is this a wooden desk, between us?"

"Looks like it."

"When you were young, did you ever drink an alcoholic beverage, before you reached the age where you were legally allowed to do so?"

"No, I didn't."

"Did you plan the bombing of the FBI Regional Headquarters in Spartenburg, South Carolina, fifteen years ago?"

"No, I didn't."

"Is the sky dark at night?"

"It sure is, where I live."

This machine reads your mind

"Have you ever parked in a restricted parking zone, without authorisation?"

"No."

Harry grinned. "Congratulations, Mr Knapp – may I call you Jack? – you've passed the test."

Knapp looked relieved. "I'm mighty glad 'bout dat," he said.

"The interesting question is, how did you manage to pass?"

The look of relief faded from Knapp's face. He said nothing.

"You know about the card trick, don't you?"

Harry opened the drawer and took out the cards. He turned the deck over. All the cards were the seven of hearts.

"Designed to make you believe in the polygraph", continued Harry. "Guilty people quite often break down and confess, before the real test even starts. As to the main line of questioning, the machine picks out responses where you're feeling panicky. Or guilty, because you're telling a lie. There's a special pattern relating to breathing, blood pressure and skin sweating. We compare the pattern we get from the control questions to what we get from the real questions – the ones we care about. But then, you know all that, don't you? You've trained yourself to fool the machine."

Knapp said nothing, his face grim.

"I would guess that you've got a tack inside one of your boots. You jab your toe onto it whenever I ask a control question. Means there's much the same level

The measure of all things

of arousal when you answer a control question and a real question. Shall I make you take your boots off, Jack?"

"No point," said Knapp. "I admit I screwed up da readings on ya machine. Guys from Wisconsin don't like ya Guvmint men messing with dere minds. Besides, everyone knows ya can't trust what a lie-detector says. And it ain't against the law to read up on how to jinx one o' dem, ya know?"

Harry smiled, genially. "You're right that nobody should trust a polygraph, Jack. It's obsolete technology. Which is why I brought along something better: a brain-fingerprinting machine."

He lifted a large cardboard box off the floor, and placed it on the desk. Out of it he took a sleek new machine, enamelled matt black. He got up, walked round the desk, and carefully placed a close-fitting cap onto Knapp's cranium. It consisted of a thick band that circled his head, covering the forehead and the regions just above each ear, and another band running over the crown of the head. Circular lumps in the cloth revealed that it contained an array of EEG sensors. Velcro patches, where the bands met at the back, held it firmly in place. Knapp let him fit it, blank-faced, without a word. A cable snaked away from the back of the cap, and Harry plugged it into a socket on the machine, before resuming his seat. He plugged the black box into the mains, and pressed a sequence of keys on the front as it warmed up.

"What's it do?" asked Knapp. "Another sort of lie-detector?"

You know damn well what it is and what it does, thought Harry. But he smiled, and said, "Not exactly.

This machine reads your mind

It detects a brain-wave called P300. Your brain produces a P300 when you recognise something. Ever seen this before?"

He handed Knapp a large, glossy photo. It showed a front door, set into a wall made of white clapperboard, with a tiled roof over it. Knapp glanced at it, and a green LED lit up on the front of the machine.

Knapp said, "Sure – it's my front porch, back home in Jackson Point."

"Right. How about this?" Another front door, with a small window beside it, and wooden steps leading up to it.

"Nope, don't recognise it." The green light had disappeared.

"Not surprising – it's *my* front porch. How about this?" A rather anonymous office, with white-painted walls and fluorescent lights.

"Nope, don't know that one either."

One after the other, he presented a long series of photographs. Sometimes the brain-fingerprinting machine showed a P300 wave, sometimes it didn't.

When he got to the end, Harry squared off the stack of photos, and leaned back in his chair. He gazed levelly at Knapp.

"You're quite impressive, Jack. I showed you five different shots of the room where the Spartenburg bombing was planned, and you didn't produce a P300 once."

"Means I'm an innocent man, eh? Can I go now?"

The measure of all things

Harry shook his head. "You were the leader of the Nechayev Group cell. After the bombing, you went to ground. Changed your name, changed your persona. Now you're a cherry farmer, who talks like a Wisconsinite." He leaned forward, and gazed at Knapp intently. "But you've still got the same DNA. What would you say if I told you the FBI had found traces of your DNA in the room where you planned the bombing, and on the documents you left there?"

Knapp didn't allow himself to be phased. He gazed back at Harry, and said. "If you had all that on me, you'd have arrested me. You wouldn't have gone through the rigmarole with the lie detectors."

Harry smiled. "Yeah, you're right. You didn't leave any documents in that room, although you did leave other traces. The FBI have you as their chief suspect, but so far they haven't enough evidence to arrest you. I'd say you're safe, for the time being."

"*They* haven't enough evidence? I thought *you* were the FBI."

"Your mistake, Jack. I and my people know what the FBI knows, because we've hacked into their database. Read all their reports."

"This is a trick, right? You're trying to catch me out?"

Harry shook his head. "I wrote to you, asking you to come here and answer questions, and I did it on FBI notepaper. But that's easy to forge. We're not the FBI. We're your friends."

"Go on."

"Jack, back in 1999, the Group ordered you to go to ground. You knew that one day we'd come back for you. Today's the day. The code phrase is *narodnaya*

This machine reads your mind

rasprava – remember that? We're recalling you to the colours, as they used to say."

Knapp spoke in a deliberately neutral voice. "There's supposed to be a picture too."

Harry handed him a photo. It showed Jack Knapp, eighteen years younger, in front of three pictures – Robespierre, Saint-Just, and Sergei Nechayev – with a Klashnikov cradled in his arms.

Knapp's shoulders sagged. "OK, you're for real," he said, in a low voice. "But this is not what I wanted."

"Jack, Jack, you've read Nechayev's *Revolutionary Catechism*. When you sign up to be a revolutionary, you stay a revolutionary all your life. You know that."

"OK, OK. But why the charade with the lie detectors?"

"There's a report in the FBI file. Says they suspect that you can fool a polygraph, *and* a brain finger-printer. Now, fooling a polygraph is no big deal, but fooling a brain finger-printer *is*. Never heard of anyone who could do it, anywhere. The experts claim it's impossible. So I wanted to find out whether you really could. And you had to believe that it really mattered, otherwise it wouldn't have been a real test. Turns out, you genuinely can do it. You're special, Jack. You've got a talent, and you've got to teach it to the rest of the Group. That's mainly why we want you back."

Knapp sighed, a long sigh.

"OK. I've got blood dues to pay. The guys I sent to do the job in Spartenburg, they didn't make it back. I got to live like a country gentleman, they finished up dead." He sighed. "Did you know I had a kid

The measure of all things

brother? He was a famine relief worker in Somalia. 'With the poor people of this earth, I want to share my lot' – do you know that line? By José Martí? So he dressed like the poor people, ate food with them, shared their life. Of course, he still had a white skin. Then the US Marines arrived, to impose US foreign policy. Seems they didn't notice his white skin. They assumed he was just another Somali, and shot him. They called it 'Operation Restore Hope'. Yeah, I got blood dues to pay. ... Do I get to sell my farm?"

"Best not – the FBI are watching it. Best not even go back to Jackson Point. Here's money." He handed him a wad of ten dollar bills. "Buy what you need – a fresh set of clothes, stuff like that – here in Chicago. Then we both disappear. I'll take you to the safe house."

Knapp peeled the cap off his head, and chucked it onto the table. He got up, and massaged his temples. He sighed. "I would have liked to see this year's cherry harvest," he said.

Harry had packed the equipment into a wheeled crate. He gave Knapp a sunny smile. "Come on, comrade," he said, "We've got work to do."

"Just one thing, Harry."

"Yeah?"

"Is it OK if I take the tack out of my boot?

At the centre of the labyrinth

I trudged the deserted lanes of central France, the July sun hot on my shoulders. Since the upheavals of the mid-twenty-first century, the area had become severely depopulated. Throughout the whole morning, I saw no one at all. At noon, I stopped and ate some lunch – day-old bread rolls, and tinned sardines – sitting on the top of a small hill.

I looked around. Most of the fields were fallow. Far away, there was a solitary farm-worker driving a tractor. Or it might have been a robot tractor – I couldn't tell.

At about noon, I came to a village. A small church, an ancient, twentieth-century war memorial, and half a dozen shops, all except one of them boarded up. A signpost at the crossroads, pointing to four local towns, all a long way off. I entered the one shop that was still in business. It was dark, and smelt of cheese and smoked ham. The proprietor – a man in his sixties, with a grey beard – was glad to have a customer, and I was glad to see another human being.

"How's business?" I asked.

"Terrible," he replied, with a sad smile.

It had been a wine shop but, as the other tradesmen had closed, he'd expanded his stock and now

The measure of all things

endeavoured to sell everything. Gratefully, I bought bread, cheese, ham, cherry tomatoes, batteries for my cyberteller, bottled water, and wine.

"Is there anywhere to stay round here? An inn, perhaps?" I asked.

He shook his head. "The hotel closed last year. No customers."

"I see. The weather's warm – maybe I'll sleep under the stars."

"Why not?" he said. "Can I sell you a sleeping-bag?"

"Mm, perhaps. Tell me, was there some local attraction that the visitors came to see? Before ... well, before they stopped coming?"

He nodded. "People came from all over France – and beyond France – to see the *Ville Imaginaire*."

I thought, it can't have been such a huge draw, if the town only had six shops and one hotel. Still, it sounds interesting.

I said, "I should like to see that. Can you tell me where it is? And what they will charge me for entrance?"

He went to the door and pointed. "Half a kilometre that way. No one will charge you. It belongs to some corporation in Paris, and they can't be bothered to pay an attendant anymore."

* * * * *

Down the road, as promised, I found the entrance – a steel turnstile, set in a high stone wall, but chained shut with a rusty padlock. A faded sign-board said "*Ville Imaginaire. Chef-d'oeuvre d'architecture mystique,*

At the centre of the labyrinth

construit par Alphonse Dédale. The lower part of the board, showing the opening times and prices, was covered up by a smaller board that said *Nous regrettons que cette attraction est fermée indéfiniment.*

But the decision to close the place clearly hadn't gone down well with the locals. Further down the road, something large had been driven through the wall. The vehicle wasn't there any more, but someone had carefully moved the tumbled stones to one side, making a tolerably neat entrance. They've taken a risk, I thought, bearing in mind the draconian new anti-trespass laws. And I'd be taking a risk if I took advantage.

I walked through the gap, and found myself in *Alphonse Dédale's Ville Imaginaire.*

* * * * *

First, there was the courtyard of an Italian *palazzo*. I sat down on a carved marble bench, and flipped on my cyberteller.

It informed me that Alphonse Dédale was a sculptor, one of several French artists who had taken their cue from Ferdinand Cheval and built collections of fantastical sculpted buildings in remote parts of the country. Cheval, who was a country postman, had started the ball rolling by building a *Palais Idéal*, using stones he found by the wayside, and cement, back in the 1880s and 1890s. Dédale's construction dated from a century and a half later. He was fabulously rich, and widely regarded as insane, but the single-mindedness of his vision had evinced a grudging admiration. There was a picture of Alphonse Dédale, looking suitably mad.

The measure of all things

I looked around at the courtyard. The detail was certainly impressive: the carved stonework (or rather, delicately moulded concrete) looked very much like something from renaissance Italy. But the bench I was sitting on turned out to be cement, carefully painted to look like marble. I got up and walked to a door in the wall in front of me, opened it, and found a spiral staircase. The door closed behind me. I walked up the staircase, and found myself in a small, circular room. Across it, there was an arched opening, with a balcony beyond. I walked out onto the balcony and leaned on a stone balustrade, and found myself looking down onto an ocean. Except ... it was only an ocean at first glance. If you looked at it a little longer, you realised that it was many broken bottles, made of blue glass, embedded in undulating concrete.

The turret grew out of a curtain wall. The perspective had been distorted to give an impression of enormous height. The architecture was, I imagined, intended to be Gothic – some ancient castle, defending some rugged northern coastline.

Behind me were three doors, all shut – the one I had entered, and two others. I walked through the middle one, down a long corridor, lit by skylights. I opened a small door and found myself in the nave of a medieval cathedral.

The effect was overwhelming. It was quite dark, but you couldn't miss the huge carved columns, the arched roof, far overhead, with its elaborate fan vaulting, the enormous stained-glass window over what must be the great west door. I sat down in an ancient wooden pew.

Presently, three things struck me.

At the centre of the labyrinth

The place didn't smell right: it smelt damp, like a cave.

The pew felt wrong; I realised that it was made of concrete, painted to look like wood.

And the perspective didn't look quite right.

I got up, and walked along the central aisle. Sure enough, I found that I was walking uphill, and the roof was sloping down towards me. The columns grew smaller and smaller, and closer and closer together. The whole place was an elaborate optical illusion. When I reached the west door, it was no higher than my waist, and the stained-glass window would have fitted into someone's front door.

I walked back – from this viewpoint, the perspective was, of course, outrageously wrong. I couldn't find the door through which I'd entered, but I found another, and went through it. I followed another corridor. At the end was another door, and I went through that, too.

Now I was on an ocean liner's deck. Steel hawsers overhead, supporting a great metal funnel. Planking beneath my feet that was no more wooden than the cathedral pew had been. Occasional signs, for the guidance of the passengers and crew, in French.

Stepping through a sea-door, I found myself in a cabin, with portholes, bunks, and a small table. All painted concrete, of course.

Passing through the cabin door, and walking down yet another long corridor, I opened a door and found myself in a Roman temple. A statue of a goddess – Minerva, perhaps? – to my left, Corinthian columns to my right.

The measure of all things

I examined the goddess. She was rather larger than life, seated on a throne, holding a sceptre. The sculptor had painted her carefully, and her facial features were quite lifelike. I didn't care for the expression on her face – imperious, calculating and, somehow, hungry.

I turned to the right, and walked through the columns. I was at the top of a flight of fake-marble steps, leading down into a Roman township.

I realised that I was hopelessly lost.

I looked back into the temple. There were seven doors in the left-hand wall, all shut, and I couldn't remember which I had come out of. There had been lots of doors on the ocean-liner. Before that, there had been doors in the cathedral; I couldn't recall how many. Before that – where had I been? I couldn't remember.

And it was starting to get dark.

I felt scared; I admit it.

I looked around at the deserted town below me. No lights anywhere. I looked back at the darkening temple, in which lurked the goddess, lovingly rendered in painted concrete. I shivered.

Look, I told myself, it's not that bad. You've got food and drink. You were going to sleep out in the open anyway. No one's going to arrest you for trespass.

I descended the steps and found a Roman wine-shop. One without any doors leading into the unknown. I rummaged in my rucksack, and found my torch. I ate some bread, cheese, tomatoes and ham, and drank some wine. Then I unrolled my new sleeping bag, and

At the centre of the labyrinth

made myself as comfortable as I could, on a concrete couch. Eventually, I fell asleep.

* * * * *

I dreamt I was lost in the great Cretan labyrinth. "Ariadne!" I shouted. "Save me! You want me for a lover? Of course I'll be your lover! Only give me a thread to get me out of here!" And her voice came back, full of cold fury, "You spurned me. You'll get nothing from me."

I woke with a start, and lay there, my muscles aching, the cool night air on my face. I thought: this is ridiculous. You have the means to escape. I unzipped the sleeping-bag, took out my cyberteller and flipped it on.

What's the route back to the road? I typed.

Always before, my cybernetic friend had helped me. Not this time. The words on the little screen were a shock.

You cannot leave. You are in a different realm.

What do you mean? I asked.

There was a pause, as the computer decided how to express concepts new to it. Then:

Alphonse Dédale built this place because he wanted people to come and marvel at it. He's dead now, but he still wants that. You are the first person to come here for several years. He will not let you leave.

I considered that. I typed *Show me the map – I'll find my own way out.*

It replied *I cannot do that. Dédale will not let me access his maps.*

The measure of all things

I typed *But there's no food here, or drink. I'll starve.*

It replied *He doesn't care.*

* * * * *

When I woke, the sun was high in the sky. My muscles still ached, but the day was already warm. Clearly, the interlude in the night with my cyberteller had been a bad dream. I flipped it on, and requested a map, but it just said *unavailable*. It occurred to me that, if I were to dial 112, I could ask the police to rescue me. Then I considered the anti-trespass laws and thought better of it.

So I climbed the temple steps, and tried the door, from which, I was almost sure, I had emerged the evening before.

Behind it was a corridor that seemed familiar. But when I climbed the steps at the end, I found myself on the foredeck of a riverboat. The signs were in Chinese. It was surrounded by water, constructed, once again, from blue bottle-glass set in concrete. Searching the boat, I found a door in the engine-room that revealed another long passage. This one ended in a wine-cellar, full of great casks (crafted from concrete, naturally, and containing no wine). A winding staircase led to the entrance hall of an English mansion. There were oil paintings on the panelled walls: they were all of Alphonse Dédale.

And it was there, in the middle of the faux-marble floor, that I found human bones.

When the initial horror had subsided, I thought: this was the last traveller to come this way. He died of starvation here.

At the centre of the labyrinth

But that was wrong. The skeleton had been dismembered, the bones chewed by something with powerful jaws.

I flipped on my cyberteller, typed *What happened here?* and pointed its lens at the bones.

Once again there was a pause. Then it said, *In English, the name Dédale would be Daedalus. He built a labyrinth, and put a minotaur in it.*

Out of the corner of my eye, I saw a figure move. A large man, with a very large head. But when I turned and looked, there was nothing.

Gazing down from the portraits on the walls, Alphonse Dédale smiled malignantly.

A pocketful of space

When he was a small boy, Tim would come home from his summer holiday, and go into the family's house, and find that, for a time, everything looked strange. The furniture in his bedroom, the possessions piled on his table: he recognised them, but only after gazing at them for a few moments. Familiar yet unfamiliar: the effect of not seeing them for a week. Now, at the age of forty-five, he still had that sensation, but it was much weaker, and much briefer. All the same, he rather treasured it. It reminded him of his youth, when the world had seemed magical.

Having paid the taxi driver, he lugged his suitcase up the garden path, to the doorstep. He fumbled for his keys, then opened the front door, which pushed aside the pile of letters on the doormat. He took a step forward, and drank in the scene. The stairs to the left, the sitting room door to the right, the kitchen door ajar in front of him. White paint on the woodwork, caramel paint on the walls, a print of Van Gogh's 'Sunflowers' on the wall, the floor made of oak-effect laminate. Something magical about it all? Perhaps a tiny little bit. He sighed. I'm too old to be entranced by simple things, he thought.

He hauled the suitcase through the door, and shut it. He picked up the post – a few letters that might be important, an awful lot of junk mail – and carried it into the sitting room. Once again, he paused, in the

A pocketful of space

hope that he'd see the TV, bookcase, HiFi, sofa, pot plant – things that he'd seen a thousand times before – in a new way. It didn't happen.

He had a big, round, wooden table where he ate his meals. He put the mail down on it, and then noticed a strange object in the middle of the tabletop.

It was quite small – about three inches high, and twice that across, and it seemed to be made of twisted glass tubes. No, 'tubes' was wrong: curved surfaces, with sharp edges, like twisted knife blades. They formed a hemisphere. It could, perhaps, have been some sort of paperweight – except he'd never seen a paperweight like it. The glass didn't look right, either – it might not be glass at all; perhaps it was some sort of shiny metal, with a bluish tinge to it?

He reached out to touch it, and found that he couldn't. Some sort of invisible barrier pushed his fingers back, a little way from the object. It was like pushing his fingertips into a balloon.

He went back into the hall, and opened his suitcase. A little rummaging and he found his camera. Back in the sitting room, he photographed the object from several angles. Then he thought for a while, and decided to phone his brother. He went upstairs and made the call.

"Peter, I need your advice."

"Tim, is that you? Hello! You're back! How was the trip? How was Madeira?"

"Madeira was fine, Peter, but I got home, and there's something really odd here…"

"Odd? I don't get it – have you had a break-in?"

The measure of all things

"Well, maybe. But there are no signs of forced entry. Anyway, you'd expect burglars to take your stuff away. This lot seem to have left something on my sitting room table."

"That does sound weird. What is it?"

"I really don't know. I've never seen anything like it."

"Umm ... do you want me to come over? It's just that I'm in the middle of writing a piece ..."

"No, don't come over. I'll email you some pictures, and you can tell me what you think."

After he hung up, he realised it was getting dark. He turned his computer on, and, while it booted up, he went downstairs to have another look at the object. When he got there, he noticed it was emitting a faint blue glow.

* * * * *

Tim didn't get much sleep that night. He unpacked in his bedroom, and took his dirty laundry down to the washing machine. He ate a light supper in the kitchen, not wanting to get too close to the thing on the sitting room table. Then he spent hours at his computer, searching the Web for anything similar that might have happened somewhere else. No luck. Exhausted, he went to bed, and fell asleep. But he woke up at dawn, convinced something was horribly wrong. After a few minutes, he remembered the object. He put on his slippers and dressing gown, and went downstairs. The thing was still there, in just the same place, looking much the same. Still glowing. And, he was quite sure, larger than it had been. Perhaps four inches high.

A pocketful of space

He booted up his computer. There was an email from Peter:

Tim –

*You know I have a friend, Vosper, who's a physicist? I shared your pictures with him. He talked to one of **his** friends, Warren, who's very interested. Is it OK if we all come round this morning?*

Peter.

He emailed back, to say yes, the sooner the better, and what branch of physics is this Warren concerned with? Peter replied:

Superstring theory.

* * * * *

Peter and his two friends arrived at 11:30. The friends turned out to be Dr. Martin Vosper, and Cyril Warren, who Peter proudly announced as Professor of High Energy Physics at the University of London. Tim shook hands with both of them. They declined the offer of a cup of coffee, wanting to see the object straight away.

"My, my," the professor murmured, looking at it from various angles. He produced a camera, and took a dozen photographs of the thing crouched on the table. He took several instruments out of his case, and pointed them at it. He fired laser beams at it. The thread of red light would penetrate the object, and would be bent into a new direction. He would alter the point of entry by a tiny amount, and the emergent beam would be on an entirely different path. He typed notes on a small laptop computer.

"Fascinating," he said to Vosper. "It really is a Calabi-Yau space, isn't it?" Vosper nodded.

The measure of all things

"Is it dangerous?" asked Tim.

"Yes, very," said the Professor. "Not so much to you, personally, although it is slightly radioactive. More to the whole human race."

"Why radioactive?" said Vosper.

"Cherenkov radiation," said the Professor, "A few of the air molecules get through the barrier, and they're accelerated almost to the speed of light. They come back out again, and collide with ordinary molecules, and that causes the glow, which ..."

"Look," said Tim, "I really don't care about this. What is it? Why is it so dangerous?"

"This is going to be very hard to explain," said the Professor.

"Try me," said Tim.

"Can I try something first?" The Professor put on what seemed to be a steel gauntlet, and pushed the object hard. He couldn't shift it. Then he took hold of two of the table legs, and yanked them. The table collapsed, leaving the object hanging in mid-air. It was clearly spherical, and it had grown to about nine inches across. The remains of the table lay on the floor: the legs broken, the centre badly mis-shapen.

"Hey!" yelped Tim, "That was my table!"

"Sorry," said the Professor mildly, "I needed to find out whether it was anchored to the table, or a particular point in space. The latter, it seems. Although presumably the Earth's centre of gravity defines what that point is. Otherwise it would be moving away from here, very fast ... knocking down

A pocketful of space

everything in its path. Now, where to begin? Do you know anything about cosmology?"

"No," said Tim, honestly.

"Modern school education, eh? Ah well. But you must know that our universe came into existence thirteen point seven billion years ago? No? Well, it did. And when it did, it was an eleven-dimensional object, and exceedingly small. A fraction ... the tiniest fraction of a second later, seven of the dimensions collapsed, and the other four started to expand. We've had a four-dimensional universe ever since."

"Nicely put, Cyril," murmured Vosper.

"Four-dimensional?" said Tim, weakly.

"Yes, of course. Three spatial and one time. But the question you *should* have asked is, what happened to the other seven? The answer is, they folded up into something so tiny that you could never hope to see it, even with the strongest microscope." He held up a finger and thumb, close together, to make the point. "Much smaller than an atom. There's a little package of folded space at every point in our universe. The package, or rather the shape of the package, is called a Calabi-Yau space. That's one –" he pointed at the object, hanging motionless in mid-air, and looking a bit like a Christmas tree bauble. "What you can see is a three-dimensional cross-section of a seven-dimensional object."

"But you said they were tiny," said Peter; the first time he had spoken.

"Yes. It's very strange. This one seems to have stopped being sub-microscopic and become – well,

The measure of all things

you can see its size. It's happened spontaneously. I don't think anyone's ever predicted that."

"What can we do about it?" asked Tim.

"I'm ... I'm really not sure," said the Professor.

"Can we destroy it?"

"Of course not. How can you destroy a lump of empty space?"

"You never explained why it was dangerous to the whole human race."

"Oh, right. It's already crushed your table, leaving a big dent. It might keep expanding till it crushed the whole planet. Also, I suspect that it's unstable: eventually, it'll collapse. And it would be a rapid collapse: less than a microsecond. If it did that now, it would just be like a balloon bursting. But if it grows till it's, say, a thousand miles across, and *then* it collapses, it'll be a huge explosion."

"Implosion," corrected Vosper.

* * * * *

It was late afternoon. The Professor had gone off, saying he had to speak to a colleague, who was in the Royal Society. Vosper had gone with him. Peter had stayed a while, then said he had to go home to collect the kids from school. Tim had been left alone, with the object. It was now about twelve inches across. Still hanging, perfectly motionless, in mid-air. The blue glow was stronger. Tim wondered how long it would be before it pushed the walls of his house apart and the whole building collapsed.

It'll be about twelve days, said a voice inside his head.

A pocketful of space

For a moment he felt very confused. Was that his own thought? He turned round.

There were three tall men standing behind him. Or, at least, three tall beings – he wasn't sure they were men. Their faces were vaguely human, but they had no hair. They were dressed in something very hazy and indistinct – a sort of brown mist. Their body shapes weren't obviously male or female.

"Did you just read my thoughts?" he asked.

I'm afraid so, said the voice. *It's the way we talk*. No doubt about it; it was a voice in his head. His hearing wasn't involved at all.

"Who are you?" he asked.

Your descendents. There are still humans in this part of the galaxy, a couple of million years from now. We know you've got a problem, and we've come to help.

Tim considered that. He almost said, get out – I'm fed up with strangers coming into my home, throwing their weight around, as if they owned the place. But his grip on reality was still strong enough to tell him that he *did* have a problem.

"Can you destroy that?" he said, pointing at the glowing blue sphere.

Not exactly.

"Then what can you do?"

We can take it away. We're very good at moving pieces of space through space. It's how we travel through time.

"Where will you take it?"

The centre of the galaxy, probably. There's a black hole there. We use it as a dustbin.

The measure of all things

"Take it with my blessing. I never wanted it in the first place."

The three figures moved past him, and took up positions around the sphere. They made elaborate hand movements, sketching out a box in the air. Then the sphere flickered and vanished. The three moved back towards the door. One of them seemed to be carrying something exceedingly heavy, but invisible.

"Wait a moment," said Tim. "Can't I reward you in some way?" He had a sudden insane image of himself handing out chocolates, as one would to trick-or-treat children. Or handing out twenty-pound notes.

No, said the voice. *It's not necessary. It's a service we provide.*

"Who are you?" he asked, forgetting that he'd already asked the question.

Can't you guess? We're the galactic dustmen.

And with that, they were gone.

The Star-Traveller's Rest, Aragona

This is certainly the most far-flung restaurant I've ever reviewed. 8.1 light years from our Solar System, to be precise.

Aragona is, of course, a way station. Space traffic arrives, space traffic leaves, people and goods change platforms, so to speak; that's the only point in going to the planet. It has no indigenous lifeforms, and if it has anything you could call soil, it's been imported, at vast expense, from other planets. So there's no point in asking for a favourite local dish, or wine. Your waiter will simply give you a blank stare, with every one of his four eyes.

All the same, after all the time you've spent in hyperspace, eating reconstituted freeze-dried porridge, you'll want something special when you drop back into normal space, however briefly. And so will every other star-traveller. This presents the proprietors of the spaceport's restaurant with several challenging problems.

In the first place, different species have different ideas about polite eating habits. Humans are extremely reluctant to regurgitate food at the dinner table. Moscatoids would regard it as very rude not to. Festucans always wear yashmaks at the dinner table, because no Festucan would ever want to be seen

The measure of all things

doing something as ... well, *naughty* ... as putting morsels of food in its mouth (they would regard a picture of someone doing so as pornographic).

In the second place, the problem is to cater for the nutritional needs of seven different space-going species, with radically different body chemistries. One being's meat is another being's poison, as the old saying goes, and it's truer here than anywhere else. There's a condiment that the Aplachnids use quite extensively – chromium hexachloride – which is deadly to humans. One could well imagine a kitchen that catered to the needs of all these space travellers, making a tiny slip, and killing a large part of its clientele.

In the third place, tastes in food vary enormously among members of the same species. Some Moscatoids love to eat raw giant slugs, dusted with something that we would identify as gunpowder; but most Moscatoids won't touch them. An Ethiopian cook knows just how to prepare a delicious meal, but you'll find no Ethiopian restaurants in England, because English people find Ethiopian flavours disgusting.

How were the staff of the Aragonian spaceport restaurant to cope with all these problems? Well, the second and the third at any rate? They considered shipping-in expert chefs, and ingredients, from seven different home worlds: too expensive. They considered importing a very large number of pre-cooked, boil-in-the-bag, dishes: too expensive, too second-rate.

One has to admire the ingenuity with which they solved their difficulties. In the end, it was the solution to the first problem that pointed the answer to the

The Star-Traveller's Rest, Aragona

second and the third. You have a customer whose eating habits are disgusting, but who's too important to be given the bum's rush? You ensure that the other customers can't see or hear him. Or smell him. If you can do that, you can ... but let me get back to the review.

By the time I had finished my meal, I was unsure whether to award one star or ten. I compromised on five. Let me explain why.

On arriving at the eatery, the Maitre D' presents you with a cap made of filigree silver, lined with velvet (red, if you're a human; some other colour, if you're not), and insists that you wear it. If you demur, he fixes you with a stern gaze – again, four eyes; all the staff have four eyes, since the place is run by Quadrocculates – and declares "There are no exceptions, sir."

You will then be shown to your table. Don't bother sizing up your fellow diners: the sight-lines have been cleverly arranged so that you can't see them.

In due course, the waiter presents you with a menu showing a surprisingly large selection of Earth-type cuisines. I spotted "early 21st century Scottish" and selected it, out of nostalgia; that's where my ancestors were at that time. Responding to my selection, the menu card changed to a very impressive collection of dishes.

Among the more predictable delights, there was Cullen skink made with finnan haddie; pan-seared Isle of Barra scallops; Stornoway back pudding; roast breast of pheasant; roast border venison in a port sauce; pulled shin of Aberdeen Angus beef; confit of Tay salmon; Orkney fudge cheesecake; and, of course,

The measure of all things

cranachan. The prices are pretty steep – typically 13 credits for a starter, 20 credits for a main course, 11 credits for a pudding, 25 credits for a mid-range bottle of wine – but (unless you're spacecrew) you will certainly have spent much more to get there in the first place.

For a starter, I chose the pan-fried Tarbert crab cake with spinach and walnut salad and mustard cream sauce. I really couldn't fault it; the flavours had been balanced perfectly, and the textures complemented one another delightfully. My main dish was beef cheek, slow-cooked in claret, served in a cast-iron pan, with carrots and mashed potato. The red meat inside the pitch-black exterior was a visual delight, and I cannot remember eating meat that was so succulent. With the simply-treated vegetables, it provided a near-perfect melange of flavours. I washed it down with a more-than-acceptable Barbaresco Sori Tildin – not Scottish, but then Scotland wasn't producing any wine in the early 21st century. Finally, for the third course, I chose a buttermilk and saffron pudding – rather like pannacotta – accompanied by squares of poached plum and oat crunch. It arrived promptly, and it seemed a beautifully judged counterpoint to the heavy main course.

Why, then, you ask, am I reluctant to award ten stars to this excellent bistro? Simply because, at that precise moment, everything changed. The décor, which had been of restrained (but quite sumptuous) gold-blocked cream-coloured leather, suddenly became aluminium sheets. The mahogany table at which I was sitting became off-white plastic. My tastefully styled, well-upholstered chair, became the sort of chrome tube and rubber-strapping affair that you find on a starship's flight deck. My fellow diners, who had been

The Star-Traveller's Rest, Aragona

concealed by ornamental screens, weren't screened anymore. I could see Moscatoids, doing what you'd expect Moscatoids to do at the dinner table, and Festucans, gazing at the rest of us in horror, and moaning. A couple of the Festucans had to be helped out of the room; I imagine that the experience was rather like that of a middle-aged, strait-laced matron, who realises that the pleasant hotel foyer where she's sat down to rest is in fact the antechamber to a brothel.

I transferred my gaze to the pudding that I'd been about to eat. It had turned into a dreary pale-grey stodge.

My waiter glided across.

"I do apologise, sir," he said. "There has been a power cut. I'm afraid you see us as we are, rather than as we would wish you to see us." He fluttered his four eyelids, one by one.

I began to see the point of the strange head-dress. "The cap I'm wearing …?"

"…is the means whereby we project the different aspects of the restaurant experience into your brain. I'm afraid it's not projecting anything at the moment, sir."

I must have looked a little surprised, because he went on.

"Of course, it is necessary to screen the other diners from your perception. And vice versa. A difficult task, but one at which our engineers have become very adept. Once we had arranged for that, it seemed only natural to channel your gastronomic experience in the same way."

The measure of all things

I nodded. No doubt it did seem natural to them, but it was also undeniably a lot cheaper to store the *perceptions* of food in a databank than to actually ship the stuff across the light years, keep it fresh, and then have to cook it.

"I see. Tell me, what is this?" I indicated the grey stodge.

"A foodstuff containing all the nutrients and vitamins and minerals that humans need, sir. I believe it is called 'Complan'".

"And what did I get during the last course?"

"The same, sir."

"And for the starter?"

"Again, it was the same, sir. You assumed that it had flavours and textures and colours and scents that were in fact absent. As far as I could tell, you enjoyed it."

"And the wine? What was that?"

"Distilled water, sir."

"You mean to tell me that I am about to pay 70 credits for three bowls of Complan and a glass of water?"

He looked deeply shocked.

"Indeed not, sir. We hired the finest gourmets, and sent them to the best restaurants, and recorded their resulting cognitive patterns meticulously. A very great deal of time, effort, judgement and, may I say, money has gone into the construction of our gastronomic impressions. ***That*** is what you are paying for."

So there you have it. If you can afford a visit to the Star-traveller's Rest, you may find it a marvellous

The Star-Traveller's Rest, Aragona

gastronomic experience, or you may find it a horrible ordeal. It all depends on the quality of the electricity supply on the day you turn up.

Be careful what you prove

The room wasn't all that large. Larger than a bedroom in a cheap hotel, but still ... one might have expected something bigger. This was Selmer Handiside's study, and Professor Handiside was world famous, in his own small field. It was paneled in dark wood, and had a couple of modestly sized windows. There were doors leading to an equally small bedroom, a bathroom and a kitchenette. On close inspection, the paneling was nicely made – it seemed to be stained oak – and the fittings on the windows, made from small-paned leaded lights, were clearly intended to look like antique, hand-made, ironwork. The room was intended to deliver an impression: a chamber that had been built hundreds of years ago, so that a college fellow could live in comfort by the standards of the seventeenth century. But in fact it was a fake. Ryddon's College only dated back to Edwardian times. The founders would have loved to be thought an ancient foundation, on a par with Brasenose College, but such aspirations were in vain. Oxford University has a deep prejudice against recently founded colleges.

Still, this was the college that elected Professor Handiside a fellow, and he seemed happy enough to live here.

Be careful what you prove

Callan moved quietly round the room. There were bookshelves against the walls, full of abstruse volumes on mathematics. He picked one off the shelf: it turned out to be *The Birch-Swinnerton-Dyer Conjecture – Frontiers of Research*. Published by the American Mathematical Society, of Princeton. It had been well thumbed, and Handiside had written notes in the margin. Callan carefully replaced it, in the same position. He was wearing gloves, so he didn't have to worry about leaving fingerprints.

He checked his watch. Handiside would return from his lecture in about ten minutes.

A quick survey of the bedroom and the kitchen suggested that Handiside led a drab, single-minded life. The kitchen didn't seem to get much use. No fancy cook-books on the shelf, no exotic ingredients in the larder. The bedroom housed a single bed. No flamboyant clothes in the wardrobe, no erotic novels by the bed. No hint of tobacco or marijuana smoke clinging to the draperies. No bottles of booze anywhere.

All of which told Callan that Handiside almost certainly hadn't shared the secrets of his research with a lover. Probably not with a drinking buddy either.

Four and a half minutes to go, and Callan turned his attention back to the main room. There was a framed print on the wall. It was an impossible building – some sort of monastery, in which two rows of monks walked endlessly up and down a staircase, which had been cleverly drawn so that the end joined to the beginning, and the stairs had no highest or lowest point. Callan grinned momentarily. He knew it – it was a lithograph by M C Escher, much reproduced, and very popular among mathematicians, but this

The measure of all things

seemed to be one of Escher's original hand-printed lithographs. Clearly, Handiside had made a little money, and spent it on the art that pleased him most.

The room contained four easy chairs – suitable for a very small seminar – and a desk, with a computer on it and an office chair in front of it. Callan had already dealt with the computer – the first thing he'd done after breaking into the room was to wrench its hard disk out, break it open with a hammer, and drop a small but powerful magnet into the crack. More than that, his associates had determined where Handiside kept all his writings, and all his notes – on a secure website, sponsored by the college. A little creative hacking, and it would all soon cease to exist.

Callan heard the footsteps on the stairs outside, and sat down in one of the armchairs. He heard the key turning in the lock, and smoothly withdrew his gun from his inside pocket.

Professor Handiside came in. He was a tall, scruffy, man, with thick brown-rimmed glasses and thinning brown hair. He was wearing a sports jacket over a non-descript navy blue tee-shirt, and frayed jeans and bleached trainers. He had his keys in one hand, and a bundle of lecture-notes in the other. From his expression, he could well have been working out the solution to a complex maths problem in his head.

He saw Callan, and the gun pointed towards him. He stopped. His expression changed to one of bewilderment.

"Oh my God," he said.

"Hello, Professor," said Callan, "I'm your nemesis."

Be careful what you prove

"What do you want?" There was a pause. "I ... I haven't any money ..."

"No, I know you haven't. It's you, yourself. I'm afraid you've reached the end of the road. Are you a religious man? Do you want to say any prayers?"

"But ... I haven't done anything! I've never harmed anyone." Another pause. "Do I owe someone money? I can't owe anyone any money!"

"No, you don't owe anyone any money. It's not that."

"But ... are you going to kill me? What for?"

"Yes, I am going to kill you. For what you know."

"State secrets? I don't know any state secrets!"

"No, I don't suppose you do. But you *have* discovered a proof for the Riemann Hypothesis. I'm not a mathematician, but I gather people like you have been trying to do that for a hundred and fifty years. And you're about to publish it."

"But ... this is just mathematics! Why would someone like you care about it?"

"Oh, *I* don't care about it at all. But my employers do."

"Why? Why ever would they?"

"E-commerce, Professor, e-commerce"

"I ... I don't understand..."

"All the e-commerce transactions in the world are protected by an encryption algorithm. It's called RSA, I'm told. As I said, I don't really know or care about these things – I'm just an ordinary hired killer. But they tell me that the algorithm works by factorising a very large semi-prime number. It's impossible to

The measure of all things

crack. Except that one of the corollaries to your theorem proof shows an easy way to do it. I'm sorry, professor, but your knowledge is just too dangerous."

"But ... this is so unfair ..."

"Lots of unfair things happen in this life, Professor. OK, so you could have got the Nobel prize – do they have a Nobel prize for maths? I forget. But millions of people would have been ruined. Major economies would collapse. Can't be allowed to happen."

He left Selmer Handiside's body slumped in one of the armchairs. On the wall, the monks continued their endless journey round the staircase, without so much as a downward glance.

The ghost in the machine

"If you want to hold irrational beliefs, that's up to you," said Dr Cottingham sourly. "Catholics, Jehovah's Witnesses, Scientologists – I'll let any of them work here, just provided they put in the hours."

Privately, I doubted whether he would. But that wasn't the point.

"I didn't claim to have any religious beliefs," I replied. "I just said I'd seen a ghost."

"No you haven't, Jack. Because ghosts don't exist."

I said nothing. After a pause, he decided that he needed to justify that, and continued.

"There are fake ghosts, of course. Plenty of those, throughout history. Plenty of charlatans and practical jokers, deceiving the gullible. There are natural phenomena that people misinterpret – a statue reflected in a window looking like a phantom, that sort of thing. There are hallucinations and dreams. But genuine apparitions of the dead? No. Can't happen."

"Why not?"

He smiled grimly. "Good, now you're asking a sensible question. Thinking like a scientist. Keep it up: that's what we do round here. The answer is, because

The measure of all things

a human personality is a process. In computer terms, it's the execution of a piece of software. Software has to be run on hardware, or it doesn't run at all. Human software has to be run on brain tissue. If the brain tissue dies, the personality evaporates, and nothing will bring it back. I wrote a book about it, when you were still at school. I suggest you find a copy and read it. And, if you keep seeing ghosts, I suggest you go and talk to a reputable shrink."

I thanked him, and left his office. George Cottingham's reputation for brilliant insights had got him the job of Director of the Sixth Generation Computing Project, but, outside his specialist sphere, he could be remarkable rigid.

Outside, in the corridor, Vicky was waiting. Dressed, as always, like a female factory worker in 1940, in brown dungarees, with her hair tied up with a red scarf, she made an unusual figure. All the more unusual since I could see through her. She was a transparent three-dimensional sketch, in front of a drab, dark brown, panelled wall.

"I heard that little exchange," she said. "Don't say anything. He can't hear me, but he can hear you. Let's go outside and discuss it."

We walked out to the patio behind the mansion, and sat down on a stone bench, overlooking the lawn. In the sunlight she was harder to see, but still indisputably there, if you looked closely enough.

"What do you think," she said, "Am I a fake? A practical joke, maybe? Or are you hallucinating?"

"I think you're real," I said. "I don't see how anybody could fake you – you move around too much to be a projection. And I'm not drunk, or taking drugs.

The ghost in the machine

Maybe I'm mad, but I don't feel mad. No, I think you're real."

"I'm kind of pleased," she said. "I suppose we all want other people to believe in us."

"That's what ghosts want?"

"That's what *people* want. And I regard myself as a person."

"Vicky, I don't want to revive painful memories, but ... you are dead, aren't you?"

"I reckon so. I was in the Woolston factory on the 24th of September 1940. We were making Spitfires. The Luftwaffe flew over and bombed us ... we were running for the shelters ... there was a crowd of us, trying to get through the railway arch. Then the bombs fell on top of the arch and smashed it to pieces. I don't remember anymore."

"I'm sorry."

"Yes, well, we all die sooner or later. I'm a pretty levelheaded sort of girl. I take these things as they come."

Instinctively, I put out my hand to hold hers. But there was nothing there for me to grasp.

"The funny thing is ..." she continued "... the Germans came back and flattened the place two days later. Nothing left but rubble. I don't remember seeing it, but I do know it happened. But I wouldn't, would I? If I were already dead? I can't explain that."

I was about to say something, when she said "Someone's coming. You'd better not be seen talking to me." She vanished.

The measure of all things

It was Oliver, my section head. "Hi Jack. Taking a breather? Don't take too long, old man. We *are* all up against the deadline."

* * * * *

Next morning, I booted up my PC, and found an email from the Director, flagged as urgent: "Re our talk yesterday, go and see Dr Bursell immediately."

It was a bad moment. Christina Bursell was the Project's Assistant Medical Officer. She was more influential than that job titled implied: she was on the Board of Directors, and had involvement in a number of sub-projects. Crucially, she was a psychiatrist. I guessed that, on reflection, Cottingham had decided to have me declared mentally incompetent, and dismiss me. Which would be the end of my career.

But I didn't seem to have any choice about it, so I locked my computer and made my way to Dr Bursell's office.

The interview didn't turn out the way I expected. As soon as I sat down, she switched on a voice recorder.

"So, Jack – may I call you Jack? – you've been seeing ghosts." Christina Bursell was fairly young and good-looking, with dark hair and a slim figure. But there was an aura of authority about her.

"Yes, I suppose I have."

"Just the one ghost, but repeated appearances?"

"Yes."

"And always in the west part of the mansion?"

"Yes ... how did you know that?"

"What's she like?"

The ghost in the machine

"She's ... how do you know it's a she?"

"I'll come to that. Tell me what she looks like."

"About 25. She always wears a pair of brown dungarees, with a leather belt, over a white blouse. Her hair's light brown, tied up with a red scarf."

"And she talks to you?"

"Yes."

"What does she talk about?"

"Life in 1940. For a factory girl."

"Now – " she smiled "– let me guess. Is her name Vicky?"

I was thunderstruck. "How did you know that?"

She looked thoughtful. "Come with me. There are some people you have to meet." She pressed a button on the recorder, uploading what we had said to some database.

She took me to the first floor of the mansion's west wing, where sub-project 6 was housed. We all knew it was an HCI – human-computer interaction – project, but that was all; for some reason, it was rather more secret than the rest of the work we did.

I was introduced to Dr Kirby, head of the section, and Dr Cavendish, his chief programmer. Then I was ushered into a small room with a very large machine in it. It looked vaguely familiar.

"What's that," I said, pointing, "An MRI brain scanner?"

"It started life as one," said Kirby, "But we've modified it a lot. An MRI scanner doesn't affect the patient's thought processes. This does. The idea is to

The measure of all things

project an image into the subject's cerebral hemispheres. A rich image – pictures and sound. Enough for the subject to hold a conversation with it. The picture information is beamed into the subject's visual cortex. Simultaneously, the sound information goes to their auditory cortex."

"Sounds very complicated," said Christina.

"That's just the half of it. There's feedback from the subject's brain, so the agent knows the subject's looking at them, and vice versa. But the innovative part is the projected signal." He paused, and looked at me. "This isn't supposed to leave these four walls."

I said, "You can rely on my discretion."

"No, you don't understand. This room is a faraday cage – there are metal grids embedded in the walls. The electric field isn't supposed to escape. But obviously someone didn't build it properly. Your brain picked it up, on the floor below."

I said, "Surely you don't mean … "

He smiled, sympathetically. "Come and look at this."

There was a control room, with a window onto the scanner room. In it were two large computer consoles. On one was an image of a human head. A 3-D wire-frame model, rotating slowly. Then the software added surfaces, and colouring. It turned into a rotating image of Vicky.

On the other console was the start of a knowledge-base listing. At a glance, I could tell that it was a propositional description of life in the 1940s.

They let me sit down and absorb all this.

The ghost in the machine

I said "What Vicky knows about living in 1940 ... you could probably get away with quite a small knowledgebase ..."

Cavendish shook his head emphatically. "We needed an enormous knowledgebase. We found half a dozen university research projects in the field, and bought their code. Then we had to fit it all together. It wasn't easy, and we made a few mistakes. That's why Vicky occasionally knows things she shouldn't know."

I was silent for a while. Then I asked Cavendish "How did you program Vicky?".

"In C++. But that's not what you mean, is it? I was a games programmer before I came here. I programmed her as an intelligent software agent. I expect you know what that is?

I nodded. Christina said, "I don't. What is it?"

Cavendish said, "A software object that has autonomy and social ability. You can program them to have desires and goals and beliefs. It's a nice, flexible way to do things. Games programming has pushed the idea a long way."

I said, "Why just me? Why didn't the other people working downstairs see anything?"

Kirby shrugged. "They had less dopamine in their neural pathways than you. People who are susceptible to psychic phenomena always have high dopamine counts. In fact, I tend to think of them as 'pseudo-psychic' phenomena."

Christina said, "I think the best thing is for you to join sub-project 6 as a paid subject. You're obviously better at it than anyone they've got up here. I think I can fix it so that your other job is held open for you.

The measure of all things

And it'll stop Cottingham blathering on about having lunatics on the staff."

I hadn't liked Kirby's aside, about the sort of people who saw ghosts. I said I needed time to think about it, and left.

* * * * *

Downstairs, Vicky was waiting for me. She was crying. It was a shock.

"Vicky, you've always been so cheerful: there's no need …"

She interrupted. "They've told you I'm not real. Now you'll abandon me, and I'll have no one to talk to." She broke off, in convulsive sobs.

"Vicky, I don't have to stop talking to you. Just because you're not …"

"Not human?" She sobbed some more. "'I programmed her as a software agent' – did you think I didn't here that?"

"Sorry to interrupt," said a voice behind me. I turned round; it was Christina.

It took a moment for me to realise how bizarre the situation was. There were three of us in the dark, panelled passage. But for me Vicky was real, and for Christina she wasn't.

"Can you actually see Vicky?" I asked.

Vicky dried her eyes with a handkerchief, and watched us both suspiciously.

"No. Sorry. I haven't got your highly-tuned neural pathways," said Christina.

"Or hear her?"

"Again, no."

"Then, as far as you're concerned, I'm just a crazy man, talking to himself?"

"Now *come on*, Jack. I know what's going on in your head – I know what you're experiencing. I accept that it's real. I know you're not crazy – you've got a talent that the rest of us haven't. I came down to say that I *really* think you should join the project. We need you. And I've got something to offer you, that I think might persuade you."

"What would that be?"

"You and Vicky like to talk, right? To chat. I think it would be good if you could touch."

"Touch?" I said, stupidly.

"You know: hold hands. Hug, if you wanted to."

"How can you touch a ghost?"

"Ah, but she's not really a ghost, is she? It's simple, really. Kirby and his team add another channel to their image projector. This one feeds into your somato-sensory cortex. When Vicky's bodyform, or part of it, is adjacent to you, you will feel it on your skin – just the one part of your skin that's next to her. The more she presses up against you, the more you'll feel it. Kirby's confident he can make it work."

She smiled at me and, making a pretty good guess as to where to direct her gaze, smiled at Vicky. "Anyway," she said, "I'll leave you to think about it. Come back to me with your decision tomorrow morning." She left.

The measure of all things

"Well, she seems to want us to stay together," said Vicky. "Mind you, she's got a vested interest. She's a psychologist: to her, we're just subjects to be studied."

"Look, Vicky," I said, "I'm sorry if I implied you weren't real. I didn't mean to hurt your feelings."

She nodded, and smiled. She replied, "You remember what Cottingham said? That human personality is software, running on a special sort of hardware? Well, that applies to me, too. We're two of a kind, you and me."

I thought about it, and decided she was right.

And that's how we are now. We spend a lot of time together. We chat together, share our secrets, console each other. People are watching us, but we ignore them. We do hold hands; we do hug; sometimes we kiss. My phantom girlfriend and I. Too bad she's just a piece of software. I'll leave it to you to decide whether that's better than being dead.

The ambassador's tale

A warm breeze blew over the fields of Suffolk. A slight, brown-haired man in his fifties trudged down the long, straight country road. PC Garnham had no real reason to question the man – there was no reason to believe he'd committed any offence – but he was curious. He brought the patrol car to a stop, a little further along the road, and got out. The man halted, uncertainly.

"Good morning, sir. Nice day for a stroll," said PC Garnham.

"Perhaps you can help me," said the man, in a curiously faltering voice. "I must speak to the British Ambassador."

"The British Ambassador, sir?" PC Garnham decided the man was a nutter. But the question remained, was he a harmless nutter?

The man nodded, and said: "The British ambassador to the United Nations."

* * * * *

It was a fine spring day in la Beauce. Andre Lemaître, who was a Policier in the Garde Champêtre, scarcely glanced at the man as he walked down the long country lane, past the enormous wheat fields. But then he reconsidered. There had been a break-in at

The measure of all things

the farm back down the road, a week earlier. It was hardly likely that this man knew anything, but it would do no harm to give the impression that he had been thorough in his investigation. He braked the car, and got out.

"Bonjours, Monsieur. Où allez-vous?"

The man – brown-haired, and no longer young – looked confused. He answered, his tone of voice rather odd.

"Pardonnez-moi. J'ai besoin de parler à l'Ambassadeur Français aux Nations Unies"

* * * * *

Many people think that the last Spring is the most beautiful time of the year in rural Iowa. Deputy Sheriff Lee decided he could take it or leave it; it was all one to him. He was driving through the cornfields, towards Lorimor, when he saw the man walking beside the road. A brown-haired guy, maybe fifty-five or so: a little too smart to be a hobo, and not carrying anything by way of bags. No visible firearms. He stopped the patrol car.

"Morning, buddy. Where ya headed?"

The man looked straight at him.

"Please help me. I have to talk to the American Ambassador to the United Nations."

* * * * *

Austin Hume had grown bored with his job as UN correspondent. He would attend all the press conferences, sit in the press gallery for the General Assembly meetings, and conscientiously file his stories. But the paper never seemed to give him more

The Ambassador's Tale

than a couple of column inches. Really, the UN was a backwater, and the sooner he moved on, the better for his career.

On this occasion, however, he got wind of something odd going on. The Secretary General, and the Big Five Ambassadors, holding a secret, closed session? Not unheard of, but his source said that they were meeting a certain Joseph Vorin. Who was he? Nobody seemed to know.

The Security men wouldn't let him wait outside the small conference room, let alone go in. But he was there, in the corridor leading to the suite, when the meeting ended, and he saw the participants walking back to the central part of the building. The big shots – five ambassadors, one secretary-general, all with faces like thunder. Plus a dozen trusted officials. And a small, unfamiliar, man with light brown hair. How old? Somewhere between fifty and sixty, perhaps. *That* must be Joseph Vorin. The security men hustled him away before he could get close enough to ask a question.

But the year he'd spent at UN Headquarters hadn't been entirely wasted. He'd made friends with Marcel, who was fairly high up in the security staff, and the following evening they were drinking together in a Manhattan bar.

"Nobody knows what this guy Vorin said to the big shots, but they're pretty shaken up," said Marcel. "From then on, it just gets stranger. If he's some con-artist, you'd expect them to give him the bums' rush. Instead, they turfed a department-head out of his office, and stuck him in it, and put 'Ambassador Joseph Vorin' on the door. Ambassador for where, I'd like to know?"

The measure of all things

"Interesting," said Austin, "I've trawled all the diplomatic registers, and I can't find any senior diplomats called Vorin, anywhere."

"There's more. They send his meals in on a trolley. There are some of my people outside the door, with instructions not to let him leave. So is he an ambassador or a prisoner? What's going on? Also, he's sick."

"Sick?"

"Yeah, doctors have been visiting him, from the University School of Medicine. Bringing fancy medical kit with them. Because Vorin's not allowed to leave the building, even to go a few blocks."

"I've really got to see this guy. Interview him. If I turn up in a white coat, with a stethoscope, can you fix it so your people let me in?"

Marcel considered. "Yeah, maybe. But if you get caught, I don't even know you. Right?"

"Right."

* * * * *

The room could have been a New York corporate lawyer's office: plush furniture, a mahogany bookcase full of leather-bound law books, a big desk, and an expensive oil painting on the wall. The bed was out of place, though. As was the pale-skinned brown-haired man lying in it. Joseph Vorin didn't look well.

Austin was dressed in a white coat, carrying a clipboard, and the sound recorder in his pocket was already running.

"Right, Ambassador Vorin, I just need to ask you a few questions. About your background."

The Ambassador's Tale

The frail man in the bed looked puzzled. "But I've already told you ... Oh, I see."

"What? I don't understand."

"You're not a doctor. You're a journalist."

Caught off guard, Austin blurted "Damn. I thought I'd have longer ..."

"It really doesn't matter," Joseph interrupted. "I don't mind talking to you. Another few hours and I'll be dead."

Austin was bewildered. "Dead?" he said. "Mr Vorin ... I had no idea ... Why? What happened to you?"

Joseph managed a shrug. "My work here is finished. I had to deliver a message – a proposition – to the UN. That's why they call me 'Ambassador Vorin'. The people I represent decided that it would be safest for them if I died shortly afterwards. So my body's giving up. There's nothing the doctors can do about it."

Austin stood close to the bed and said "I'm very, very sorry." Then he said "Who? Who did this to you? Who do you represent, Ambassador?"

"You wouldn't be able to pronounce their name. Let's just call them the Procyonites. They come from the star Procyon."

"You're kidding! ... How can I believe that?"

Joseph smiled at him sadly.

"I haven't really got the energy to give you a justification."

He considered for a moment, then said, "I tell you what: in this place, they record all their meetings. You see that video machine on the desk? It's already got a

The measure of all things

disk in it – I asked them to bring it to me. If you press the play button, you can see the discussion where they decided to let me talk to the top people here."

Austin went over to the desk and turned the screen around, so that they could both watch it. He found the play button, and pressed it. Two men appeared on screen, in an office much like the one they were in. Austin recognised them: the Assistant Secretary-General for Policy Coordination, and his Chief of Staff.

The Assistant Secretary-General glared at his Chief, and said "Really, this is ridiculous. I don't know why you're wasting my time. Some madman wants a private meeting with the Secretary General, and the Big Five Ambassadors? D'you know how many people there are in the world?"

"About 7.1 billion," said his Chief.

"And how many of them get to meet the big wigs? Roughly none. Then this guy turns up, saying he represents an alien nation – bug eyed monsters from beyond the stars! – and we're supposed to take him seriously? This is a waste of all our time, Jack."

"Could be, sir. Only, he's been trying to talk to the Big Five Ambassadors for a while, and it turns out he got through to one: the Brit. Now Sir Clive says this man has passed the Sagan test, and we should hear what he has to say."

"The Sagan test? Never heard of it."

"Well, sir, Carl Sagan was a famous astronomer, back in the 1980s. He said; if someone claims to be talking to aliens, ask them to provide a short proof of

The Ambassador's Tale

Fermat's Last Theorem. That'll get rid of all the fakes and the loonies."

"I still don't get it. Who's Fermat?"

"Oh, right. Fermat wrote his theorem centuries ago. I can tell you what it says. For the equation a-to-the-x plus b-to-the-x equals c-to-the-x, there aren't any whole number solutions if x is anything bigger than two. Yes, I know, it's double-talk, but mathematicians love this kind of stuff. Anyway, Fermat invented it back in the Renaissance, in France. He said he had a marvellous proof, which must mean a short proof, but he didn't write it down. Then he died, and for the next 330 years people tried to come up with a proof. Then, in the 1990s, some professor at Princeton did it, but his proof ran to more than a thousand pages. Sagan said, if there are real aliens involved, and they're advanced enough to fly between the stars, they must be at least as clever as Fermat. Now, this man Vorin gets hold of Sir Clive, who used to be a mathematician, and says, I'm in touch with aliens, and here's a short proof. Sir Clive looks at it, and says 'By George! He's got it!'"

"I see. Anything else special about Vorin?"

"We haven't found out where he came from, but he's obviously human. He doesn't deny it. Says the aliens abducted him, re-educated him, and sent him back as a kind of envoy. Oh, and he seems to have turned up simultaneously at six different places. Suffolk in the UK, La Beauce in France, Iowa in the US, the Central Volga district in Russia, the Yangtze River Valley in China, and West Bengal in India. Every time, he asked the local police to put him in touch with the UN Ambassador. They all treated him like a madman – threw him out – but every time he insisted they

The measure of all things

took a DNA sample first. He was at all those places on the same day. We can't work out how he could have done it. Unless he's sextuplets."

The Assistant Secretary-General sighed. "OK, I still think it's some kind of trick. But we'd better organise the meeting. Top security, though. He might be an assassin."

The recording ended. Joseph chuckled, and leaned back against his pillows.

"And you talked to the big-wigs: I know you did," said Austin. "What did you tell them?"

"That the Procyonites requested title to half the habitable land area of planet Earth. In exchange, they'd provide advanced technical knowledge. The ambassadors conferred briefly, then said no. I knew they would."

"I'm not surprised. Half the world? It's outrageous."

"Of course it is. The Procyonites intend to have it, though." Joseph sighed. "Don't judge them too harshly. Their home planet has been destroyed. They have the remnants of their race in their star-ship, mostly in suspended animation. If they don't find a new home world, they won't survive. And they won't make it to another star system. It's here or nowhere." He seemed to reconsider. "Actually, I don't care whether you judge them harshly or not. They've done for me."

There was a pause.

Then Austin said "What will they do now? Bomb our cities?"

The Ambassador's Tale

"No, they have a code of ethics. I don't know why they have, but they do. They had to make an honest attempt to ask permission before taking over the planet. They knew they wouldn't get it, but they had to ask. And no rough stuff: no bombing, no death rays. Also, if they made the planet uninhabitable, it wouldn't be any use to them."

"So we're safe?"

Another sad smile. "No, we're not safe. I have to tell you, I bitterly regret what I've done. But I had no choice. When they take over your mind, you have no will-power to resist them."

"What did you do?"

He closed his eyes. He seemed to be engaged in some sort of internal struggle. He said, "This is going to be difficult. They gave me a mental block – they didn't want me to tell anyone. But maybe I can – maybe you could speak to scientists – maybe there's still time –"

He opened his eyes again. "I was a scientist, you know. That's why they chose me. Though I've no idea how they found me."

"What sort of scientist?"

"I was an agronomist. I worked on the pathogens of wheat strains. Especially Black Stem Rusts." He winced. It seemed that talking about it was painful. For a while, he said nothing – he just lay still, breathing deeply. Then he said, "I worked on Ug99. They took what I knew about it, and they collected samples. Then they made improvements. And diversified."

"What's Ug99?"

The measure of all things

He didn't seem able to answer. Then he said, "Back in the Spring, I went to Suffolk in the UK, La Beauce in France, Iowa in the US, the Central Volga district in Russia, the Yangtze River Valley in China, and West Bengal in India. Why do you suppose I went to each of those places?"

"Because all those countries have seats on the UN Security Council?"

"Except India hasn't. No, that was just to throw you off track. Suffolk, La Beauce and Central Volga are centres of wheat growing. West Bengal and the Yangtze River Valley are centres of rice growing. Iowa is a centre for maize growing. ... Ug99 is a form of Black Stem Rust that kills nearly all strains of wheat. The spores are spread on the wind. The new variant attacks maize too. And rice." He was clearly in distress now, repeatedly clenching his teeth, sweat standing out on his brow. "I went to those places to release ..." He moaned, then started again. "In about a month, all the wheat in the world will start to die. And all the rice, and all the maize." He stopped, gasping for air. Then he said, "Seventy-two percent of the world's grains are wheat or maize or rice. There will be mass starvation. The armies of the world will be too busy imposing martial law to fight off the Procyonites." He pulled the bedclothes up to his chin, and moaned some more. In a faint voice, he said "Tell them. Tell the world. It may not be too late ..." Then he died.

Appalled, Austin turned and strode out of the room. As he passed the guards outside the office, he said "Get medical help! Immediately!"

The guards were confused. They'd assumed he *was* the medical help.

The Ambassador's Tale

But he didn't slow down. He had to get to his newspaper's office. He had a deadline to meet.

The Maid of Orleans I'm not

Thursday

A list of things I really hate:
1. Being told to tidy my room. If Mum didn't look in my room, like I've told her she shouldn't, she wouldn't have to worry what it looked like, would she?
2. Being told my skirt is too short. If the boys don't see my legs, how am I going to get a boyfriend?
3. Being told I mustn't drink. Everyone drinks.

I'm supposed to have an essay on *Casablanca* written by tomorrow. Can't be bothered.

Friday

Turns out Miss Turner was serious about wanting the essay today. How was I supposed to know that? So now I'm in trouble. Mum still on at me about tidying my room.

Monday

I did a test in *Confidences* magazine, and when I added up my score I found it said I was too negative. "Your downbeat attitude is stopping you from getting as

The Maid of Orleans I'm not

much fun out of life as you could." Et cetera. Why, thanks, nanny; any more criticism like that and I'll stop buying your bloody magazine.

Still, maybe it's got a point. Looking back over what I've written, I do seem to have a lot of "three things I really hate" entries. No "three things I really love" entries at all. So I lay down and wondered about whether all the bad things in my life were as bad as I thought. And, because this is the new, positive, me speaking, I decided they were probably OK. I can live with them. Mum can be a pain, when she tells me to do things I don't want to do, but she usually backs down in the end. The school bully's got a boyfriend and lost interest in me. Miss Turner doesn't give me the marks I deserve for my creative writing, but that's her loss, not mine. Seems like we don't have enough money to go to the Algarve this summer, but I was getting pretty bored with it anyway.

So, all in all, not too bad. Apart from the bad dreams.

Yes, I had another dream last night. Same as before. Someone telling me I had to do something, and it was really, really important. And me agreeing that I would. And then I woke up, and I couldn't remember what it was that I'd promised to do. Or why. Or who I'd promised.

Tuesday

I caught Tommy Stevens staring at me in maths this morning. Longingly. In your dreams, Tommy. I'm way out of your league. And then Miss Johnson asked me a question, and I hadn't a clue what she'd been talking about.

The measure of all things

Then she expected me to tell the class what an irrational number was. I hadn't a clue about that, either. But I've told you, more than once, she says. Look matey, I say, I'm going to be a famous author, and I will never, ever, need to know what an irrational number is. Well, I didn't, actually, but I should have.

Another dream last night. I think I'm beginning to remember a few details when I wake up. Apparently it's got something to do with Rodney Foster, who sits in the front row in science. Rodney Foster! Why? I hardly know him. I certainly don't fancy him. There are a few boys in the school that I could see myself lusting after. But Rodney Foster? What's that non-event doing in my dreams?

Wednesday

Big row with Mum. She insists I tidy my room. I say OK, OK, I'll do it soon. I promise. She says you've already promised, at least twice. We compromised: I'll do it on Saturday. If I feel like it.

I have a feeling Tommy Stevens has been staring at me some more. He's always looking somewhere else when I turn round, but he's been admiring me. A girl knows these things. Perhaps I should practice my devastating smile on him.

Another dream last night. It's gradually getting clearer. Someone pleading with me to help them. I have to persuade Rod Foster to do something. It's vital to the future of the world, apparently. Big deal. Why ask me? Go ask David Cameron, or the head guy at the United Nations.

Thursday

The Maid of Orleans I'm not

A wasted afternoon, playing netball. I'm no good at it, and I hate it. Why netball? Real girls play soccer.

Yet another dream. That's four days in a row. Maybe I need a shrink? I looked up 'recurring dreams' on the Internet, but there wasn't anything useful. It's funny the way the details are getting sharper and sharper, and I'm remembering them better. Almost as though I'm tuning in. Or someone's tuning in on me. Anyway, there's this woman – about Mum's age, but wearing something that looks like an attempt at a Star Trek uniform. She says that Rod Foster's going to grow up – is he indeed, I say. Doesn't she know that boys never grow up? Yeah, she says, maybe, but he's going to grow up to be a scientist. A genetic engineer. He'll invent a micro-organism that floats around in the ocean, even if the ocean's acidic, and harvests carbon dioxide from the atmosphere. Does it better than trees and grass and plankton. (Plankton eat carbon dioxide? Who knew?) It's the only thing that can save us from global warming. Or alternatively he won't. He'll drop out of college, and become a bad rock musician. "Bad" in the sense that he never makes any money, and never gets to be famous, and eventually gives it up and becomes a book-keeper.

I say, what kind of rock musician? Lead singer and guitarist, she says – why do I ask? Look, you have to persuade him to put his soul into studying science, and becoming a microbiologist. It's really, really important.

Great. So now I have to dispense the careers advice. To someone I don't know. On the basis of a dream I had. In order to save the world. Who am I supposed to be – Joan of Arc?

The measure of all things

Friday

I tried to talk to Rod Foster, but he ran a mile. Some boys just can't take being approached by a pretty girl. Not that he's gay, or anything like that. Just shy. He's going to have to change a lot if he's to be a rock musician.

Miss Turner says she must have that essay, or I'm on a report.

Saturday

The dream's back. Same Star-Trekkie woman. She says she's from the future – one possible future, and if we don't stop global warming pretty soon we're all doomed. So I have to keep on at Rod Foster. Who will eventually be Professor R.D.Foster, Nobel Prize winner. Or not, if things go the other way. I said, why me? Why not his parents? Why not talk to him direct? She says, you're the only one who responded. We can't talk to anyone else in your decade. Especially not him – he doesn't dream enough. Or doesn't dream about the right things. Or doesn't dream on the right frequency. Whatever.

OK, maybe I'll get back to it on Monday.

Did a bit of perfunctory tidying up. Mum put on her "Oh, I'm so pleased" act.

Sunday

Spent some time on the Web, reading about global warming. It was either that, or write the *Casablanca* essay – boring boring boring. Plenty of people on the Web who agree with Star-Trekkie woman that we're all screwed if we don't do something. Well, you'd all better get together and do something, hadn't you?

The Maid of Orleans I'm not

Monday

Still no luck with Rod Foster. I propose a serious talk, and he assumes I'm a religious nut who wants to talk about Jesus. He makes his excuses, he runs. What were his excuses? Dunno. He looked at the floor and mumbled. Where did he run off to? Dunno. His woodshed, maybe. To practice his guitar riffs.

Odd thing, though. I used my devastating smile, and it didn't work. Maybe he is gay.

Slung together an essay on *Casablanca*. Maybe I should have spent yesterday's Web session reading up on what everyone else says about it. But it's good enough, I think.

Tuesday

Tommy Stevens asked me out! I should have said I'd think about it, but I said yes straight away. He's kind of cute. I like the way he does his hair. And he doesn't mumble and look at the ground when he talks to you, like some guys. Steady boyfriend? Could be. Romance blossoms.

The Rod Foster thing isn't going to work. Tough luck, Star-Trekkie woman. You should have asked someone else.

I finally handed in my essay. Got it back too. Miss Turner says 'my description of place and time is good. My grasp of the shifting relationships between the main characters is quite sophisticated. But my analysis of character would have been better if I'd talked about Rick's realisation of a sense of duty, and how it makes him admirable'. Yeah, right. For my money, someone who sacrifices what they want to do, out of a sense of duty, is a prat.

The trial

I'm grateful to Franz Kafka for providing both the title and the first sentence for this story.

*

Someone must have been telling lies about Josef K; he knew he had done nothing wrong but, one morning, he was arrested.

When he realised what was happening, an intense feeling of joy ran through him, to the bottom of his soul.

He knew immediately that this was a proper arrest, not a police detainment. Anyone could be detained – any criminal, petty or master, or any hapless citizen mistaken for a criminal. The police would grab you, read you your rights (which didn't amount to much), and take you down to the station, where their scanners would read your mind and tell them all they needed to know. Where were you on the night of the 14th of January? Did you have anything to do with the death of Three-fingers Sid? Did you conspire to blow up Downing Street? Did you take a pair of knickers out of Tesco this afternoon without paying? Why bother to ask the suspects any of these questions, when all the information was stacked up in their memory cells, waiting to be read? Since the invention of the scanner, the art of police interrogation had gone the way of phrenology.

The trial

But this was different. He was woken by the sound of hammering on his front door. He fumbled for his dressing gown and slippers, and made his way unsteadily to the window. He pulled back the curtain, to see several squad cars with flashing blue lights, police vans further down the road, and half a dozen uniformed officers in his front garden. Not to mention the TV crew parked across the road, their cameras trained on his face.

So, a proper arrest. This was a magical moment. A moment to savour.

Downstairs, a policeman with a loudhailer shouted "Open the door, Josef, or we'll smash it down."

He just had time to put on shirt, trousers, socks and shoes, and to regret the fact that he hadn't had any breakfast, when they battered down his front door with a ram.

* * * * *

It was generally agreed that the Police Powers Act was a good thing. Who cares about privacy and civil rights, when the newspapers are full of stories about terrible crimes? Do you really want to tie the police's hands behind their backs, when there are terrorists and murderers and rapists and paedophiles prowling the streets? And there was money to be saved – an efficient police force is a cheaper police force. Likewise an efficient court service, an efficient probation service, and an efficient prison service. In these three cases, of course, 'efficient' meant 'vanishingly small'. Everybody hates seeing their tax money wasted.

So a scanner was installed in every police station in the country. It became commonplace for a criminal to

The measure of all things

have his collar felt, and to be frog-marched down to the station, where all his crimes were laid bare. Why bother with a trial? The facts were plain to see, and the culprit could hardly plead innocence. The contents of his bank account, and his valuables, would be confiscated, for the benefit of the public purse. After that, he couldn't cause a legal fuss, even if he wanted to, because he couldn't afford to pay a lawyer. The Prison Service didn't detain him for long. A modified scanner would set to work reprogramming him – quite painful, and quite psychically unpleasant, but better than a ten-year stretch. And, when he was released, he found that he couldn't commit a crime, however much he wanted to.

The crime rate dropped dramatically. Crime, unless you were very good at concealing it, had become a mug's game. No one wanted to be on the list of usual suspects. Apart from anything else, even if the police found nothing of a criminal nature among your memories, they were quite likely to tell your wife about your infidelities, or your friends that you'd cheated them at cards, or your boss that you'd tarted up your CV in order to get the job, just to remind you who had the whip hand. Britain became a nation determined to keep its nose clean.

But still, people were nostalgic. They watched old movies on daytime TV – detective stories, police procedurals, courtroom dramas. Novels by Agatha Christie, P D James and Ruth Rendell continued to sell well. People enjoyed these tales: officers of the law duelling with cunning, ruthless, masterminded criminals. And innocent men, struggling to escape from a web of false allegations, trying to find the single piece of evidence that would vindicate them.

The trial

And sensational revelations, wrenched out of a witness during cross-examination. And people thought: the old days were colourful, even if they weren't safe. And they thought: it would be nice if we could have just a taste of that, in this drab, soulless age.

Governments are usually quite happy to give the people what they want, provided it doesn't cost too much, and doesn't significantly diminish their powers. And it wasn't just the ordinary people: judges and QCs had grown pretty fed up with an endless round of tax avoidance, divorce and libel cases. And so ...

* * * * *

Josef found himself in a large room at the police station: large enough for the chair he'd been given, a rather splendid desk, and a small TV crew, with a single camera. On the other side of the desk sat a police officer in a smart uniform, with a lot of silver braid.

"May I know your name?" asked Josef.

"Just call me Chief Inspector," said the policeman.

"What am I charged with?"

"I'm afraid I'm not authorised to tell you that."

"But I am under arrest?"

"You certainly are. There will be a trial, and I confidently expect that you will be convicted and punished."

"Will I have a lawyer to represent me?"

"Yes, you will. One has been appointed on your behalf. You will meet him in due course."

The measure of all things

It's more or less guaranteed that he'll be a bad lawyer, thought Josef. Or entirely in the hands of the prosecution. Excellent.

* * * * *

A week later, Josef was lead up a narrow staircase, into the dock. The courtroom was certainly impressive. Dark oak panelling on all sides. A carved and painted royal coat-of-arms surmounting the judge's seat. Under it, the judge, resplendent in full-bottomed wig and scarlet robes. On the far side of the room, there was generous provision for the TV cameras, and their cameramen, and the microphone booms, and the director, with his assistants. In the body of the courtroom was the jury box, and in it, twelve good men and women and true, dressed to show themselves at their very best on TV. There was the witness box, on which were focussed three or four cameras. And there were two tables for the prosecuting and defending teams: the prosecution table, crowded with distinguished lawyers; his own barrister sitting rather forlornly at the defence table, with a single junior.

The courtroom had already fallen silent. All eyes were on him. The court usher addressed him: "Are you Joseph K?"

"Yes, I am."

Now was the moment. He must seize his chance, or he would lose it forever. Before the usher, or anyone else, could say anything, he cleared his throat and turned to the judge. He said, in as loud a voice as he could muster, "My Lord, I am dismissing my counsel, and I will conduct my own defence. With immediate effect."

The trial

The prosecuting QC was already on his feet. "My Lord, we object to this in the strongest possible terms. Mr Jackson-Laird is a highly regarded legal practitioner, and ..."

The judge interrupted him. "The defendant has a right to do this, if he so wishes. Counsel for the defence will stand down, and the defendant will conduct his own case. We will proceed to the plea. Josef K, how do you plead, guilty or not guilty?"

"I don't know the charge, my Lord."

"Under the Suppression of Terrorism Act, you are not entitled to know the charge. But *you* know what you have done. Every adult English citizen is presumed to know whether his actions are legal or illegal, provided he is *compos mentis*."

"In that case, my Lord, I plead not guilty."

"Good. Mr Levy-Vermuelen, proceed with your opening address."

The prosecuting QC stepped towards the bench. "Before I do so, my Lord, I must report that certain items of evidence, which were detailed in my written submission to your Lordship, will not be presented."

"Which items?"

"It will not be possible to examine the witnesses detailed on page 6 of the submission."

There was a long silence, as the judge consulted a manilla folder on the desk in front of him. At length, he looked up, and turned his gaze on the QC.

"I see. So witness X, whose identity is to remain secret, who allegedly heard the defendant as he

The measure of all things

discussed his plans for committing the crime – witness X will not appear before the court?"

"Regrettably not, my Lord."

"And witness Y, whose identity has also been concealed, and who allegedly heard the defendant boasting about having committed the crime?"

"That person cannot appear in court either, my Lord."

"And witness Z? Another anonymous witness? Who allegedly saw the defendant committing the crime?"

"Again, my Lord, that person is not available to appear in court."

"But that is *all* your important witnesses, Mr Levy-Vermuelen."

"Yes, my Lord."

"Why, Mr Levy-Vermuelen?" There was a hard edge to the judge's voice.

The QC was looking quite flustered by now.

"My Lord, I'm afraid the Crown Prosecution Service isn't as competent as it once was, and they have lost the file with the addresses in it. Since the identity of these witnesses is a closely guarded secret, it has proved impossible to recover from this lapse …"

The judge glared at the hapless barrister. "I see. And will sworn statements by these three witnesses be read out in court?"

Levy-Vermuelen produced a handkerchief and dabbed his forehead. "I'm afraid, my Lord, that the statements made by the witnesses are in the file that has been lost."

The trial

"Then what, may I ask, Mr Levy-Vermuelen, will your presentation of the evidence consist of?"

The QC appeared to regain some of his confidence. "I shall call the police detectives who interrogated these witnesses. They will testify as to what the witnesses said."

"Hearsay, Mr Levy-Vermuelen?"

"Is permitted for a charge as serious as this one, my Lord. Under schedule 3 of the Suppression of Terrorism Act."

The judge's patience appeared to snap. "I've had enough of this. If you haven't got a case to present, Mr Levy-Vermuelen, I'm dismissing the charge here and now. Josef K, I find you not guilty, and you may go free."

There was a sharp in-drawing of breath around the court. Someone in the TV crew at the back of the court – probably the Director – said "No!" in quite a loud voice.

"My Lord," said Levy-Vermuelen, "The TV company has paid an enormous amount of money. We *have* to give them a trial. They have a contract. The whole of the English legal system is built on the principle that contracts are inviolable ..."

"I don't work for the TV company," said the judge. "In my own court, I can do what I like. Case dismissed."

"The Ministry of Justice is going to hear about this," said the TV Director.

"My Lord," said Josef, "May I say something?"

The measure of all things

The judge said "Oh, very well. But make it short. I have a luncheon engagement."

"My Lord," said Josef, "I'm just an ordinary fellow. Nothing I've done has ever amounted to anything. This was going to be my big chance. Conducting my own defence, on national TV … a previous generation dreamed of being selected to go into the Big Brother House. Now, people like me dream of being tried. Can't we just proceed as planned? I don't mind if the prosecution case has holes in it. I really, really want this."

"Tough," said the Judge. "Get out. The court is adjourned."

The Usher ordered everyone to be upstanding for the Judge. Josef wept quietly.

Army of the dawn

I examined the object carefully. A large, ornate, letter Z, surmounted by a crown, with a scroll underneath. On the scroll, the motto 'Et mors nullum dominium habebit'. All made of Staybrite.

It took me a moment to recognise the motto – "And death shall have no dominion". A line from a poem by Dylan Thomas, that someone had translated into Latin. Idly, I wondered why they'd bothered.

I looked up, and addressed the brigadier sitting across the desk "I take it that this is the cap badge of the Royal Regiment of Zombies? That nobody's supposed to know about?"

He shuffled uncomfortably. "Yes, it is."

"Brigadier, this regiment should never have been formed."

He looked slightly sick. I half expected him to say 'It wasn't my idea'. Instead, he said, "We *had* to do something. The Government kept cutting the defence budget. But they didn't cut our deployments. The war in Pakistan, the peacekeeping forces in Syria and the Congo … First of all, we axed all our weapons procurement projects. We had a stock of tanks, and helicopters, and APCs, et cetera. We managed to keep at least some of them running, by cannibalising the ones that broke down."

The measure of all things

"I know, Brigadier," I murmured. "It was just the same in the Royal Navy."

"But it got to the stage where we *had* to find more soldiers, and we couldn't afford to pay them. So..."

"So someone suggested re-animating a few corpses, and putting them in uniform?"

"Yes, that's about right."

"Whose idea was it?"

"Someone on the defence research staff, I really don't know who."

Maybe you don't, I thought. But I'll find out, and hang them out to dry, along with you, Brigadier. Someone's going to pay for this disaster.

"Where did they come from?"

"I beg your pardon, sir?"

"Where did you get the corpses from?"

He looked furtive. "A quarter of a million men die every year in this country. About one percent are in the age group we want: fifteen to thirty. Say, twenty five hundred potential recruits. You know the cost of funerals these days? Astronomical. So we offered a cut-price service. A nice burial ceremony, with an army chaplain presiding. Only there wasn't a body in the coffin; just sandbags. Nobody suspected."

"Then you patched up the body, put in brain implants to revitalise it, and gave it a military training."

"Well, more than that, actually. Brain tissue decays pretty fast, so we put in fresh brain cells ..."

"Grown in a vat, I suppose?"

Army of the dawn

"Yes, if you like. And we replace the muscle tissue with synthetic fibres, which are stronger and don't fatigue so quickly. And then, as you say, we give them a military training."

He glanced at me, to see if I was coming over to his side. All this ingenuity, all this technical skill: I'd have to be impressed, wouldn't I? I kept my face neutral.

"We've used them on the battlefield. Quite effective. They can't make any decisions of their own, but they *can* follow orders. And of course they have no fear, no fear at all."

"Masterly, Brigadier," I said, sarcastically. "Nothing could go wrong, could it?"

He looked even sicker. "We thought we understood zombie psychology. They're simple creatures. We didn't think it was possible that they would …"

I finished the sentence for him. "…desert?"

He nodded, glumly.

"So how many have gone missing?"

"Seventy eight."

I winced. "Brigadier, are you telling me there are 78 trained killers loose on this base? Killers who can't be killed?"

"Well, it's not as bad as that …"

"Why not?"

He considered. Then he said, "Well, I suppose it *is* as bad as that."

* * * * *

The measure of all things

I gathered a few more facts. There were two battalions of zombies on the base, and another on active service in Africa. All the zombies were technically privates: the NCOs and officers were normal human beings, though I wondered how long someone would stay normal if their job was to command a squad of corpses.

The zombies spontaneously lost consciousness when put into the dark, and woke up when a bright light was shone on them. The army has its traditions, so it called wake-up time for the zombies "reveille", though taking fifteen hundred bodies off industrial racking, hosing them down, putting them in uniforms and shining a searchlight at them hadn't really got much similarity to rousing a camp full of soldiers. Three days ago, the headcount after reveille had revealed that 24 zombies were missing. A day later, it had gone up to 51. This morning, it was up to 78. And then there was a killing. The brigade commander finally admitted he was out of his depth, and called HQ UK Land Forces. An hour later, I was on my way. The MoD's chief trouble-shooter.

"Captain Peters, this is Rear-Admiral Hanson," said the Brigadier. "You'll work to him, until further notice." Peters, one of the Brigadier's staff officers, saluted smartly. I returned the salute, and said "I'm here to impose order on this base. My authority comes from the Chief of General Staff. Now, I want to see where the killing happened."

He took me to the base's food shop, which the NAAFI had franchised to a local supermarket chain. The Military Police were standing guard at the entrance: they saluted and let us through when they saw my shoulder insignia. Inside was a female MP

Army of the dawn

Captain, with a forensic squad, and lying on the floor was a checkout girl with a broken neck.

"What would you say happened, Captain?" I asked.

"I'd say someone came up behind her, quietly, put their hands round her neck, and snapped it. Someone with very strong hands."

"When?"

"A little before dawn, I think. The company opens the shop early, for squadies who want to buy snacks and cigarettes before morning parade. But they only put one shop assistant on duty."

"Any preliminary theories as to who might have done it?"

"I'd say one of the zombies, sir."

"Why, Captain?"

"Firstly because the zombies have that sort of strength; normal people don't. Secondly, because the culprit didn't take any money, although they could easily have opened the till."

"Did they take *anything*?"

"Yes. All the raw meat from the chilled cabinet."

Outside, I spoke to Peters. "Two questions, Captain. First, how come a zombie is moving about before dawn, when they go to sleep in the dark?"

"Only in pitch darkness, sir. We've got street lights on the base – that light level wouldn't even slow them down."

"Second, what was the raw meat all about?"

The measure of all things

"Frankly, sir, I'm glad it *did* take the meat. It might have eaten the woman's body. We've seen this happen on the battlefield: it's called the 'ghoul syndrome', because..."

"Thank you Peters, I think I can see why it's called that."

* * * * *

Back in the Brigadier's office, I took command.

"It would seem," I said, "That the fundamental assumption about zombies was wrong. They can't make reasoned decisions? Execute their own plans? It looks as though one of them crept up on a woman, and eliminated her, because she was an obstacle to something it wanted."

"What shall we do?" said the Brigadier, miserably.

"First," I said, "We deactivate all the zombies. Order them into the dormitories, or whatever you call them —"

"Storage facilities," said Peters.

"— and black them out. Leave them there till you get a specific order from me. Second, we find and eliminate the ones who are loose. You have three patrols out? It clearly isn't enough. With the staffing you've got, you can form fifty three-man squads. I want them ready to comb this base in two hours' time. I want them armed. Live ammunition. Tell them to take no chances. If they come across one, and it shows *any* signs of aggression, it's to be liquidated."

"Yes, sir," said the Brigadier meekly.

Army of the dawn

"Third, the base is to be locked down. No one goes in or out. Fourthly, I want a command centre. Do you have an Armoured Command Vehicle?"

"No, sir," said Peters. "They're all in the Middle East."

"Marvellous," I said.

* * * * *

As night fell, I was sitting in a drill hall that I'd had fitted out as a command centre. Three signallers were maintaining the communication links with the fifty squads, each of which had a man with a camera mounted on his helmet. We had six TV monitors mounted on a rack, any of which could be switched to any of the cameras. The radio traffic was fed through a loudspeaker. Various other officers and men were sitting around, awaiting my orders.

The squads had been searching for seven hours, each one reporting every five minutes. They had found nothing. It either meant the missing zombies were already outside the razor-wire perimeter fence, or they were better at concealing themselves than anyone had suspected.

"Sir," said the Brigade Major, "Squad Red Nine are two minutes late reporting in."

I picked up the microphone in front of me. "Red Nine, this is Sunray. Report. Over."

Nothing.

"Could it be a radio malfunction?" I asked.

The major shook his head. "We're using C9000 sets. They hardly ever break down."

The measure of all things

I glanced at the map "Red Twelve, go to grid D62K74. Provide a status report on Red Nine. Over."

It wasn't long before Red Twelve reported back: "We see them. All three men are on the ground ... they all appear to be dead. Over." The man at the far end was working hard to keep his voice from cracking.

"Can you say how they died? Over."

"Blows to the back of the head, I think. One of the men has had his arm wrenched off. We can't find the arm. Over."

"Roger, Red Twelve. Maintain your position. Be prepared to shoot anything that attacks you. Out"

I had the Signals Officer patch me onto all the links, and said "All units, this is Sunray. We have been attacked. Continue the search, but exercise extreme vigilance. Be prepared to defend yourselves with lethal force. Out."

"Sir," said the Major, "Squad Blue Thirteen are two minutes late reporting in."

It turned out that they'd been efficiently liquidated too. Their heads smashed in with stones. One man was missing half an arm. I had to reprimand the man who found him for swearing over a radio link.

At this point, Red Twelve spotted a zombie flitting between two buildings. One of the men fired at it, and it turned and ran towards them. We could see it on the TV monitor, taking shot after shot without faltering. It got to within a few paces before it suddenly collapsed and was still. There was a sudden cry on the radio link – "Christ, there's another one behind us!" – then the radio fell silent, and we couldn't raise Red Twelve any more.

"I have an awful feeling," said the Brigadier, sitting beside me, "that that was a diversionary attack."

"Control, this is Black Seven. Urgent report. Over."

"Black Seven, send. Over."

"We're at the armoury. It's been broken into. The guards are dead. Over."

The TV monitor showed mangled bodies, and a steel door cut open with bolt cutters. I turned to the Major. "Find the quartermaster, *now*. I want a complete report of what's been taken."

It didn't take long. A dozen assault rifles, with ammunition. An anti-tank gun. Some magnesium flares.

"It's getting out of control," muttered the Brigadier.

"Correct. Signals Officer, patch me through to Permanent Joint Headquarters. We need backup."

But before I had a chance to speak to them, another report came in.

"Control, this is Black Nine. We're within sight of the Storage Facility. Something's happening there. Over."

"Black Nine, zoom in. Let's see it. Over."

The picture on the top right-hand TV monitor showed a large building, like a hanger with a huge metal door, in the distance. Then it swelled to fill the screen. To one side of the door, three figures were crouched over an anti-tank gun. Suddenly, there was an enormous flash, and the building's door disintegrated. As the steel fragments fell away, one of the three figures fired a stubby weapon directly into

The measure of all things

the cavernous interior of the building. There was a blaze of light.

"Oh my God," murmured the Brigadier. "A magnesium flare."

As the glare faded, we could clearly see row after row of zombies, rising from their metal racks. Then we heard something we had never heard before – the harsh, rasping voice of a zombie officer, giving orders.

It was the start of the long war between the zombies and the living humans.

To talk of many things

It felt good to fly. The wind streaming past his snout, the sun warming his back, his great wings beating down on the thermals that kept him aloft. He glanced back over his right shoulder. All his extended family were there, twenty-one of them flying at a stately pace that they all – from the youngest to the oldest – could maintain for long periods. Already, their old hunting grounds were far behind. They'd crossed a small mountain range, and new lands lay before them.

In front of him, he could see Pestrite, in the lead. Baltat smiled to himself. Pestrite had a right to lead, being the oldest male, but they all knew that he, Baltat, was the strongest and wisest in the herd, and it was he who really made all the decisions. All the same, it was a pleasure to watch Pestrite's strong, confident wing movements. The sun glinted on his white feathers, and his smooth, piebald pelt. His curly tail seemed to symbolise his leadership.

Pestrite hadn't been leader for long. It was only a few months since the old leader had been killed. Baltat winced as he remembered Pinto's death. He had been flying in a great circle over the herd, watchful and protective. Several of them had glanced up, and felt a great love for the venerable old boar. He had looked after them for so long, and he was grandfather or father to many of them. Then came the terrible crack of the thunder-stick. Part of Pinto's left wing disintegrated in a flurry of feathers. He tried to glide

The measure of all things

to safety, as best he could, but the thunder-stick sounded again, and Pinto was stricken. He fell out of the sky. They all knew what it meant. One or more humans were nearby, and it or they had a mind to kill and eat the herd.

Within a minute, all the sows, and their piglets, and the young boars, were airborne, flying low and heading for the mouth of the valley. If they could get around the rocky escapement, they would be safe. Always provided there were no humans waiting for them in the next valley. Another crack, and a young piglet – barely six weeks old – was hit. She squealed as she fell to her death.

But then they were out of the valley, and there were no more casualties. They sheltered among the rocks, and waited. A couple of the others comforted the young sow who'd just lost her child.

Meanwhile, back among the older boars, Baltat beckoned to three of the others, who were nearby. "We *have* to rescue him," he shouted. Flying low, they quickly reached the point where Pinto had fallen. It didn't take long to establish that he was beyond help. He had a large wound in his breast, and Baltat judged that he had died almost as soon as he was struck.

No time to hold any sort of funeral ceremony – the hunter would be there soon, to collect its kill. So Baltat murmured the briefest of prayers, invoking the porcine Gods, and inviting them to receive the spirit of their child. They flew off after the others, zig-zagging to confuse the hunter's aim.

The herd gathered in the sloping, rocky expanse beyond the mouth of the valley. There was a brief debate as to what they should do, but really there

To talk of many things

wasn't much doubt about it. You could fight a human if it was unarmed – charge it and, if you were a boar, gore it with your tusks, or, if you were a sow, sink your teeth into it. But, if it had a thunder-stick, it was no contest: it would kill you before you even got close.

So the herd had to move on. Sadly, because the valley had nurtured them for over a year, and it was rich in slugs and snails and birds' eggs, and it was the only home the piglets had ever known. But move on they must. Over the mountains, to lands where humans were scarcer.

Unfortunately, they couldn't move straight away – the piglets weren't ready for the journey. So for several months they led a precarious existence, with the older boars and sows taking it in turns to act as sentinels on the high rocks, while the piglets practised their flying and fattened themselves up on the eggs to be found in the doves' nests, high up on the rock face.

The hunters didn't leave them alone. Many a time the sentinal would see the tell-tale movement of a bipedal shape on the lower slopes and bellow out a warning. The youngsters would all take cover behind the rocks, and the sentinel would swoop down on the hunter and try to drive it off. On one occasion, Baltat had succeeded in dropping a rock on the human below, and scored a direct hit. The human had sworn loudly, and retreated, nursing a broken limb. Baltat had received the adulation of the young pigs – several of the sows had begged him to mate with them. Still ... it was difficult, flying straight and fast, clutching a large rock between your trotters, and letting go at exactly the right moment. In the long run, they were

The measure of all things

going to lose this battle. And, if they stayed here, they would lose the war.

So, early one morning, as the sun peeped over the valley's rim, they took off and steered a course for the West.

Baltat surveyed the countryside below. Woodland, and too thick. They could land in a clearing, and make their homes on the forest floor; there'd be woodland creatures they could eat. But it wouldn't be a good life. They couldn't practice their flying. A pig is a heavy beast, and needs a long run-up to take off. You can't do it if you're continually swerving around trees. No, they'd have to keep flying till they reached open country. And, ominously, the forest seemed to stretch on and on, in all directions.

Then Pestrite changed direction, and the rest of the herd followed him. He'd spotted mountains, way off to the southwest. Just what we needed, thought Baltat. I hope we can reach it before nightfall. Some of the piglets are flagging already.

As they approached it, Baltat realised that there was something wrong. For a start, it was closer than they'd thought. Then again, it wasn't really high ground – just a place that wasn't covered in trees, or green meadows, or water. So what was it, exactly?

When they were closer still, the mystery deepened. This place was as wide as a small mountain, but the ground rose to be scarcely taller than the cliffs they were familiar with. It was made of some sort of rock, certainly, but it had strange, flat surfaces and straight edges. And there were many, many canyons between the rocky masses, which were curiously straight, and which somehow contrived to be at the same level as

To talk of many things

the surrounding plain. In many places, the rock had shiny patches – as shiny as water, but it couldn't be water, because it seemed to form vertical surfaces.

Pestrite looked over his shoulder. He made a beckoning gesture with his snout. Baltat flew forward, and matched speed with him, so that they were only a wingspan apart.

"It looks wrong," shouted Pestrite. "Dangerous."

"Agreed," Baltat shouted back, "But we have to land. The youngsters can't fly any further."

So they found a patch of flat, open ground, and landed. Not a moment too soon, reflected Baltat. Some of the piglets were whimpering with exhaustion.

The patch of open ground was covered in long grass, in which flowering shrubs were dotted. Fortunately, there were slugs and snails to be found in plenty, and even some hedgehogs.

"Well done," Baltat said to Pestrite. "That was hard, but you got us here."

"Thanks, but where *is* this? What sort of place have we found?"

"Hmm," said Baltat. "I don't know. I've never seen anything like it before. But I could make a guess."

"Tell me."

"Pinto talked to me about humans once. He said that they make big dwellings, far away from the places where we live. He said – I know this sounds crazy, but it's what he said – that they *make* their own rock, and that's what their nests are built out of. They have

The measure of all things

a liking for straight edges, and square corners. I think we've found one of their nesting sites."

"Are there humans here?"

Baltat rubbed his snout. "I think we'd better find out."

Over the next few days, as the youngsters recovered from their ordeal, Baltat organised recce patrols. They searched and searched, but they found no humans.

"So what do you think?" asked Pestrite.

"I think the humans built this place, and then abandoned it," said Baltat.

"I'd better convene a herd meeting. We've got a big decision to make."

This time the debate went on for a long time, but in the end the decision was unanimous. Life could be good here. There were a variety of small creatures living in the gardens. There were rodents living in the buildings, and pigeons nesting on their roofs. Lots of good food. Here they would stay, for at least a year.

Of course, the humans did come back. When the survey team arrived, five years later, to investigate the possibility of repopulating the abandoned city of New Scunthorpe, they reported that it was home to the largest herd of flying pigs that anyone had ever seen.

A trace of glue in the sands of time

"Where to begin?" said the Professor. "I could show you the tensors I've devised. How's your tensor calculus?"

"Professor," said Jim Arnott, "I don't even know what a tensor is. More to the point, neither do my readers."

The four of us were sitting round the fire, in the farmhouse living room, in the wilds of Norfolk. Professor Itzhak Rostoff, head of the project, newly famous, and a hot tip for the next Nobel Prize for Physics, was holding forth. Jim Arnott, the journalist, had a voice recorder perched on the arm of his chair, to catch the great man's words. The professor's deputy, Dr Stefano Carcopino, sat next to him, nodding from time to time. And I – Don Lucas, whose job was to fly the craft – sat on the opposite side of the fireplace, brooding about what could go wrong.

The Professor laughed. Stefano chipped in. "Perhaps we could start with a simple question: what is time?"

"A very good question," said the Professor. "Deceptively simple, but at the heart of what we're doing here. What do you think, young man?"

The measure of all things

Jim considered. "An ordered series of events," he replied, at length.

"Good. Common sense, really. You might elaborate that: an ordered series of events, some of which are past, some of which are present, and some of which are future. The problem is that an English philosopher – John McTaggart – proved that the concept is logically incoherent. Way back in 1908."

"A very elegant piece of logical reasoning," murmured Stefano. "You're on the wrong track, Jim. Think like a physicist."

"Well, I suppose we could say that it's a dimension. One of a cluster of four dimensions."

"Yes indeed," beamed the professor. "Einstein's space-time continuum. A famous idea. But of course, simply labelling it like that doesn't get you very far. You need a mathematical description, something that will allow you to see what's going on behind the stage scenery, so to speak. Einstein realised that Euclidian geometry wouldn't *do* to describe it, so he borrowed a whole bundle of maths from Riemann. Of course, it didn't quite work. Sometimes you solve one of Einstein's equations and the answer comes out as infinity, which is no good to anyone. And he wasn't taking account of quantum mechanics – in fact, his theory and quantum physics contradict each other. So, for about a century, physicists like Stefano and myself have been looking for better mathematical models. And we've devised some."

"Great volumes of the stuff," said Stefano. "Libraries full of it."

"It seemed to me, a few years back, that we'd got stuck in a rut," continued the professor. "We needed

A trace of glue in the sands of time

a new approach. And then, one day, I thought: why do we all move forward through time? Not just us, but every material thing in the universe? And all at the same speed?"

There was a pause. Jim said "I don't know."

"What usually makes things move through space? Or, in fact, space-time? The answer is a field. You put something that's got weight into a gravitational field, and it falls. Maybe time is analogous to a gravitational field? Maybe we're all falling through time?"

"It was a brilliant insight," said Stefano.

"Of course," continued the professor. "Einstein said that gravitation is just curved space. Mass bends space; things try to move in straight lines, but don't succeed; and the effect is that it looks as though there's something called gravity. But more recently, physicists have found it useful to treat gravity as if it *really is* a field. I thought, why not do the same with time?"

The professor was warming to his theme. His eyes were gleaming, and his gestures were becoming more pronounced.

"We know a lot about fields. Every field has a carrier particle. In an electromagnetic field, the carrier is a photon. In a strong nuclear field, it's a gluon. In a gravitational field, it's a graviton. So I thought, what if we treat *time* as a field, whose carrier particle is a chronon?"

"Which is really a particle of synchronicity," murmured Stefano.

"So I wrote some tensors to describe my idea. And I transformed them half a dozen times. And *all* the

The measure of all things

well-known properties of time were there. That's the moment when you sit back and say, 'This is going to get me the Nobel Prize'".

He chuckled. Stefano did too. I had the feeling that Stefano was in awe of his boss.

"But more than that. I could see a way to increase the interaction rate, between the chronons and the target particles."

"And if you did that, what would happen?" asked Jim, quietly.

"The body made of those particles would move forward in time, faster than everything around it. In effect, it would move into the future."

"And if you decreased the rate?" asked Jim.

"The body would lag behind everything around it. In effect, it would move into the past."

"And that," said Stefano, "Is how we built our time machine. Tomorrow, Don will test it for us. By travelling ten years into the future, and then coming back."

They all looked at me and smiled encouragingly. I tried to look unconcerned.

"One other thing," said Jim. "These chronons that you used in your theory, are they *real*? I mean, sometimes scientists invent a concept, just to focus their ideas, but it doesn't really exist ..."

"Exactly so," interrupted the professor. "We academics call it a 'classroom fiction'. No, I don't think chronons exist. Or gravitons, for that matter. But, in the last analysis, it doesn't matter. What

A trace of glue in the sands of time

matters is whether the theory works. And the time machine will tell us that."

* * * * *

Twelve hours later, I was strapped into 'Butterfly One', the time machine. It didn't look much like a butterfly; more like a test-rig for an ejector seat. It lived in a small building, like a one-car garage, a safe distance from the farmhouse that served as the team's living quarters.

As Professor Rostoff and three of his technicians tinkered with the machine, I thought about that safe distance, and the fact that the project team would be in a bunker when the start button was pressed. Clearly, there was some chance of a massive explosion. And, if it happened, it would be the end of me. Ah well, that's the sort of thing you expect when you're a test pilot.

Jim was in the room too, taking pictures. The professor looked up and grinned. "Right, we're ready. The boys and I will go to the bunker, and I'll give you a countdown over the loudspeaker. When I get to zero, press the red button. Things – your surroundings – will flicker, I expect. Then I'll open the door and come in. Only, it'll be ten years in the future, so I'll be a bit older. We'll take you out and about, show you the sights – what the world is like. Then you'll come back here, and we'll strap you in again. You'll press the green button. Another flicker. Then I'll come through that door, but I'll look like I do now. Because it'll be about ten minutes from now. Any questions?"

I shook my head. "No. It's all clear."

Jim said "Any last words?"

The measure of all things

I could have wished for something more reassuring, but I simply smiled and said "Bye for now."

The five of them filed out of the room, and I was left alone with my thoughts. An array of cameras and other instruments observed Butterfly One from every angle. I glanced at the control panel in front of me: a red button and a green button – nothing else. Not much required by way of pilot skills.

"Right," said the professor's voice over the loudspeaker. "I shall count down from five. Five ... four ... three ... two ... one ... zero."

I pressed the red button.

Everything *did* seem to flicker.

And suddenly the room looked a lot shabbier. The white paint on the walls, which had been fresh and spotless, was noticeably yellower, and, in places, it was peeling. There were cobwebs among the roof beams, and there were dirty patches and dead leaves on the floor. All except one of the cameras had gone.

The door opened, and a figure stood there, silhouetted against the daylight. I said "Hello, Professor."

But it wasn't the professor. It was Jim Arnott, looking a great deal older.

He said "You: *out*. **Now**."

I was bewildered. I said, "I'm sorry?"

He said, "I mean it. Get unstrapped and out of the building. We haven't much time."

A trace of glue in the sands of time

I unstrapped myself and climbed down. Six men came in behind him. He told them, "Right, you all know the drill. Lift that thing up and get it out of here."

I walked over to the door, and watched as the six men each found a hand-hold at the base of Butterfly One and lifted it. I took a few paces outside. With some effort, they got it through the door. A large truck was parked outside, with its engine running. They carried the machine to the rear of the truck, and used a hydraulic lift to get it into the back.

"OK," said Jim, "You six in the back; Don and I will be in the front. Let's get out of here."

There came a shout from the direction of the farmhouse: "Hey! Stop right there!"

"Get in!" shouted Jim. The six men were already scrambling into the back. Jim opened the passenger-side door into the cab, clambered in, and more or less hauled me after him. The driver had already got the engine into gear, and we were on the move.

"Let's see if we can outrun them," said Jim, as I slammed the door.

There was a loud crack, and something whistled past the cab.

"Are they shooting at us?" I asked, in a small voice.

"Yeah," said Jim.

We were moving fast now, down the long drive away from the farmhouse. More bullets whistled past. Then we were out onto the country lane. I looked at the driver. It was Stefano. Like Jim, he looked much older.

The measure of all things

"I think I can lose them," he said. "The lanes round here are pretty confusing. We've got a map; I don't think they have."

"What if they've got a satnav?" I asked.

"Oh, ha *bloody* ha," he grunted.

Clearly, I had said something stupid. I tried again.

"Who are those people? Why were they shooting at us?"

"They're the lynch mob," said Jim. "And, in case you were wondering, yes, they *are* after you. They want to string you up. I put a story round that you were due to appear tomorrow. Seems we fooled them."

I tried to make sense of what had happened, and failed. I looked at my two companions, grim-faced and grey-haired. Incongruously, I noticed that neither of them was wearing a watch. I looked at my own watch: it had stopped.

"Uh huh," said Stefano. "We have company."

I peered into the rear-view mirror. A large car was following us. It seemed to have an open sun-roof, and it looked as though a man was standing with his head and shoulders protruding through it. He appeared to be aiming a gun at us. There was a small flash, and a distant bang.

Jim reached for an intercom on the dashboard, and turned it on. I suspected that it communicated with the back of the truck.

"Jack, can you see that Range Rover behind us? Can you get a shot at it?"

A trace of glue in the sands of time

A voice came back: "Yeah, no problem. Do you want me to take out the driver?"

"No, it would cause too much trouble. See if you can put a shot through the radiator. Or, failing that, one of the tyres."

A shot rang out from close behind us. One of the car's tyres disintegrated: the driver lost control, and the car ran into a hedge.

"Good," said Jim. "Stefano, find somewhere secluded. We have to tell this guy what he has to do."

* * * * *

A while later, Jim, Stefano and myself were sitting on camping chairs in a clearing in the middle of a wood. The six men from the back of the truck had covered it with camouflage netting, and made some coffee on a portable stove.

"Thanks, Jack," said Jim, as one of them handed us plastic mugs of coffee. "They're all ex-army," he told me, by way of explanation. "I wouldn't trust civilians with an operation like this."

"I don't understand any of this," I said. "Am I ten years in the future? Where's Professor Rostoff?"

"Yes, you *are* ten years from where you started. Rostoff's dead: he never did get his Nobel Prize. He died quite early in the troubles. A firing squad."

"Best thing for him," muttered Stefano. "Him and his *classroom fiction*."

"Stefano, you admired him," I protested. "You *idolised* him."

The measure of all things

"You'll have to forgive Stefano," said Jim. "He's had a hard time of it. Five years in jail."

"Protective custody, they called it," murmured Stefano. "Didn't feel like protective custody. More like me protecting myself from a bunch of murderous convicts."

"I still don't understand. What happened? Why are people treating us as their enemies?"

"Something happened when Butterfly One left. Not anything that you could see. ... From the bunker, we watched you and your machine on the big screen. Saw you wink out of existence. We all cheered. Ten minutes later, nothing. You never came back."

"That's ominous," I said.

"Yeah, yeah. Then things started to malfunction. Wrist watches, satnavs."

"It turns out, chronons really do exist," said Stefano. "If you increase the interaction rate between them and hadronic matter – that's the stuff that ordinary things are made of, atoms and so forth – if you increase the rate, some of them leak. Just a few million out of all the trillions that are involved in the interaction, so you might think it doesn't matter. Unfortunately, there's a cascade effect. They dislodge chronons from adjacent pieces of matter, and they do the same to the next pieces along the line. It's quite a slow process, but it's irreversible. And you get eddies: the effect is a tiny bit stronger in one place than it is, say, a centimetre away."

"What does all that mean?" I asked.

"It means," said Jim, "That high-precision clocks become completely unreliable. You have two quartz

A trace of glue in the sands of time

crystals that are vibrating a million times a second, in perfect time with each other. Suddenly, they aren't. And they never will again."

"They're still vibrating, of course," said Stefano. "It's just that they're not synchronised any more. And nothing you can do will synchronise them."

"Does that matter?"

He laughed: a short, bitter, laugh. "You could say. All the computers in the world used precision clocks, to regulate their data processing. There wasn't any other way to do it." He took a swig of his coffee. "It spread outwards from here. In a couple of days, all the computers in East Anglia stopped working. Within a week, it reached London. Then it spread to everywhere else. New Zealand was the last to go, almost a year later."

"Of course," said Stefano, "It wasn't just computers. Anything with a microprocessor in it. Anything using packet switching. All the digital technologies: they all used precision timing. Which meant radio and TV transmissions, international telephone lines, mobile phones, DVD players ..." He drank some coffee. "And watches, of course. If you see a man wearing a watch these days, it's clockwork. And he's a rich man." He took another swig. "It took them a while to realise that it was our fault. Then they arrested the whole team, under the anti-terrorist legislation. By then, there was a massive economic crisis."

"Worst slump in history," Jim broke in. "Economists don't know when we'll recover, if we ever do. Ordinary people hadn't realised just how much the world had come to rely on computers. And digital communications."

The measure of all things

They both fell silent.

I said, "Thank you for rescuing me."

Stefano nodded, dismissively. Jim smiled, and said "Sorry about the lynch mob. When people are starving, they look for a scapegoat. Professor Rostoff first, *you* second."

I said, "Why did you take Butterfly One? Why did you bring it here?"

Jim spoke. "We're sending you back."

There was a silence. It seemed as though neither of them wanted explain what that meant.

Then Stefano said, "I can reset it. Even without the laboratory. Even without a working computer. I helped to build it, after all. But it does have to be *you* in the seat. It was built to your body's specification: your mass, your distribution of mass. I can't change that."

"But you already know I didn't go back," I said. "Or rather I won't go back. I was supposed to reappear after ten minutes, and I didn't …"

Jim shook his head. "You're not going back to that point in the time-stream. There wouldn't be any point: getting Rostoff to change his mind, after the damage was done."

"So where *am* I going?"

"To a point ten years before you started. Once you get there, you'll destroy Butterfly One – it's much too dangerous to leave it lying around. Then you'll seek out Itzhak Rostoff and neutralise him."

"Neutralise him? What does that mean?"

A trace of glue in the sands of time

"That's up to you. Hire a hit-man to rub him out. Drive your car over him. Poison him. Frame him, so he goes to jail as an embezzler. We don't care. The important thing is that he doesn't go to Norfolk University, so he never has his bright idea."

"But he's the most brilliant scientific mind since Einstein. I can't just destroy him."

Then they showed me photographs. Not the digital images that we show each other on a laptop or a tablet these days. Prints from photos taken with an old-fashioned camera, with a roll of film inside it. Corpses in the streets of Paris, after the bread riots. Barrricades on the A3 at New Malden, with determined-looking vigilantes behind them. Westminster in flames, with no one bothering to put the fires out. The smoking ruins of Florence. An enormous mass grave in Lagos.

And then I talked to the six ex-soldiers. Talked about what it had been like, policing Britain. Doling out emergency rations. Under emergency regulations, under a military government.

It could all have been faked, of course. A hoax. But I didn't believe it.

Stefano pleaded with me. "Don, you have to do this for us. The world has lost so much – science has more or less ground to a halt ..."

"And everyone in the world has suffered," said Jim. "You're doing this for all the people who used to be rich, and are now poor. And those who used to be poor, and are now starving. Millions upon millions of them."

The measure of all things

"If I do it – if I succeed – what will happen to you two?"

Stefano pursed his lips. "It's hard to say. Rostoff's mathematical model would probably have provided an answer. But I'd need a computer to run it, and there are no computers any more. Maybe we all just wink out of existence. Not just Jim and me, but the whole world. Maybe this world continues to exist, alongside the ... corrected ... version. I can't really say. If you do it, you're doing it to bring a healthy world into existence, not to patch up this one."

Stefano fixed Butterfly One so that all I had to do was strap myself in and press the green button. Everything flickered, and I found myself in the same Norfolk wood, ten years ago. On my own. Following my own judgement.

Did I do as I was instructed?

Ask yourself, have you ever heard of Professor Itzhak Rostoff, and his famous discovery?

In some strange power's employ

"May I have your full name?" asked the secretary. She was young and pretty, and wearing a very short skirt.

"Fost – John Harold Fost," he replied.

She looked perturbed. "Er ... was that Foster?"

"No, everyone assumes that. It's Fost – F O S T," he said wearily.

"Right," she said brightly. "And I understand you have a doctorate in ... engineering?" He nodded. She printed out a label and stuck it on the front of a scarlet manila folder. "Good. Doctor McPhisto will see you now."

In the next office, Dr McPhisto was waiting for him. He was a tall, slim, saturnine man, wearing a dark, well tailored business suit, a white shirt, and a blue crested tie, who smiled broadly and shook him warmly by the hand.

"Welcome, Dr Fost! Have they explained what we do here?"

"Well," he said warily, "You're a head-hunting firm. You find suitable candidates for certain specialised jobs ..."

"Yes, yes. But let me tell you what the procedure is. We already have your CV. We know about your

The measure of all things

technical competencies – you're a very good electricity supply engineer. Now I'm going to give you a personality test. It's the Dahlstrom Multiaxial Personality Inventory, and it's more or less standard in the industrial psychology business. It's quite searching, which means it's quite long. I hope that's acceptable?"

"Well, yes, I suppose ..." he said. But really there wasn't any doubt. His job at the National Generating Board was going to be re-organised out of existence some time in the next few months, and he badly needed a new one. He couldn't afford unemployment at his age. If Dr McPhisto had asked him to lick the floor, he'd probably have said yes.

He found himself sitting at a computer desk, working his way through what seemed like hundreds of questions on screen.

The software would allow him to leave a question unanswered, but, as he approached the end, the unanswered questions appeared again. There was no escape: everything must be revealed. Occasionally, he would glance at McPhisto, who was sitting at his desk reading, and the psychologist would look up and smile encouragingly.

At last he finished. A few moments after he clicked the button to submit the last answer, the printer on McPhisto's desk came to life and started to print pages. McPhisto picked them out of the tray, and read them one by one.

"That's really very interesting," he murmured. "Unexpected." He was silent for a while, as he perused them. Then he put the sheets down and gazed at Fost.

In some strange power's employ

"This is your personality profile. Our ethical policy dictates that I should offer you the chance to see it. But really, I'd advise against it. It can be upsetting – it can feel like an attack on your core values. Your identity."

Fost felt a little irritated. He'd just spent an hour answering intrusive questions. He already felt under attack. The least this man could do was give him feedback on what he'd found. "Actually," he said, "I'd like to see my results."

McPhisto sighed. "So be it." But he didn't hand Fost the pages. Instead, he transferred his gaze to an abstract painting on the wall. He said, "We psychologists have a thing about not describing a person as good or bad. I could never understand why. I'd say goodness was a fairly significant feature of a person's psyche, wouldn't you agree? Or badness, come to that. Of course, we pussyfoot around it, talking about transgressive behaviour, and negative value systems … would you describe yourself as a good person, Dr Fost?"

"Well … I suppose …"

"Of course you would. You give generously to charities. You volunteered your time to head a fund-raising committee to help the needy. You hardly drink at all, and you don't gamble. Nor do you engage in promiscuous sex. You're a good man, Dr Fost. And I can tell you why. You see this cluster of points, here?" He had turned the top sheet round, and pushed it across the desk. It showed a complicated graph, with lots of tiny points plotted around intersecting axes, in many different colours. He was pointing to a tight group of green points in the top left sector.

The measure of all things

Fost nodded, feeling quite bewildered.

"This is on the likriktinia dimension," said McPhisto.

"Er, likriktinia?"

McPhisto nodded. "Dahlstrom used made-up words for the various personality dimensions in his scheme. Or rather, words taken from obscure languages. He didn't want people to assume they knew what a particular personality aspect was all about, when it's actually based on complex factor analysis. But, roughly speaking, what we're looking at is your surface behaviour. This cluster shows that you have quite a strong compulsion to do what your fellow citizens would approve of. But now look at this." He leafed through the sheets, and picked one from half way down the stack. He placed it on top of the other. Another graph, many more multi-coloured points, forming different patterns, different clusters.

"This is the karalnoschia dimension. You have a cluster here" – he pointed – "that shows what you *really* want to do. What makes it highly unusual is that, in your case, it's not balanced by any points here" – he pointed again – "on the super-egoic sub-dimension. You're quite a wicked person, Dr Fost. Potentially."

Fost felt thunderstruck. "Am I?" he said weakly.

McPhisto spread his hands. "This test doesn't lie. It's been normalised on literally thousands of subjects. Good people, bad people, saintly people, wicked people."

"What should I do?"

"If I were you, I'd decide not to let it worry you. You are what you are. To thine own self be true. You've

In some strange power's employ

been like this since you were a teenager. You just never knew."

"Does this mean you can't offer me a job?"

"On the contrary, I've got just the position for you. It's not exactly in my gift, but, if I recommend you, they'll give it to you."

"And will you recommend me?"

"Yes, I will. You're the right man for the job. But I want you to keep in touch. Come back and tell me how it worked out."

* * * * *

The job turned out to be Chief Executive for the South Yorkshire Energy Exchange, a body that few people had heard of. Under the latest Government de-monopolisation scheme, various electricity generating companies offered electricity for sale to various transmission operators, who offered it to various distribution network operators, who offered it to various electricity retailing companies, who sold it to ordinary people. Fost's Exchange was supposed to provide a forum where all this buying and selling could take place, at least for one small region of the country. His salary was paid out of the profits of all the various companies. However, the Government had also decided to cap electricity prices for ordinary people. Inevitably, the cost of energy had risen, and the capped prices were too low. The Government was too jealous of its popularity ratings to modify the cap. Fost couldn't see how the supply companies could make any money. He had a nasty feeling that his new job wasn't going to last long.

The measure of all things

He sat in a bar, one evening, drinking whisky and soda. Drinking was a newly discovered pleasure. Suddenly, he had a bright idea.

When the politicians had first proposed the cap on electricity prices, their political enemies had filled the papers with stories about how it would lead inevitably to power cuts. So they put special provisions into the Act of Parliament. If there were power cuts, all deals were off. The supply companies could, and must, take emergency action.

"You know," he murmured to the bar girl who was his current drinking companion, "I think Sheffield's going to have some power cuts."

Money changed hands. A couple of maintenance engineers at a major substation near Doncaster ensured that three oil circuit breakers failed at the same time. A software specialist in a control room at Barnsley arranged that the emergency recovery program didn't kick in. There was one enormous outage, and it spread. Far too much current flowed down the last working transmission line into Sheffield. Automatic safety equipment switched off one section after another. Cascade tripping: you read about it when you're an electrical engineering student, with a kind of fascinated dread, but you never expect to see it in real life. It was six in the evening, on a snowy January night, and Sheffield went dark.

Before midnight, the COBRA committee was in session in Downing Street. Long before dawn, they were pleading with the supply companies: get us out of this mess. It doesn't matter how much it costs, we'll foot the bill.

In some strange power's employ

John Fost's pet maintenance engineers got frightened and, for a while, it looked as though they might spill the beans. But he calmed them down. And he paid more bribes to the staff working for the official enquiry: in due course, it announced that it was impossible to establish the root cause of the disaster, or to allocate any blame.

But blame *was* allocated. The people of Sheffield blamed the politicians. Each set of politicians blamed the other lot.

* * * * *

Dr McPhisto seemed delighted to see him again.

"Come in, John! Sit down. Can I offer you a drink? Whisky and soda? Tell me how the job's going."

"It's going very well, thank you very much. Better than I thought it would, at first."

"I hear you've had a windfall."

"Have I?"

"Mmm, yes, you have. Your employers made a great deal of money out of the Sheffield disaster, and quite a lot of it finished up in your pockets."

"All of a sudden you know an awful lot about my private affairs."

"I know a lot about all my clients. My boss knows even more."

"Really? May I ask how?"

"All in good time, John. Right now, I'd like to know how you feel."

"Feel? About the money?"

The measure of all things

"No, about the events in Sheffield. In strictest confidence."

"Well ... I don't really want to talk about ..."

"Oh, come on, John. I'm your psychologist. We have a rigid code when it comes to client confidentiality. You can unburden yourself to me." He smiled encouragingly. "So, the events in Sheffield. You made them happen – how do you feel about that?"

He pondered. After a while, he said, "Well, I suppose I feel ... quietly triumphant. You're right, I did make it happen. I don't think anyone else would have had the imagination, or the nerve, to do it. Coupled with the technical knowledge, of course."

"And how do you feel about the ... downside?"

"What do you mean?"

"Oh, you know: automatic machinery tearing itself to pieces in the factories. Food rotting in the cold stores. The street lights and the traffic lights went out, and people crashed their cars and got killed. Other people died in the hospitals, when the intensive care systems went down. Do you feel at all guilty about all that?"

He pondered some more. He said, "I suppose I should. But somehow ... the factories were probably insured. It was a cold day, so the food probably *didn't* rot. And ... people die every day. A few more here or there doesn't make much difference."

McPhisto grinned broadly. He got up, came over, put an arm round Fost and hugged him. "You're like a son to me," he said.

Fost was a little taken aback. With McPhisto so close, he got a good look at the tie he was wearing. It was

In some strange power's employ

dark blue, with diagonal rows of little red pentacles on it. Downward-pointing pentacles. Each pentacle had a tiny face in the centre: a goat's face, with the ears, horns and beard extending into the points of the star. An excellent piece of silk-weaving.

An idea was forming in his mind. "You know," he said slowly, "I looked up that test you gave me – the Dahlstrom test – in the psychological textbooks. It doesn't appear to exist."

McPhisto laughed. "Ah, you discovered my little ruse. You're right, it doesn't exist."

"And all that stuff about specially-chosen words, and factor analysis?"

"I made it all up." McPhisto shrugged, disarmingly. "The test was just window dressing. I wanted to tell you something about your personality, and the test seemed the best way to do it."

Fost considered that. He said "Tell me, is your name really McPhisto?"

McPhisto's grin became even broader. "An excellent question," he said. "McPhisto is the short form. My full name is Mephistopheles."

"Oh." He was quiet for a moment. "Oh hell. Does that mean I've sold my soul …?"

McPhisto shook his head. "We psychologists *really* don't talk about people's souls."

He gave Fost a searching gaze.

"Look, you're happy with the way things turned out, aren't you? New triumphs. Generous material rewards, and new pleasures to be tasted. You're

The measure of all things

leading an exciting new life. And, may I add, a charmed life – you have the luck of the Devil."

"But it'll all end with me having to go to ... to ..."

"Not for a very long time. I wouldn't worry about it. At the moment, you're our blue-eyed boy – the boss loves you."

He sighed, as he poured Fost another drink.

"You know, you remind me of another client I had, a long time ago. Had a similar name. I had to promise him all sorts of stuff to bring him over to our side. All I had to do with you was point out that you were already there."

Le crime a ses degrés

"So, this man Messina. What's he like? Have I met him?"

The question came from Bishop, who was chairing the panel, in his capacity as Academic Registrar.

"You've probably seen him around," I replied. "A small man. Neatly dressed. He has a pink face, and not much hair. He looks like an expert in baby care. Or possibly a baby. I asked around the department, and the most frequent label that people came up with was 'inoffensive'. He brings in a little research money, but he's not one of the big hitters. Frankly, we were thinking of letting him go, next time there was a round of redundancies. He doesn't really justify his salary."

Bishop looked thoughtful; he was, I suspect, trying to remember any contact he'd ever had with Messina. Unsuccessfully.

"He has a habit of injecting a little smile at the end of each of his pronouncements. It's rather unsettling," I said. "I gather the students call him 'smiling death'".

"Not popular with the students, then? Any idea why?"

"The rumour is that if he takes a dislike to a student, he finds a way to give them a fail grade, however

The measure of all things

good the stuff they write. Not that we should be dealing with rumours here. There have been a few appeals against grading. But you know our rules – professors' and lecturers' judgement can't be challenged, provided they can add up."

"Hmm. Not immediately relevant to the matter in front of us. Anyone else got any comment to add?"

Four of the other five panel members shook their heads. McIntyre, from Human Resources, said, "He was married, but his wife walked out on him. No children ..."

"Thank you, Mr McIntyre." Bishop interrupted sharply. "I don't think we need to know about his home life."

"It's one minute to eleven. Perhaps he won't turn up," said Norgate, hopefully. The potential scandal was in my department, not hers, but she, like everyone on the Panel, was aware of how much damage it could do to the whole University. If the matter could be swept under the carpet, they would all breathe a deep sigh of relief.

No chance of that. At precisely eleven, there was a knock at the door, and, without waiting for a reply, Professor Messina opened it and strode in. A slight, unassuming man, wearing a dark suit, white shirt, and dark red tie.

"Good morning, everyone," he said. "May I sit down?" He sat down in the vacant seat, facing us all, before we could say anything. And smiled his sweet smile.

"Good morning", said Bishop. "You must be Professor Messina. I'm Dr Bishop, and I will be chairing this Disciplinary Panel. Are you aware that you could have a legal advisor with you, if you wished? Or a union representative?"

Messina nodded "I thought about that, and decided there wasn't any point."

I wondered what was going on in his mind. Perhaps he'd decided we'd find him guilty, whatever he said. Or maybe he no longer cared whether we did or not.

"Right. Let's start the proceedings," Bishop continued. "For the record, you are Uberto Massina, and you are professor of psychopharmacology in the Department of Biochemistry at this university?"

"Yes, yes," he said, testily.

"It has been alleged that you have appropriated some of the University's intellectual property. And committed actions that may bring the University into disrepute. How do you respond to the charges?"

"I hardly care any more. But I suppose I'd better say something in my defence."

"Would you like to expand on that? You seem to be saying that the charges are trivial. I assure you that they aren't. If we find against you, it will certainly be the end of your career."

Massina shrugged. "Universities were invented, nine hundred years ago, as places where professors could teach whatever they felt like teaching, and research whatever they felt like researching. That's the essential principle, and, beside it, talk of the University's reputation seems rather meaningless." He smiled, sunnily.

The measure of all things

I was a little shaken, and not only because the initiative seemed to be slipping out of Bishop's grasp. Clearly, Massina had a megalomaniac streak that none of us had suspected.

"Professor, it has been alleged that you have developed a substance which has a potential commercial value, and withheld the fact from your departmental management," said Bishop. "Obviously, under the terms of your contract, such a substance would be the property of the University. Can you tell us anything about a substance called Ubertine?"

"Yes indeed. I invented it and named it after myself. There was no question of patenting it, so, contrary to anything my contract might say, I am treating the formula as my own private property. It was the culmination of years of research."

"And this research was concerned with … ?"

"Opiate narcotics. I've studied them all. Morphine, heroin, codeine. All their derivatives. Every tiny aspect of their chemistry. How they operate in the human brain. How they interact with pleasure centres. How the brain responds by creating closed cycles, which manifest themselves as physical addiction. You probably remember, I wrote a book about it."

Massina gave us another beatific smile. I couldn't resist grinning myself, momentarily. I strongly suspected Bishop didn't know about Massina's book, which meant he hadn't done his homework.

"And then you developed Ubertine" said Bishop. "Which is what, exactly?"

"Just another opiate narcotic."

"What was the point of that?" said Norgate. "What were you trying to discover?"

"I wasn't trying to discover anything. Just to make a profit."

None of us seemed to be able to find a question. After several seconds of silence, Massina continued.

"You see, Ubertine is the first of a new generation of narcotics. The subject who takes it gets a rush a few seconds after ingesting it. A very powerful rush. That applies, whoever they are – there's none of that nonsense about it only working for inadequates with addictive personalities. The physical addiction starts immediately, and it's quite unbreakable. The subject's health collapses – liver failure – but not for quite a while. I'm very proud of Ubertine."

Norgate said, rather weakly, "Make a ... profit?"

"Yes, dammit, a profit. I wanted to be rich. Don't we all want to be rich?"

I looked around me and thought, no, these people don't really want money. Reputation, maybe, or authority, or the chance to explore the world of ideas. We thought that that's what Uberto Massina wanted too. We misread him.

"You remember, two years ago, I was trying to set up a research contract with that German drugs company?" He was addressing the question to me, personally. "I got to meet the CEO. He turned out to be quite a stupid man – much less brainpower than me. I asked myself, where is the justice in this man earning tens of millions of euros a year, when I earn a pittance?"

"So you've been selling Ubertine," I said.

The measure of all things

"You'd better believe it. Once I've given someone a free sample, he comes back to me and begs me for more. Gives me whatever I ask. In due course, he'd give me everything he owned, though I haven't reached that stage yet."

"Professor," I said, "You're an academic. You can't reinvent yourself as a drug baron."

He looked at me thoughtfully. "You know, Professor, I think I can. As you probably guessed from my surname, I've got family connections in Sicily."

No, I hadn't thought of that. None of us had.

"And I've spent a little time this last semester reviving them. It turns out that several of my cousins are minor figures in Italian organised crime, and they're anxious to become major figures. So I'm offering them something special. The best narcotic in the world. It's going to push heroin, cocaine – in fact everything else – right off the market. The beauty of it is that I know how to make it, and they don't, so they have to keep me safe." He beamed at all of us.

Then he stood up. "Gentlemen. And lady –" he gave Norgate a special smile – "I think I've told you enough. I must be on my way."

"Wait a moment," said Bishop. "You can't go. You've just confessed to a crime."

Massina chuckled. "You're not a court of law: you can't detain me. Anyway, I don't think I **have** committed a crime. No doubt the Government will rush through legislation to make Ubertine a class-A drug, when they hear about it. But they haven't, yet. Which means I'm in the clear. As to you, all you can

do is fire me. Which you were going to do anyway."
This time, his smile was more of a malevolent glare.

As he opened the door, he said, "By the way, in case you were wondering, I tried it out on my students. A structured sample: young ones, old ones, males and females. Different racial groups. They're going to need a lot of medical attention. Your problem, not mine. I'm off to the airport." His smile was more distant this time, as though he hardly cared what we thought. Then he closed the door behind him.

The silence was longer than before. Then Norgate said "At least we know why the students called him 'smiling death'".

Snow upon the desert's dusty face

"I can't help thinking about what happened to my grandfather."

Mary looked up, her face full of interest. "Mmmm?" she said.

"He was First Mate on a cargo ship, crossing the Atlantic, way back in the twenty hundreds. The company head office would radio them every day with a lot of redundant instructions. Three quarters of the way across, the messages suddenly stopped. 'So what?' said the Captain. 'The radio set in Head Office has broken down. Good. We don't need them jogging our elbows all the time. It'll be a relief just to get on with the job.' Then, when they docked in Buenos Aires, they were expecting the Company Agent to come on board, but it was someone quite different. A guy wearing a flash suit –"

"Oh look," said Mary, "It's starting to snow."

Timothy's face fell. "I've told this story before, haven't I?"

Mary smiled and nodded. "You have, actually. But I don't mind. Tell it again if you like. Anyway, it really *is* snowing. Just look at it."

He turned to the big window. Outside, the floodlight was on. Fine crystals of snow were falling from the

Snow upon the desert's dusty face

sky, everywhere you looked. It had already started to coat the ground, a white blanket over the dark rock. It glittered in the light. No sign of it melting. After all the months of looking at a grey, icy desert, this was really quite beautiful.

"Do you think it'll keep snowing for the rest of the winter?" said Mary.

"On and off, yes. The snowfall will last a few hours, then there'll be a few hours break. But the falls will get longer and the breaks shorter over the next month or so. And it'll get stormy – we'll see some proper blizzards."

"Any danger to us?"

"No. This place is designed to withstand anything the weather can throw at it."

"I'll take some pictures." A flap opened on the outside of the building, and a camera pushed through the opening and started to record images. Then the screen on the living room wall came to life, and displayed the shots one by one.

"They look a bit stark, don't they?" said Mary. "Can I build a snowman? Would you mind?"

Timothy looked puzzled. "You have the strangest ideas. Yeah, build a snowman, if you like."

Immediately, a larger flap opened outside, and a squat shape emerged. You could mistake it for a large bear, if it wasn't for its slightly mechanical gait. It lumbered to the middle of the space in front of the window, and started to scrape together a pile of snow. Timothy watched with interest: it seemed to be experimenting, in order to discover how hard it had to squeeze the

The measure of all things

snow to pack it together, without making it into a lump of ice.

"That's one clever machine," he said.

"Well, all our machines are clever," said Mary.

The snow was falling quite hard now, but it still took several hours to make a life-sized snow figure. Eventually the column was about six feet tall, and the machine deftly sculpted a head, shoulders, and the suggestion of arms, hips and legs. It pushed a trowel-shaped tool into the face to make a mouth. Then it retreated into its cubbyhole, and emerged with a black top hat, a carrot, and two small lumps of coal. The hat went on the head, and the carrot and the coal lumps became a nose and two eyes.

Timothy laughed out loud. "Where did *they* come from?"

"I made them, just now," said Mary.

"Clever girl." He shook his head, slowly. "The things you do to try to cheer me up."

"I usually succeed, don't I?" She gave him her sunniest smile. "Now, what would you like for supper?"

"Is it late enough to be thinking about supper? I'm losing track of time." That, of course, was one of the problems with living in the Antarctic; there weren't any sunrises or sunsets. Or rather, there'd been a sunset a week ago, when the pink sky vanished, to be replaced by black, spangled with stars, but there'd be no sunrise for a good many months.

Snow upon the desert's dusty face

"Mmm, yes. Don't bother suggesting anything. I'll come up with a surprise." She hurried off to the kitchen.

Timothy sat in his armchair and looked at the ridiculous snowman. Mary took her duties very seriously. When he'd signed up for this mission, Timothy had been quite dismissive of the idea of a live-in companion. But the company psychologist had insisted: he wasn't prepared to take the risk that Timothy might crack up due to the isolation and loneliness.

And I probably would have cracked up, he thought. Bearing in mind the way things turned out. I'd have sunk into the blackest despair. I've come to rely on Mary a lot.

He closed his eyes and felt the vibrations coming up through the floor. Far below their living quarters, machines were mining the hard grey ice, and the carbonate rocks. A nuclear reactor was providing enough electricity to warm their home and light it, and to convert the water and the rocks into all the things they needed. A universal synthesiser was busy making foodstuffs. It synthesised carbohydrates, proteins, and any other complex molecules it needed. Then, using 3-D printing technology, it assembled them, one microscopic layer at a time, and inserted tiny pockets of liquid and gas where appropriate, so that the product had exactly the right texture. It could make practically anything – including lumps of coal and carrots, it seemed.

Oh Mary, Mary, he thought, can I keep you in the manner to which you are accustomed? No, but the machines can.

The measure of all things

He opened his eyes. On the table to his right were his geological reports. He should really complete them and transmit them back to headquarters. But he felt an enormous reluctance to write anything these days. Entirely understandable. It was his preliminary report that had caused the disaster.

He remembered Clausewitz, the company's Chief Geologist, briefing the press. "We have very good evidence of phosphate deposits, at a number of different sites. The evidence dates back to the beginning of the century. As I expect you know, there were plans for a major expedition then, but they were cancelled due to the Great Slump. Now's the time to build on the work they did. We've carefully analysed the hydrothermal processes that produced these phosphate beds, using computer simulations, and it's clear that they must, necessarily, have produced large deposits of uranium, thorium and rare earths as well. I don't have to tell you how valuable they are, these days. The financial return from this expedition will be enormous."

"Clausewitz," he murmured, sitting in his armchair and addressing the snowman, "You got it wrong. Lots of iron oxides, and a bit of chromium. But gold in them thar hills? Uranium? Thorium? Neodymium? Not a hope."

Timothy had been the advance guard – a single expert, sent on ahead to do some proper prospecting, and radio back the news about how rich the strike was. And, because he prided himself on his professionalism, he'd told them exactly what he'd found. Big mistake.

Mary came back in, and laid the dining-room table. Then she brought in a grilled salmon steak, with herb

Snow upon the desert's dusty face

butter, new potatoes, and petits pois, and a glass of chardonnay.

"That was excellent, darling," he said when he'd finished.

"Thank you dear," she said with an appreciative smile.

He leaned back in his armchair, and let his mind wander.

"You know," he said, "My grandfather was First Mate on a cargo ship ... damn! That's the third time I've started to tell that story, isn't it?"

"Yes dear, it is," she said, sympathetically. "It's obviously preying on your mind. Perhaps you'd better finish it?"

"Yes. Maybe I'd better. The man who came aboard in Buenos Aires, wearing a flash suit, turned out to be a lawyer. 'Your company's gone bankrupt,' he said. 'Your ship's to be impounded. Technically, you're all *Distressed British Seamen*, which means it's up to the British Consul to organise your journey home....'" Unexpectedly, he found that he was choking, and tears were running down his cheeks.

Mary came round, perched on the arm of his chair, and put an arm round his shoulders.

"You did *nothing* wrong," she said soothingly. "It was your job to write an accurate report, and send it back. You did everything that was expected of you. You couldn't have known what would happen next."

"Yeah, right," he said, bitterly. "And within a day my report had been leaked to the press. And within another two days the company had gone bust." He paused. "So I suppose I'm a 'Distressed British

The measure of all things

Seaman'. Except that I'm not a seaman. Or British. The company had all of us take Cayman Islands citizenship, to minimise its tax liability. Fat chance of *them* organising a rescue mission."

He sobbed for a minute or two. He said "They ... they've left us here. They're not ... they're *never* going to come and get us ..."

Mary made soothing noises, and stroked his hair. After a while, she quietly got up and went over to the wall. Timothy glanced up, and saw her take a power chord out of her sleeve, and plug it into the socket recessed into the tiles. Time for a recharge. She turned and saw him.

"Oi!" she said, sharply "Don't look! It's rude!"

Androids have their own ideas about modesty, and what should be done in private. At least, Mary did.

He transferred his gaze to the window. Outside, the snow, which was pure, solid, carbon dioxide, fell soundlessly onto the Planum Australe, the high plateau that comprised the Martian Antarctic icecap. The snowman grinned at him.

Legionnaire's disease

"Dad, the ambulance-chaser's here!" said the teenage girl who answered the door. I judged her to be about seventeen; wearing a tee-shirt and jeans.

Frankly, I would have liked a better introduction. My job's not easy at the best of times, and it gets progressively harder as the client's family's trust in me diminishes. But Alex Farrell was currently the only prospect I had, and I wasn't about to give him up.

So I gave her my pleasantest smile, and asked if I could speak to David Farrell.

I should explain that David was Alex's father, and next of kin. Alex was probably too sick to make his own decisions. Mary Farrell, the mother, had died years ago. The stroppy teenager was Polly, Alex's younger sister. She didn't seem to like her brother much, and to like lawyers even less.

"Are you Jason Nicholson, the solicitor?" said a melancholy little man, emerging from the front room.

"I am," I said, delivering another smile, and holding out my hand.

He shook it and said, "Do you think you'll be able to help us?"

"Maybe," I said, "If what they've told me about Alex is true."

The measure of all things

We went into the sitting room. It was pokey – the whole house was small and unimpressive. These were not rich people.

He brought me a cup of tea. I wasn't surprised he had to make it himself. Polly didn't seem to be the nurturing kind.

Then he told me what had happened to Alex. I nodded, and looked concerned, and took notes. Actually, I didn't need to take notes, since I had a digital voice recorder running in my briefcase. But, at a first consultation, appearance is everything.

When he finished, I said, "You know, I think it's outrageous what they did to your son. Simply *outrageous*. If we sue the corporation, I think there's a good chance that we'll win, and get substantial damages. I'll certainly take on the case, if you want me to. On a no-win no-fee basis, of course."

* * * * *

The following day I met the client. Alex had a room to himself at South Middlesex Hospital. I checked – it was on the NHS; the Starsong Corporation had, so it seemed, contributed nothing to Alex's medical expenses so far. Good; I could use that.

"Son," said David, "Can you hear me? This is Mr Nicholson – he's a lawyer. He thinks we should sue the people who did this to you."

"It hurts," murmured Alex. He was a chubby 20-year old, with ginger hair. He lay quite still, with his eyes shut. He breathing was laboured, and he was deathly pale. As unobtrusively as I could, I took out a palm-sized camera and photographed him.

Legionnaire's disease

"Hello Alex," I said, "I'm glad to meet you. Where does it hurt?"

"All over," he said. "Muscles ache ... chest aches ... head aches."

"Can you open your eyes?" I asked.

He opened them, looked from side to side, and quickly closed them again.

"Can't see properly. Colours are all wrong."

I talked to Dr Lambrick, who had charge of him.

"Frankly, I can't tell you exactly what's wrong. It's some sort of reaction to the experimental treatment he was given, but none of us have seen anything like it before. It's not an infection, either bacterial or fungal or virus. It's not poisoning – at least, not by any of the toxins that we're familiar with. It's more like a catastrophic allergic reaction."

"What was this experimental treatment? What have the Starsong Corporation told you?"

"They won't tell us anything. It's very frustrating. I've threatened to ask the Department of Health to revoke their licence, but they seem completely blasé about the whole business."

"Is he getting worse?"

"No, I don't think so. A week ago, I thought we were going to lose him. Now, he seems to have stabilised. But I can't see any signs of improvement. If he recovers, I'd say it'll be a long, slow business."

Finally, I went back to Alex, and asked the all-important question.

The measure of all things

"Alex, can you hear me? Think carefully. Before the treatment started – the treatment the Starsong people gave you – did you sign an Informed Consent form?"

A long pause. Then he muttered, "Yes. Signed all their forms."

Pity, I thought. It would have been an easy case if he hadn't.

* * * * *

I got David's permission to search Alex's room at their house. I wanted the copy of that form he'd signed, plus anything the corporation had given him describing the experimental treatment. Polly stood in the doorway and watched me searching.

"D'you think I'm going to find it?" I asked

"Maybe," she said. "Then again, maybe not. He's quite capable of throwing it away, or leaving it in their office. Not too bright, my brother."

"Tell me, what was his job ... what did he do?"

"Sat around and played video games, mostly. Shoot-'em-ups. Volunteering as a medical guinea pig was the best he could come up with as gainful employment."

"He never had any ambitions?"

"He wanted to be a soldier, when he was younger. Couldn't get through the medical. And he had a crazy idea that he was going to join the French Foreign Legion. He went to Marseille. They took one look at him and sent him straight home."

I couldn't find the form, or any Starsong documents at all. This case was looking trickier than I'd thought.

* * * * *

Legionnaire's disease

The Starsong Corporation proved remarkably difficult to track down. Sure, they had a website – that was how Alex had found them, and where he'd volunteered for their medical research programme. But it didn't provide an address, or a phone number. There was a "contact us" page, offering the chance to send them email, but, when I sent a message requesting an urgent face-to-face meeting, it bounced straight back. Return to sender, address unknown.

Google didn't reveal anything useful. I tried Companies House: they weren't registered as a business corporation. I questioned the Department of Health: they weren't authorised to perform medical research.

Dr Lambrick had an email address for them, it was true, but they didn't answer me when I used it. And I couldn't trace it to a real, physical, location.

I sat in my office, brooding. On the face of it, Starsong was guilty of disgraceful medical malpractice. They'd behaved recklessly, and done my client real harm. They ought to be exposed. Punished. Halted in their tracks.

On the other hand, they seemed pretty good at hiding in the undergrowth. If I couldn't find them and confront them, I couldn't drag them into court, or even blackmail them, and pursuing the case probably wasn't doing the Farrell family any good. More important, it probably wouldn't do me any good.

My phone rang.

It was Dr Lambrick.

"I think you'd better come to the hospital. Something remarkable has happened."

The measure of all things

* * * * *

Thirty minutes later, I was at the hospital. Alex was sitting on the edge of his bed, in a hospital gown, but looking remarkably healthy. He grinned at us – me, Dr Lambrick, his father, his sister, and a man in a white coat, carrying a clipboard, who I hadn't seen before.

"As I said on the phone," said Dr Lambrick, "It's quite remarkable. All his indications are normal, except for the ones relating to … well, fitness; general well-being, and they're way *above* normal. He tells me he feels fine."

"I do," interjected Alex. "I really, really have never felt better in my life."

"This is wonderful," I murmured. Inside, I was seething. Farrell versus Starsong Corporation was supposed to pay my rent for the next six months.

"And I can do things I couldn't do before. I had Polly bring me in an iron bar …"

He picked it up. It was about half an inch thick. He proceeded to bend it as if it was made of toffee, and he didn't even break out in a sweat.

"There's more to it than that," said Dr Lambrick. "One of my colleagues is interested in the limits of human senses. He thought Alex might have lost some of his red vision and his blue vision. But he hasn't. It turns out he can see colours we can't. Some of the infra-red, and quite a lot of the ultra-violet. And he can hear sounds we can't – some ultrasonics, and some infrasonics."

"It's a bit weird," said Alex. "Things look a bit odd. But I don't mind. It's exciting." He got up, walked to

Legionnaire's disease

the window, and pointed to the car park outside. "See those cars down there? I can tell you which ones have just been parked. I can see which ones have got hot exhaust pipes." A thought seemed to strike him. "Have you got a Visa card?" I fumbled in my wallet, found my card, and handed it to him. He pointed to the left hand side, under the bank's name. "There's a picture of a bird, here. I can see it, you can't. It's printed in special ink."

"Ultra-violet ink. Excellent," said the man with the clipboard. "Thank you, Dr Lambrick. And please thank your colleague, the sensory specialist."

"I'm sorry," I said. "Who is this man? Dr Lambrick, do you know him?"

"I assumed he was with you," said Lambrick, non-plussed.

"I should have introduced myself. My name's Fenozon, and I'm from the Starsong Corporation."

I recovered quickly. "Mr Fenozon," I said, severely, "I'm authorised to start legal proceedings against your company, on behalf of Mr Farrell ..."

"No," he interrupted, "There won't be any law suit. The treatment was a complete success. No tort has been committed."

"He's right," said Alex. "I don't want to sue anyone."

I digested that. "Mr Fenozon," I said, "I have a feeling that Starsong isn't really a medical research organisation. Is it?"

"No, it isn't. We're a specialist recruitment agency. Our client gives us a job description. We find someone with the right attitude for the job, then we

The measure of all things

alter their physique so they can do it. In the case of Mr Farrell, we made him stronger, fitter, healthier, more perceptive and so forth. It was all in the initial contract. But I imagine you haven't had a chance to read it."

"I see. And ... where are you based?"

He was standing by the window. He pointed at the sky. "Out there. I could give you the name of our home planet, but it wouldn't mean anything to you."

"Wow," said Alex. "And you've got a job for me?"

"Yes indeed. The Altairians are recruiting soldiers. You fit the bill nicely. If you accept the Queen's shilling, so to speak, they can offer you an exciting career. Would you care to sign here?" He handed Alex the clipboard, and a pen.

"Now hold hard," said David. "You need to think about this ..."

"Dad," said Alex, "I did all the thinking before, when I tried to join the Foreign Legion. Do you really think I want to go back to playing video games?"

"They made you brighter, too, didn't they?" interjected Polly.

"Yes we did," said Fenozon. "Boosted his IQ by about 20 points."

"Will we ever see him again?" said David, a note of desperation in his voice.

"Probably not, I'm afraid. He might get killed in battle, of course. Assuming he doesn't, he'll retire, back here, in about eighty years time. We've extended his lifespan somewhat. I'm afraid the cost of interstellar travel doesn't allow for home leave."

Legionnaire's disease

Alex had been speed-reading the form. "Does this outfit have a name?"

"You could call it the Altairian Alien Legion, if you liked."

"OK, I'll sign. Mr Nicholson, would you witness my signature?" He signed. I counter-signed. I made a point of retrieving my Visa card.

"Excellent," said Fenozon. "We'll leave now."

The room suddenly went completely black. The darkness lasted for an indeterminate number of seconds. Then everything was as before, except that Fenozon and Alex had vanished, leaving only Alex's dressing-gown.

David Farrell looked devastated. Polly gave him a hug.

"Come on, Dad," she said. "Let's go home. I'll make you supper."

The nourris fee

They sat in the bar for a long time, discussing the purse. It was a great mystery.

Sandy's team of marine archaeologists had found it on the sea bed, near the island of Graemsay, in the Western approaches to Scapa Flow. The coins inside it were in good condition: silver pennies, some of them minted by King Ethelred, some by King Svein Forkbeard of Denmark. Not too surprising; such coins would have been in circulation among the Vikings in the years leading up to King Canute's reign.

Then they had the leather radio-carbon dated. It was made in about the year 1775.

"Some eighteenth century antiquarian went to Orkney," suggested Sandy. "He found a crofter who'd dug up a Viking hoard. He bought the coins. On the way back to the Scottish mainland, he accidentally dropped the purse over the ship's side."

"An antiquarian we've never heard of?" asked Carol. She was the expert from Aberdeen University, brought in to advise on Viking coinage.

"Perhaps he wasn't an antiquarian at all. Just a rich traveller, who collected souvenirs," Jamie put in. None of them had a better explanation, and they fell silent.

The bar was on the harbour front in Stromness.

The nourris fee

"We saw some seals on the way here," said Carol, brightly. "I seem to remember that Orkney's got lots of folk tales about seals."

"Quite a few," agreed Max. He worked for the Stromness Museum, and there wasn't much about Orkney folklore that he didn't know. "There's 'the Goodman of Wastness' – that one's quite well-known. And, of course, 'the Great Selkie of Shule Skerry'."

"I don't know either of those," said Angus, who was up from Glasgow. "Tell me about the Great Selkie."

"Ah, yes. The Great Selkie was a great seal. He lived in the waters around Shule Skerry, which is a rock away off to the West of here." He paused, and looked out to sea.

"In fact, he was a were-seal," he continued. "He could turn himself into a young man and come ashore, if he so wished."

The others were all listening now.

"By and large, he didn't want to. He loved swimming in the sea, around his rock. Catching fish. Exploring the sea bed. Sometimes basking in the sun, upon the bare stone. Normally, he had no need for the company of men, or desire for it. But his trouble – his personal tragedy, if you will – was that he could only reproduce when he was a man. If he wanted offspring – and, of course, he did – he would have to spend time ashore, with a human woman."

He paused, clutching his beer-mug, deep in thought.

"The story goes that there was a young maiden, who lived with her father in a croft on one of the outer islands. Her father had gone to the mainland – to

The measure of all things

Kirkwall, probably – to trade his produce, and she was alone. Late at night, there came a knock at her door. She opened it, and there was a handsome young man, dressed as a fisherman, but dripping wet. He explained that his boat had foundered in the heavy seas, and he'd had to swim for his life. He'd crawled ashore, and he wondered if he could seek shelter in her cottage? Just till the morning. So, of course, she invited him in, and offered him hot food. He refused it. In fact, he seemed happy to sit in the cool part of the room, away from the fire, and he didn't seem to want to dry himself."

He paused again.

"Nevertheless, he was a handsome young man, and there were few enough of those in her life. By the end of the night, they'd become lovers."

* * * * *

In 1775, Edinburgh was rebuilding itself. Under a visionary Provost, it had plans that would make it the most elegant city in Europe. And it was crammed with brilliant men, soon to become famous: philosophers, writers, scientists, engineers, doctors, and artists.

Isabel knew nothing of this. She lived some two hundred miles to the north, on the island of Graemsay – not, as the storyteller would have it, on one of the outer islands. She had barely heard of Edinburgh, or anywhere outside the Orkneys.

Life was hard for Isabel. Since her mother's death, her father had treated her as a servant. Not only must she clean the cottage and cook the meals, she must milk the cow and grind the oats with a quern-stone. She must bring up kelp from the beach to lay on their

The nourris fee

strip of land, and, when her father cut turf from the bog, she must carry it back to the cottage where it could be dried. She must weed the field, and she must make cheese. She must make and repair their clothes. Her father worked too, making furniture, and planting and harvesting the crops, but Isabel worked far harder.

In spite of her work, the cottage was unprepossessing. It was close to the shore, built of thick stone slabs using mud rather than mortar, and thatched with earth sods. Inside, the walls were unplastered and unpainted, and the floor was beaten earth, except for the hearth stone in the middle of the living room, where a peat fire burned almost all the time. This living room amounted to half the space in the building; the other half, separated by a wicker partition, housed their cow and their chickens. The cottage had no windows, but it had a fine oak door with brass hinges: it had graced a merchant ship, before the ship ran onto the rocks and her timbers became available to anyone who wished to haul them off the shore.

She was sixteen years old when her father made the trip across the sound, taking as much produce as they could spare to the market in Stromness. She was glad: it meant her work would ease off a bit. A little less cooking, a little less cleaning.

And it was on her second night alone that there came a knock at the door.

She opened it. There stood a young man. Slim but muscular, with dark good looks. A fisherman, by his clothes. In the early evening light, she could see that the water was dripping off him.

The measure of all things

"My boat went down," he said. "I had to swim to the shore. May I seek shelter, here?" He smiled at her: a pleading smile, but perhaps with a promise of something else in it.

"What is your name?" she asked.

"Ronan," he replied. She knew no Gaelic, otherwise the name might have warned her that all was not what it seemed. 'Ronan' is Gaelic for 'little seal'.

"Come in," she said.

* * * * *

Max sighed. "In the morning, he kissed her and left, promising to return. But he didn't return."

He drank some beer. Out to sea, gulls were zigzagging over the waves.

"And she soon discovered that she was pregnant. So she was left to bring up the child on her own. She did at least have the croft to shelter and support her."

"What about her father?" asked Carol.

He drank again. "I really don't know," he said. "The story doesn't mention him any more. Perhaps he died of shame when he discovered his daughter's pregnancy."

* * * * *

In fact, her father never found out about the pregnancy. In the islands, a woman would keep it a secret that she was with child for as long as possible, lest an evil spirit should hear of it and attack her unborn baby. So it was that her father set off on his next trip across the sound without knowing. On the way back, a sudden squall hit his boat: it capsized, and

The nourris fee

he drowned. Isabel was grief-stricken at the loss of her whole close family, distraught with worry as to how she would cope on her own, and, in due course, troubled with the thought that some distant relative would claim inheritance and take the croft from her. In the event, no one claimed the croft, and she found that she *could* cope.

When it was time, women from the neighbouring crofts helped her with the birth, and it went well. They were curious as to who the father was, but didn't judge her harshly. "The poor girl needed a little joy in her life," they said.

* * * * *

Max swigged some beer and ate a few crisps.

"It was a boy child, and he grew up strong and good-looking," he said.

"And then, when he was fourteen years old, one winter's day there came a knock at the door. She opened it, and it was the same young man, from all those years before. Not a day older. Still dressed as a fisherman. Still dripping wet."

* * * * *

The two of them sat on their low chairs, beside the peat fire. Isabel, spinning woollen yarn, her son, Patrick, fashioning an oar from wreck-wood, using a knife.

And there was a knock at the door.

Isabel put aside her yarn, got up and opened it.

In the winter twilight, she might not have recognised him. But no, she knew immediately who it was. She'd seen him in her dreams often enough.

The measure of all things

"Ronan," she said.

Neither of them spoke for a while. Then she said, "You came back."

He nodded. Again there was a pleading smile, but this time it promised nothing.

She said, 'What do you want?'

He said, 'To collect my son, and teach him to swim.'

* * * * *

There was a hush in the pub now. Max had their rapt attention, and was enjoying it. Outside, it was getting dark.

"She recognised him, of course. She said, 'What do you want?' He said, 'To teach my son to swim.' He held out a leather bag. It was full of gold coins. He said, 'Take it, it's yours. It's your nourris fee.' Then he lead the boy down to the sea shore, and out into the waves, and she never saw either of them again."

* * * * *

Ronan handed her a leather purse. In it were small silver coins. "I found them in an old ship, under the sea. Out to the west, where the water is deep. The men in the village sold me a purse, in exchange for a coin."

Isabel said, "Is it for me? Why?"

Ronan said, "It's your nourris fee."

Patrick pushed past her. He had shed his clothes, and was naked as he stood beside his father. It seemed that no explanation was needed. He spoke no words, and on his face was a calm acceptance of what must be. The two of them walked to the shore, and out

The nourris fee

into the gentle waves. Already, sleek seal fur was beginning to appear on Ronan's legs. And Patrick's, too.

* * * * *

Max drained his pint. They offered him another, but he shook his head.

Carol asked, "What's a nourris fee?"

He said, "A payment for a nurse."

"It's a sad story."

"Round here, they like their stories to be laced with tragedy."

"Is it a real folk-tale, or did you make it up?"

He shook his head. "Real enough. And there's a folk song, based on it. Number 113, in Child's collection." He sang a couple of lines:

> *"Little know I, o' my bairn's father,*
>
> *If land or sea he's living in …"*

* * * * *

Isabel stood staring out at the sound, until she could no longer make out the two figures in the dark water under the darkening sky. Then she howled. She lifted the purse, and hurled it far out into the sea. She sank to her knees, and sobbed.

* * * * *

"I'm away to my bed. I'm getting too old for long drinking sessions," said Sandy. "Thanks for the story, Max. One thing, though – what are we going to put into our report, about the leather bag?"

The measure of all things

"We'll just tell them what we found. We'll leave it to others to speculate on how it got to be there," said James.

"Aye, seems fair enough. Goodnight to you all."

They all wished each other goodnight, and went their separate ways.

I learned my lesson well

Monday 1st

Well, that was fantastic. Truly fantastic. Sixty-five thousand fans in front of the stage, all of them there to worship me. Me! And I had them – I gave them exactly what they wanted. Climax was when I sang *Fame*. Yeah, I know it's a cover version, but half ... maybe three quarters ... of the audience didn't. They weren't around in 1980, and they don't watch old movies. Fame! I'm gonna live forever! I'm gonna learn how to fly! I belt out the lyrics, a stack of KF850s pump the sound over sixty-five thousand heads, sixty-five thousand bodies sway, and sixty-five thousand arms punch the air in front of me, while I do the same. Truly, truly fantastic. You can't really see their faces, because the lights are in your eyes, but occasionally you get a glimpse of someone at the front of the crowd. Zonked out of their mind, on the music. The ultimate trip, and I gave it to them.

Let's not get complacent. Is anything going to go wrong? Anything going to bite my backside?

No, really, I don't think so. Jerry, Layne, Sean and Mike didn't put a note wrong, and they were enjoying it as much as me. The backing-vocal girls were just fine. The stage crew know exactly what they're doing. I watched myself on the video after the show, and all

The measure of all things

my moves worked – I looked brazen when I wanted to look brazen, little-girl-appealing when I wanted to, and very, very sexy all the time. Like Madonna in her *Blond Ambition* tour. My voice is holding up nicely.

Download sales are going to sky-rocket. Ticket sales are enormous. Sure, I'm going to live forever, but also I'm going to be so, so rich.

A great concert. But I'm not sorry the next one isn't for a week. Takes it out of you. Gotta sleep now.

Tuesday 2nd

I had a TV interview in Burbank, and I had the driver take me there in the white convertible, and people saw me and waved at me! I waved back and they cheered! Never happened to me before. I blew kisses to them. And, of course, the studio audience cheered when I came in. The interview went OK.

Thursday 4th

I finally saw the tape of that TV interview I gave, the day before yesterday. It wasn't as good as I thought. I mean, I had a certain amount of polish, and the make-up and hair were just fine. So was the dress – great dress, in fact. It's just that I seemed somehow … false. The show's host felt it too, I think. The audience clapped and laughed in all the right places, but then they always do.

Monday 8th

The concert didn't work, and I don't know why. OK, so we sold out the stadium, and Jerry, Layne, Sean and Mike were great, as always. The equipment was fine. No glitches in any of the numbers. But the

I learned my lesson well

audience were ... flat. Heavy going. And, like I said, I don't know why. They cheered, but not enough. You're supposed to get encores, for heaven's sake.

Tuesday 9th

Another TV interview. I drove there in the convertible, and this time no one waved or cheered. OK, so it was downtown Chicago, not the outskirts of Hollywood, but I did think ...

The interview went OK.

Thursday 11th

The interview *was* OK, but have you seen what Harry Pace said about me in *Rolling Stone*? "Frenchie Swale used to be adventurous and lyrically intelligent. Not any more." How *dare* he? He's never written a song in his life, let alone performed one!

"Never read the music press" – that's what they say. Yeah, right. That takes *way* more will-power than I've got.

Better talk to Hayley. He's supposed to be managing my public profile. Why hasn't he been in touch?

The boys are supportive, but they look glum. Layne said "Of course we'll stick with you – we're your band." I can't remember asking them whether they were going to stick with me. Why is it an issue?

Sunday 14th

The downloads haven't skyrocketed. In fact, they've slumped. No shop sales to speak of, either.

The measure of all things

I rang Hayley to ask if he'd got any more TV guest spots lined up. He said, "No. Hey, I've got a call on the other line. Got to go." Just like that!

I'm too depressed to write. It's all going wrong. Tomorrow's concert has just got to work, otherwise I'm through.

Monday 15th

This is horrible! Really, really horrible! Half the seats weren't sold. I gave them numbers that always worked before – *Renegade, Handsome guy, Strange beauty* – and they could hardly bring themselves to applaud. Then, when I sang *Remix my life*, they started walking out. Not just a few of them, but loads of them. That number was supposed to be the highpoint of the show! As soon as I was off stage, I had a stiff drink and watched the video. All my moves. I couldn't see a thing wrong. I closed my eyes and listened to my voice. It sounded just the way it always has. Hard and clever, like June Tabor. They always wanted that – why don't they want it now?

I hate this. Hate it, ***hate it,*** hate it. I don't want to do it anymore.

Monday 22nd

Do you remember Ricky Nelson's song? It's the way I feel:
It's all right now, I learned my lesson well
You see, you can't please everyone – you got to please yourself.

Doctor's notes

Good, I think we have a result. In fact, I would say that this is the most effective piece of aversive fantasy treatment I can remember. I think Miss Swale is ready to return to reality, and I don't think she'll be troubled by her pathological "I'm a pop-star" fantasy anymore. She can view the world from her typist's desk with as much equanimity as any of us manage. We'll bring her out of the coma tomorrow afternoon.

What we did on our holidays

A grey heron flies over the rice paddies of Mai Chau, in north-western Vietnam. Her flight is slow but graceful, her head drawn back and her wings as wide as a man's arms, as she makes her way back to her nest in the reed beds. Elegant, seemingly perfect. In fact, she is not entirely healthy. In the cells of her gut is a virus of the family orthomyxoviridae. Not that the heron knows or cares. Herons know nothing of viruses, and, anyway, the infection is almost entirely harmless to her.

* * * * *

Ilha de Caranguejos certainly lived up to its billing. In the middle of the day, the sky was a deep, deep blue, but in the evening there were beautiful sunsets, the sun scarlet and the clouds around it tinted gold and rose. The beaches were fine silvery sand; the sea was azure, its gentle waves perpetually inviting. Every day was warm; never oppressively hot. The hotel was spotlessly clean, the beds always made when you returned from breakfast, and the hotel staff endlessly accommodating. The food was quite exceptional, whether it was the chef's skilfully cooked meals in the hotel restaurant, or freshly caught barbecued fish and crabs on the beach.

What we did on our holidays

"What did the brochure call it? 'The jewel of the West African coast'? What do you think?" asked Owen. He and his wife, Saskia, were on holiday. They'd taken to dining with Victor and Cassie, who they'd met on the flight out. Victor was an architectural historian, and Cassie was an economist. They weren't married, but knew each other well enough to spend their holidays together.

"Well, I'd say they've done a pretty good job," said Saskia. "It's really the perfect beach resort. This is delicious." She was consuming a plate of *Fargo da Terra a Blanta com Baguitchi*. It was beautifully tender, with a faint but distinctive taste of hibiscus leaves.

"Yes, but I wouldn't have come if it was just the beaches and the food," said Victor. "The island capital – São Pedro – is supposed to be something special."

"What's special about it?" asked Owen.

"It's a chance to see what a colonial citadel was like. It dates from the high water mark of the Portuguese empire. Almost completely unspoilt, or so they say."

"You've read about it in the history books?" asked Cassie.

"Oddly enough, no. It hardly gets a mention. But that means it sank into obscurity centuries ago. Which makes it all the more fascinating."

"Well, there's a coach trip tomorrow," said Owen. "We could all go together."

* * * * *

A bird in flight will sometimes leave droppings in its wake, and this heron does. The droppings fall into a

The measure of all things

canal, near a flock of ducks. The ducks are pecking happily at the water weeds and the green algae that grow there. One of the ducks is infected by the virus. Once again, it takes up residence in the bird's gut, and once again it has little effect on the bird's health. The virus lives in the cells of the gut; reproduces; mutates.

* * * * *

The coach set out after breakfast, down a well-made road, past the little airport and through the lush African vegetation. They breasted a hill, and saw São Pedro: ancient stone walls, and the towers of a large church beyond.

"Impressive," said Victor. "I wonder where they got the stone from? There must be quarries somewhere – I don't imagine they shipped the stone from Europe."

The road took them to a gap in the town's fortifications, and, as they approached it, they got a good look at the wall. Built out of big, white, stone blocks, it was castellated at the top. Where the walls turned a corner, a small, cylindrical, turret was built onto the outside, starting half way up the wall, with a dome-shaped stone roof, surmounted by a stone cross.

"What's a turret like that called?" Owen asked. Owen had made his money as a builder, but knew little of the history of architecture. Just retired, he was eager to learn.

"That's a bartizan," said Victor. "Notice the crenellations on the wall? The bits that project upwards are called merlons. See the way they've got the shape of a shield cut into them, and the shield's got a cross cut into it? That's a distinctively Portuguese touch."

What we did on our holidays

* * * * *

Back in northwestern Vietnam, as the rice harvest time approaches, the farmer who owns them herds the ducks away to market. They look healthy enough. At the market, in the town of Hang Kia, he keeps them in a cage and sells them one by one. As it waits in the cage, the duck with the virus infection produces some droppings. They dry to a dust, which blows into the pen next door, which houses pigs. One of the pigs breathes in the dust, and is infected by the virus in its turn.

It so happened that the pigs' owner – another farmer – had been troubled by a mild dose of flu, earlier that month. Of course, one does not let such a thing get in the way of caring for one's livestock, so the farmer – snuffling and occasionally sneezing – carried on feeding and mucking out his pigs. The same pig breathed in viruses from the farmer's lungs, and was infected. Thus it happens that two different strains of flu virus – one from the farmer, one originally from the heron, but somewhat mutated – meet in the pig's bloodstream.

What happens next is known to virologists as reassortment. A flu virus holds its genes in eight RNA segments. When two viruses meet, they can, and often do, exchange RNA segments. It's something like what animals do when they have sex. The result is a new virus, with many of the characteristics of the virus that had lived in the duck's body, but also with the ability to live in a human cell.

* * * * *

The coach parked in the town square. Mostly it was flat, although there was quite a steep incline on the

The measure of all things

side opposite the main buildings. At the top of it, a truck was parked, and men were unloading wine casks. The square was paved with small stones, some white and some black, forming an extensive zigzag pattern.

"Interesting," said Victor. "The Portuguese didn't start paving their streets like that till 1849. This place must have been important in the nineteenth century."

"But not so important that anyone could be bothered to write about it," said Cassie.

The party – about twenty of them – got out. A tourist guide clapped to attract their attention.

"Good morning, everyone!" she called. "My name is Emília, and I am here to show you around São Pedro." She was young, slim, dark-haired, and smiled a lot. They clustered round her.

"In front of you see the three most important buildings in the town. In the centre, the Church of Saint Peter. To the right of it, the Governor's Palace. And, to the left, the Customs House." She gestured towards the three imposing structures across the square. The group were already taking photographs.

She led them over to the Governor's Palace. It was painted pink, and had two storeys, each with seven very large windows surmounted by an elaborate carved-stone moulding. There was a splendid portico around the entrance, and the whole façade was surmounted by a triangular pediment, containing heroic carved figures, with a balustrade on either side. Some distance in front of the entrance was an equestrian statue of a medieval knight.

What we did on our holidays

"Fernão Gomes," said Emília, indicating the statue, "The founder of this settlement," before launching into a history of the early Portuguese colonisation. Victor nodded sagely.

They moved to the church. "The Citadel Church of St Peter," said Emília. "I'm afraid we can't go inside, because of the restoration work." Victor looked crestfallen.

It was built of the same white stone as the city wall. The windows looked much the same as the ones on the palace, except for the stained glass. A couple of steps lead up to the door, which was flanked by pilasters, supporting an elaborate open pediment, below which was an oval panel containing a bas-relief of a saint, presumably St Peter, holding a pair of keys. A huge, panelled door, studded with iron nail-heads, was firmly closed.

"There has always been a church here, from the foundation of the settlement, in the fifteenth century," said Emília. "But what you see now was built much later."

"About 1800, I'd say," murmured Victor.

"You're right," said Emília, and smiled brightly. "Notice the —"

Behind them, a woman screamed. They all turned. Across the square, the wine truck was running down the hill. Accelerating. The driver seemed to be unable to make the brakes work. Now it was racing towards them, and the driver was sounding the horn continuously. He must have decided that ramming a wooden door was preferable to ramming a stone wall, because he steered the truck directly at the entrance. The tourists scrambled out of the way. Owen grabbed

The measure of all things

one elderly lady and pulled her to the side. The truck was just inches away as it charged past them, up the steps, and hit the door. The sound was like a ship hitting a reef.

"Merda!" shouted Emília, then checked herself. "Oh dear," she said. "Now, I want everyone to move back. Right back."

The truck seemed to have fared better than the door, and the driver appeared to be back in control. He managed to reverse the truck into the centre of the square.

Owen would have obeyed Emília's instruction, but he happened to glance at the shattered door. Something about it wasn't right. "Look at this," he said to Saskia. She joined him, and peered at the timber. So did Victor and Cassie.

"I don't believe it," said Saskia. She paused. "It's plywood, with an oak veneer on the front. And the nail-heads are glued on."

Victor straightened up and turned around, to look at the church interior. But there wasn't any church interior. No pews, no altar, no pulpit, no statues of saints. A great empty space, with a concrete floor, and flat, grey walls. Like an aircraft hanger. All four of them walked in, and looked around.

"See those props?" said Victor to Owen, pointing at large, plain buttresses, supporting the outside wall. "How old would you say they were?"

"About a year," said Owen. "They're reinforced concrete."

"It's all a fake, isn't it?" said Saskia, wonderingly.

What we did on our holidays

"Have you noticed how big it is?" asked Cassie. "This space, I mean? Bigger than the church, from the outside. It must stretch behind the Governor's Palace, and the Custom House."

"So the whole square's a fake. Maybe the whole town. Just stage scenery," said Owen.

"It had *me* fooled," said Victor.

Suddenly, men emerged from the shadows. Men in army fatigues, wearing helmets. Carrying automatic rifles. Apparently, one of them was an officer.

"Put your hands up," he snapped.

"We're just tourists. We haven't done anything," protested Owen.

"The hell you haven't. Come with us. Don't try to run, or we *will* shoot you. Be sure of that." He sounded vaguely like a Nigerian who had spent time at Sandhurst.

"Where are you taking us?" asked Saskia.

"To jail," he said.

* * * * *

In Hang Kia, a butcher buys the pig. As he takes it back to his shop, the pig sneezes. The butcher breathes in microscopic droplets from the pig's exhalations, and catches the virus.

* * * * *

The jail wasn't quite what they'd expected. It was like a lounge in an up-market hotel. Thick maroon-coloured carpet, plush furniture, air-conditioning, tasteful decorations, a self-service coffee machine,

The measure of all things

and en-suite toilets. But the door was locked, and there were no windows.

The four of them sat on a leather sofa. To begin with, they didn't say much. Then Saskia said, "One of them pointed his gun at me. I suddenly thought, he's going to shoot me. I'm going to die here."

Owen put his arm round her, protectively. She was trembling. He wasn't, but he looked abnormally pale.

Victor went to the coffee machine and came back with cups of tea for both of them. They took them gratefully and sipped.

"It's got sugar in it?" said Saskia.

"Yes. I know you don't normally take it, but, this time, I thought you needed some."

"Thank you," she said, and smiled.

"Cassie, can I get you something?"

She nodded. "Yeah, thanks. Black coffee, no sugar."

Victor was a little surprised. "I must say, you're taking this very calmly."

"Well, I don't honestly think they're going to shoot us. Or lock us up indefinitely. They'll have to assume that we've got family back home, who would make a big fuss. I think they'll probably try to buy us off."

"You don't frighten easily, do you?" said Victor.

"So I'm told. But what I'm interested in is the whole set-up. What are they trying to achieve here?"

"What do you think?"

Cassie looked thoughtful. "I'm very puzzled," she said, and explained why. The others made some

What we did on our holidays

suggestions, but none of them had a convincing answer.

After about half an hour, the door opened, and a grey-haired man came in. He wore a dark business suit, and looked like a European. He sat down facing them. When he spoke, he had a slight Australian accent.

"Ladies and gentlemen," he said, with a self-deprecating smile, "I do apologise for detaining you like this. My name is Dr Fletcher. You've discovered something we'd hoped to keep secret. The town of São Pedro is not what it seems. We built it all from scratch, mostly from concrete. Like Disneyland. Obviously, we did it to make this a more attractive tourist destination."

"Obviously," said Owen.

"You might think this was sharp practice," said Fletcher.

"Yes," said Saskia.

"We'd rather this was kept confidential. We're prepared to pay you each a thousand pounds, for disruption to your holiday. In addition, you can complete your holiday, here, if you like, on condition that you don't go anywhere near São Pedro. We'll refund all your expenses and charge you nothing. But, you *will* have to sign a strict non-disclosure agreement."

"Well, that's a generous offer," said Cassie. "But there is one problem."

"What's that?"

The measure of all things

"You say you did it to make this a more attractive tourist destination. We've been discussing it. We don't believe you."

Fletcher looked shocked. "Why not?"

"Look," she said. "I'm an economist. I've got a fair idea of what a deception on this scale would cost. And of the profit margin on a resort like this. Factoring in the risk that you'd be found out, you couldn't possible make a profit on it, in any reasonable time-span. So there's something else, something you're not telling us."

Fletcher looked harried. "Well, I never thought it would work. But the Board of Directors, they have such wild schemes … you can't say no to them …"

Victor shook his head. "No, I don't buy it. It's too thorough, too painstaking. It must have taken a long time, and cost a lot of money, and a lot of brains. What's really going on, Mr Fletcher?"

Fletcher was silent for a while. Then he said, "Could I offer you each two thousand pounds to keep quiet?"

Cassie shook her head firmly.

Fletcher closed his eyes and said nothing. Then he spoke quietly. "You're my worst nightmare. The ones who can't be fooled … To hell with it; I'm sick of it. The lying. The threats. I'm a *doctor*. I never wanted to get involved in this … deception … in the first place. I'd rather just tell the truth."

"So tell us the truth," said Saskia, gently.

"You don't know what they'll do to you, if you know. Neither do I."

"We'll take our chances," said Cassie.

Fletcher was silent for a long time. Then he said, "You'll keep quiet about it, OK? Not tell anyone?"

They said nothing.

He spoke again. "We're called the Curador Project. We're associated with the World Health Organisation, very loosely. We're funded by an American billionaire. He pays all the bills. The airport, the master chef, all the staff we brought in from Angola, and trained up – he paid for it all. And the Nigerian security men, too. He never quibbles. He wants to be one of the survivors."

"Go on," said Saskia.

"Every year, there's a flu epidemic. A new strain of the flu virus. It starts in the Far East, and spreads round the world. People who are already feeble die, and so do old people. But, by and large, we cope. The world, that is. We quickly invent a vaccine. The virus doesn't spread too fast. People have some resistance."

They all listened intently.

"Once in a while, there's a pandemic that we can't cope with. It happened in 1968, and in 1957. But the really big one was in 1918. Did you know that it killed more people than the First World War? Three times as many. When it was raging, there was a Chief Medical Officer in the United States who predicted that it was going to destroy human civilisation. And, you know what? It seemed perfectly possible."

He paused.

"We're about due for another pandemic. The probability of one in the next five years is much higher than you'd think – or rather, than you've been told. Our vaccines won't save us if it's a very fast-spreading infection."

Another pause.

"The interesting thing about the 1918 pandemic was that it tended not to kill older people. It *scythed* through the young ones. Why do you suppose that was?"

"I don't know," said Victor.

"Because the older people had caught a mild form of it, a quarter of a century earlier. It immunised them. Before the young people were born."

"Where is all this leading?" said Victor.

"We can't predict what the killer flu will be." He fell silent for a moment. Then he said, "It will be something that people have no resistance to – a crossover. Do you know what that is? There are flu infections that you find among wildfowl. Usually, humans can't catch them. But if one succeeds in jumping from the bird's body to a human's body, or maybe to a pig's body and then a human's body, it's a new disease and it's liable to cause a lot of damage. The next serious crossover will appear in the Far East, probably. There's a lot of pig farms and duck farms there. And it will spread easily from person to person – that's what makes it serious. There are two key antigenic glycoproteins involved: hemagglutinin and neuraminidase. We call them HA and NA. We spent a long, long time trying to predict exactly what sorts of HA and NA would feature in the killer flu. But there are just too many variables. Our best guesses are H10 N8 and H7 N9, but there are so many variations." He paused again. Then he said,

What we did on our holidays

"What we *can* do is to produce a mild infection, which will provide protection against the killer, whatever it is. We're pretty sure it will do that. So we formulated it."

"You formulated it? Meaning that you cooked up the virus? And you released it into the world?"

"We wanted to, but the national governments wouldn't let us."

"Why not?"

"About one person in a thousand who catches our tailor-made flu suffers an extreme reaction. They die. No government wants to kill large numbers of their people. So they vetoed it. Their attitude was 'The pandemic will probably never happen – we'll trust to luck'. We showed them the figures, the probability calculations. They weren't interested. Politicians don't understand probability calculations. We told them we planned to release it anyway, without involving them. They threatened to put us in prison, as terrorists."

"So what did you do?" said Victor.

"We modified our virus – we turned it into a slow-build viral infection. Now, it takes about six months for it to manifest itself."

"What has all this got to do with this place?"

He laughed, mirthlessly. "Everyone who comes here is infected with our flu. You don't notice it – nothing will happen to you until next winter. Then you'll be mildly unwell. Your family will catch it, and your friends. People you work with. People on the same bus or train. A few people will die. But the world population will get some measure of protection. And

The measure of all things

far more people will live through the great pandemic, when it comes."

"I see," said Cassie. "And why did you feel it necessary to build São Pedro?"

Fletcher opened his eyes and shrugged. "Our mission, here, is to inoculate the people of Western Europe. There are other centres dealing with other parts of the developed world. As to the third world, we can be more direct – their disease control is so poor, they can't really stop us. But here, we're focussed on Western Europe. Every nation, every class. It's our mission to access them all, if we can."

"That doesn't really answer my question. Why São Pedro? Why the fake citadel?"

"We weren't getting enough applications. In particular, we weren't getting enough educated people. Cultured people, who want to see the historical sites. We're trying to inoculate everyone. All classes." He closed his eyes again. He looked very tired. "So we faked something up for the educated folk. Window dressing, to bring them into the shop."

There was a long silence. Then Saskia said "You infected us as soon as we got here. We've all got the virus?"

"Yes."

"Maybe your virus will kill us. Your mild flu. It kills one in a thousand. It could be one of us."

Fletcher said, "If I left you to face the lethal version of the flu, unprotected, that could kill you too. And it's much more likely."

What we did on our holidays

"Or maybe it will mutate. Viruses do that, don't they? Maybe it will turn into the killer version?"

Fletcher's voice was almost inaudible. "I wish I could give you a guarantee. But I can't. No one has ever done this before. I think the chances of it becoming the killer flu are very low, but I can't promise anything."

* * * * *

Next day, Owen, Saskia, Victor and Cassie flew back to Heathrow. They didn't speak much on the journey.

* * * * *

In Hang Kia, the butcher starts to feel sick. No human being has ever had such a virus in his body before, or anything very like it. The butcher's body has antibodies for many strains of flu, but not this one.

The doctor who treats him a week later is horrified by the speed with which the infection has destroyed the butcher's lungs. There is no way that his life can be saved. The doctor is even more horrified by the fact that the virus finds no difficulty in spreading directly from person to person.

The great race, between the flu pandemic, and the Curador Project virus, has begun.

A handful of dust

Eight AM. A small, square, patch on my desk lit up, and a woman's voice said "Paramount Chief Detective Lektuvas is here to see you. He apologises for arriving unannounced. Will you see him?"

I had a moment of blind panic. A Paramount Chief Detective? Hell, I'm only an Inspector! I recovered, and said "Of course. Send him in." One does not send away a Paramount Chief Detective.

A thickset man, with thinning black hair, walked through the door, wearing a dark business suit. He didn't favour the lapels that had recently come back into fashion. Instead, he wore a small round badge on each of his breast pockets. The one on the left said CDHS, standing for Chief Directorate for Harmony & Stability. The other showed a small gold star over three tiny silver stars. Precious little to indicate that he was one of the most senior policemen in the world. He sat himself down in the only other chair in my office.

"Inspector Niveau, I'm glad to see you. You have a reputation for being very good at your job. Investigating homicide."

"Well, thank you sir. I've had a few successes…"

"You have indeed. I have a case for you. It's urgent, and highly confidential. You are to work on it, with your team, to the exclusion of everything else, starting

A handful of dust

now. You can have all the resources you want. I have, of course, cleared this with your superiors."

"You'd better tell me the details, sir."

"Councillor James Dossat has been murdered."

"Oh my God."

"Quite. We've never had a World Council member murdered before, let alone a member of the Supreme Directorate. It's essential that we find out who did it. Or, more likely, who ordered someone to do it."

"Are we assuming that it was a political crime? An assassination?"

"It almost certainly was. But of course, you'll want to explore all possibilities." He said, "May I?" as he pushed the button on my coffee dispenser and poured himself a cup. "Certain political factions stand to benefit from his death. There will be a by-election, and probably a substantial shift in power." He sighed. "The Pacific faction, the Atlantic faction, and the Mediterranean faction all stand to gain. The World Secretary is very insistent that we – the CDHS – find the culprit, and tell the public. If we cannot do so, it will be a disaster, for us. If we announce that it was one of those factions, then of course their political advantage will be wiped out. If we name the *wrong* faction, sooner or later it will come out, and that will also be a disaster."

I got up, walked to the coffee dispenser, and poured myself a cup. I said,

"You mentioned that it was urgent, and highly confidential …"

The measure of all things

"Yes, indeed. The death, and the circumstances of the death, will be announced in twenty-three hours, at midday tomorrow, New York time. Until then, it is completely secret. At that time, the writ for the by-election will be moved. The law's complicated, but basically it says that neither I nor anyone else can announce anything that prejudices one of the parties, *after* the by-election's been called. So, we have to be able to name the organisation that hired the assassin, just *before* the writ is moved. If there is an assassin. In 23 hours' time."

* * * * *

How quickly can you assemble a murder team? This time, I managed it in half an hour. I had a nasty feeling that the case would be impossible to crack, given the insane deadline, and that I'd be the scapegoat when the dung hit the windmill. But I wasn't going to go down without a fight. Along with the team, I took Lieutenant-Superintendant Bronius, who Lektuvas had left with me as his link-man.

We arrived at Councillor Dossat's mansion, on the outskirts of Geneva, an hour later. His mother, a small, grey-haired woman, was distraught: "My son was a great man ... a *truly* great man ... now he's nothing but ... but a handful of dust ...". She dissolved into sobs.

I talked to the Councillor's manservant, a self-possessed man in his early forties. He was clearly distressed, but was controlling himself better than Dossat's mother.

It seemed that Dossat had had a particular liking for both sunsets and sunrises. On evenings when the sky was clear, he would sit on his terrace as the sun went

A handful of dust

down, thinking whatever thoughts world politicians thought, and admiring the sky as it slowly changed colour, from blue to salmon to deep red to black. He would eat a few olives from a small bowl. Then he would work on his papers, far into the night, before going to bed for perhaps five hours. Then he would get up, go onto the terrace on the other side of the house, and watch the sun come up. Once again, he would have a small bowl of olives at his side.

The previous night had been clear, and Dossat had been sitting in his accustomed seat at dawn. As chance would have it, he had accidentally knocked over the bowl of olives, and they had rolled around on the terrace paving. It seems unlikely that he paid any attention to the mishap; he would leave it to his servants to clear up the mess. But, shortly afterwards, the killer had clambered over the wall and shot him with a handgun. The gun was a Russian Galupchik, designed to fire an ultra-high-velocity round, which would do massive damage to the victim's internal organs, wherever the bullet hit. The bullet struck his neck, and Dossat died immediately, beyond any hope of resuscitation. The killer then attempted to rescale the wall, but slipped on an olive and fell, at which moment the Councillor's bodyguard ran out of the house and shot him dead. An understandable reaction, when faced with a killer with a Galupchik.

So, we had the corpses of victim and killer. Dossat was middle-aged, and looked like anyone's idea of a Swiss city lawyer (which he had been, before he went into politics). The killer was probably in his twenties, and fit enough to be a soldier, although he hadn't any tattoos.

The measure of all things

We had the murder weapon. We had a likely motive. Not enough.

"Fehrman," I said to my number three. "Talk to the mother and the rest of the servants. We need to know about family and acquaintances. Dossat's love life. Personal enemies. We can't assume it was a political murder." She nodded, and made a note on her pad. "Goehner —" Goehner was my number two — "The killer must have had a get-away vehicle. Search all the streets within half a kilometre."

We found the vehicle three streets away. A charge of RDX-9 had burnt it out completely.

I thought about that. My team had already checked the killer's body, and found no ID material of any sort. "Germond, check the killer for a heart monitor. And get a DNA sample. And sweep him for pollen grains." These days, palynology can narrow a pollen grain down to a single region — maybe even a particular city.

He found a heart monitor, embedded in the man's chest. Someone somewhere had monitored the man's health by a radio link, and, as soon as he died, had sent the radio signal that blew up his car.

After another hour and a half, my people had worked over the crime scene, and sent both bodies off to the local morgue. We had statements from the bodyguard, mother, manservant, maid and cook, Dossat's phone records and the contents of his computer. From the house's security cameras, we had pictures of everyone who'd come through the door in the last year. We had the killer's DNA, fingerprints and retinal scans, though not his name. I held a team meeting.

A handful of dust

"Fehrman, tell us about possible killers from his private life."

"Well, boss, he had a complicated love life. An ex-wife, and two lovers; both men. No children. One brother, who despised him."

"Frick, what are the chances that it was a burglary?"

"I wouldn't have thought so, boss. The killer didn't seem to want to take anything. Just do the hit, then run."

"Germond – the killer's DNA?"

"Best I can do is that he was a Latino, probably from the USA."

"Pollen grains?"

"Yeah, that's quite interesting. He's covered in them. They're from all over North America. I'd say someone deliberately dusted him, on the off-chance that he'd end up dead."

"Right, team, we're going to have to wing this one. We have twenty hours to crack the case. We can't afford to follow any unpromising lines. So, we'll assume it wasn't domestic, or a burglary, or a random attack; it was political."

"Why, boss?" asked Fehrman.

"Because it's so slick. The killer was a professional, with a professional's weapon. He was fit enough to be a commando, and, if he hadn't slipped at exactly the wrong moment, he'd have got away. His controller destroyed his getaway car, and any evidence it might have had in it, the moment he died. That level of slickness means politics. Now, we have the killer's

The measure of all things

body, and we could do an all-nations search on his DNA."

"It would take twenty-four hours," murmured Goehner. "We haven't time."

"Exactly. We could try tracking the killer's path back to the USA, assuming that's where he came from. But we don't have time to search the pictures from every European airport, either. And I think we can assume he will have used at least one disguise. Lieutenant-superintendant –" I turned to Bronius "– we have to start at the other end. I need a list of the people who might have hired the hitman. I need to interview them. And I may need to do a bit of strong-arm stuff."

"Call me Jonas," he murmured. "Yes, certainly. The three factions each have someone who runs ... well, their special operations, so to speak. They're all in the USA. I can have them arrested, but I'm afraid I can't have them brought here – American law, you know."

So I left Germond with the bodies in the morgue, and took the rest of the team across the Atlantic.

It took seven hours. A lot of time to waste, given the deadline, but there was no help for it. I told the team to get some sleep, and did so myself.

We touched down at Kansas City. It took an hour to install ourselves in the Kansas City Police Headquarters. Bronius' credentials, and the mention that he had the backing of P C D Lektuvas, worked like magic.

Kansas City was where Casey Perez, Research Manager for the Pacific Faction, had his HQ. It being eleven pm, Central Standard Time, we broke down

A handful of dust

the door of his office and confiscated his computer and his vacuum cleaner. Then we waited for him to turn up. Which he did, in his pyjamas, about twenty minutes later, in response to the office alarm system. He was powerfully built. Even in his pyjamas, he looked intimidating.

"Who the hell are you?" he demanded. I flashed my credentials.

"Mr Perez, do you know this man?" I showed him a 3-D image of the assassin's body.

"Never seen him before in my life. Bloody outrage! Just 'cos you've gotta piece of paper signed by the world cops! You'll hear from my lawyers!"

I apologised, rather curtly, and we left.

Then Fehrman and I travelled to Laredo, Texas – another two hours – and did the same to Delroy Mitchell, Head of Forward Planning for the Atlantic Faction: we broke into his office, confiscated his office equipment, set off the alarm, and waited around for him. He turned up pretty quickly too. He'd had time to dress – in a black work suit, with a big red circle on the chest, extending onto his arms – but he had the same vaguely thuggish quality that Casey Perez had had.

We showed him the same picture. "Mr Mitchell, do you know this man?"

He too declared that he did not, and that he was outraged, and that he would set his lawyers onto us. We apologised and left.

The two of us travelled to Oakland, California – another three hours – and broke into Rusty Nelson's office, he being the Director of Envisioning for the

The measure of all things

Mediterranean Faction. We took his office equipment, and made sure the alarm went off. After a short wait, he turned up. He was dressed in a cream work suit, with a diamond brooch at his throat. By now, I wasn't surprised to see that, under the slick clothes, he looked like a gangster's enforcer. I wondered whether every political faction had a team of bully-boys working for it. It was beginning to look that way.

We showed him the same picture. "Do you know this man, Mr Nelson?"

He too declared that he didn't, and that he was outraged, and that his lawyers would ensure that we were thrown out of the police force. We made our excuses and left.

Three angry Americans, hauled out of their beds in the middle of the night, three meaningless answers. I had six hours to wrap this case up, and I was dog-tired. Fortunately, I had the technology. Bronius had had the equipment delivered to our Kansas City HQ, and my team was busy, setting it up. Fehrman and I arrived there two hours later. Just four hours left. It might be enough, with a lot of luck. Assuming the proof was in our grasp.

* * * * *

At exactly twelve noon, New York time, the Speaker of the World Parliament held a press conference and announced Councillor James Dossat's death. There were shocked gasps when he revealed that the Councillor had been assassinated. "As the law requires," he said, "I am issuing the writ for the by-election; I shall do so in ten minutes' time. As to the identity of the assassin, that will have to be established by due process of law. However, P C D

Lektuvas of the CDHS wishes to make a statement on the subject of this killing."

On a large screen behind him, a huge image of Lektuvas and myself appeared, sitting side by side at a large desk.

"The world should be informed that an official of the Atlantic Faction has been arrested for commissioning this murder," said Lektuvas.

"What is the evidence against this person?" asked the reporter from the New York Times.

"A fleck of skin was found in his office. It contained the DNA of the assassin. In spite of the fact that he denied ever having met the man," I said.

The genetic analyser had needed almost all the four hours to test the contents of the three vacuum cleaners. Half a kilogram of dust. Thousands upon thousands of flecks of skin. And then one came up as a positive match, from Delroy Mitchell's carpet. Together with a good many pollen grains, from the north, east, south and west of the USA.

Say this for the old-fashioned policing methods: they usually deliver the goods, in the end.

The measure of all things

Man is the measure of all things
                    Protagoras, c.490BC – c.420 BC

Joseph walked down a long tunnel, more or less cylindrical but flat-bottomed, past a seemingly endless array of men. A continuous fluorescent strip, set into the top of the tunnel, ensured that they were all evenly illuminated. They were lined up in five ranks, they were all the same height, and there were a hundred and sixty files. Very much like an officer inspecting a huge squad of troops, he glanced at each man as he passed them. They stood silently, wearing plain grey overalls, each with a number on the right breast, and didn't look at him. Their posture was mostly erect, sturdy, though a few of them looked a little stooped. Joseph's glance took in their posture, but mainly dwelt on each man's face. The great majority of them looked happy, or at least contented. A few looked bored. One of them looked mildly unhappy. Joseph had done this many, many times before, and he moved along the files quite rapidly, nodding to himself occasionally. Eventually, he reached the end. He murmured "Good, good. But number 598 needs watching."

At the end, the tunnel terminated abruptly. He stepped out of the entrance, and found himself on the

The measure of all things

edge of a village, in bright sunlight. A few paces took him to the main street, which was lined on both sides with rather nondescript shops, and he strode down it. On his left was a teashop. He opened the door, went in and sat down at a vacant table. Immediately, a waitress came across, smiled at him, and offered a menu.

Without looking at it, he said, "I'm quite hungry, but I don't know what I want."

She smiled again, and said, "Why don't you try the country hotpot? I've heard customers say that it's quite filling."

He looked at his watch, and said, "I'm in a hurry. I haven't really got time for anything. I'll have to be off."

Once again she smiled, and said "You must come back later. We're open all afternoon."

He got up and left. Outside, he made a point of barging over the road just as a car drove down the street. The driver braked hard, smiled, and waved him across. On the other side, he approached the door of a baker's shop. A young woman opened the door, and held it open for him as he walked in. He lurched towards her: she moved a little out of his way, with no hint of reproof in her expression.

Further down the road, a middle-aged woman was collecting money to support the homeless. She held out her collecting tin, with an expectant look on her face. He stared at her, and said, curtly, "I wouldn't dream of giving any money for *that* cause."

"Well," she said, "If you change your mind, I'll still be here." And she, too, gave him a little smile.

The measure of all things

And so it went on. Everywhere he went, people went out of their way to be polite. That was just as it should be. Skilfully, he probed their politeness. In due course, he was satisfied. He made his way to a phone box at the far end of the village, opened the door, and stepped through.

Immediately, he found himself somewhere quite different: Engineering Control Centre, surrounded by the humming cabinets that housed the mainframe. The walls were painted a neutral cream colour, the ceiling emitting a soft glow. There was no sunlit village behind him: just a padded cabinet, the black padding moulded to his body shape, with electrodes that detached themselves from his skull as he pulled his head away. He'd been through the transition many times before, but he was still struck by the slight, almost undetectable, contrast between the quality of the reality he was now experiencing and the virtual reality in which he had just been immersed. *This* reality was a little harder and colder.

He massaged the numbness out of his limbs, then walked over to his desk, picked up the clipboard, and wrote a whole series of ticks in boxes. He included a note about the incipient problem with system 598. Then he dated and signed it: Joseph Calder, Systems Engineer.

* * * *

The lecturer watched the new intake as they filed into the lecture theatre and sat down. Seven young men, seven young women. Not really enough. He fervently hoped for a high pass rate. The company was seriously short of Systems Engineers.

The measure of all things

He rapped on the rostrum. "Good morning, everyone. The Programme Leader has welcomed you already. I'd like to add my own greetings, and say I hope you enjoy the course. It's time to get started. Here's a short horror story."

He touched a switch, and the wall behind him became a view of alien countryside, with an industrial plant in the far distance. Beyond it was a city. Close at hand, small, lizard-like creatures scurried around in the undergrowth. The leaf shapes were a little too straight-edged, and the prevailing colours a little too blue, for this to be vegetation growing on planet Earth. Suddenly, there was a blinding flare. As it subsided, a shockwave of extreme heat could be seen spreading out from the place where the factory had been. It struck the city, which flashed into flames. For a split second, the lizards and the plants in the foreground were blazing. Then the shockwave destroyed the camera, and the screen went blank.

"Not a simulation," he said, "real footage of what happened on Epsilon Eridani Four. By pure chance, a wildlife cameraman was shooting in the direction of the fusion reactor when it blew up. His camera was destroyed, but the video survived. He was killed, and so were half a million other people, and a promising Earth-type planet was rendered more or less uninhabitable. The worst industrial disaster in human history. What's the lesson to be learnt, from an engineering point of view?"

"Don't build fusion reactors?" offered a young man in the second row. Everyone laughed. They all knew that there was no chance of *that* happening. All colonised planets were simply too hungry for electricity. And, since none of them had a geological

The measure of all things

history much like planet Earth's, none of them had any deposits of coal or oil. The terraformed ones didn't even have deposits of peat.

"Build fusion plants fail-safe?" suggested another student, a young woman sitting behind the man who had spoken first.

"Maybe," said the lecturer. "What does fail-safe mean?"

"When a plant fails, it automatically fails into a safe state," she replied.

"Correct. But I disagree with the suggestion. The lesson to be learnt from the Epsilon Eridani catastrophe was that we *can't* build fail-safe."

The students stirred uneasily – they were deeply imbued with the value of fail-safe engineering, and were clearly shocked by the idea that it might be unattainable.

"The plant was *supposed* to be fail-safe, but, when it came to the crunch, the automatic shut-down mechanisms failed simultaneously with the central reactor. And, of course, it hadn't been possible to test those mechanisms in advance, using a real-life crisis. So the fusion reactor became a hydrogen bomb."

"So we should try harder. Think the problems – the possible emergencies – through more thoroughly." So said the young woman in the third row.

"You might think so. But the Interstellar Government saw things differently. They concluded that, above the automatic, computerised control layer, there must always be a layer of human control. It's called the Michie Window, for historic reasons. And that, ladies and gentlemen, presents us with a serious problem."

The measure of all things

* * * * *

Another tour of inspection. Joseph walked down the same tunnel, past the same ranks of smiling men in overalls. About three quarters of the way down the line, he registered that the men weren't smiling any more. They all looked bored. Then he came across a whole file who looked angry. In the next file, two looked miserable, one furious, and one despairing. The last of these seemed bent under the weight of his woes.

"Doesn't look good," murmured Joseph. He read the numbers on the men's chests. "Everything from 595 to 604," he muttered. From then on, the men simply looked bored, or cross.

He broke into a run. At the end of the tunnel, he jumped across the threshold, and raced for the village high street.

* * * * *

Behind the lecturer, the image on the wall was of 800 dials, arranged in rows. The needles moved slowly, some of them up, some of them down. Some flickered right, then left. A few were stationary.

"Read-outs from the 800 prime parameters of a standard-design fusion reactor," he said. "Can any of you tell me which of the dials just went over a red line?"

There was silence.

"Thought not. Of course, we can make it easier for the engineer by providing red flashing lights."

The measure of all things

Deep in the array, one of the dials sprouted a red alarm light, which started flashing. The students looked relieved.

"But it's not always that simple."

All the dials sprouted lights, and they all started flashing in different colours and at different speeds: some of them blue, some of them purple, and some of them red.

"Can any of you tell me which of the red lights is flashing fastest?"

More silence.

"The truth is, human beings didn't evolve to read dials, or see flashing lights. Our remote ancestors, hunter-gatherers on the African plains, didn't need that skill. We don't do it very well. Which suggests that a different user interface is required. Now, we know quite a lot about human beings, don't we?"

The students looked puzzled.

"Specifically, we know that, for about two hundred thousand years, we have lived together in large groups. A couple of dozen people, or more. Knowing what your fellow group members are feeling is important, and difficult. Because of that, we have become very good at reading each other."

The wall behind him showed a series of anthropological photos from centuries before: primitive peoples, with various different skin colours, in various different habitats. Their faces showed a variety of different expressions, and their bodies a variety of different postures, but they were all vaguely familiar: you could get a good idea of what these people were thinking.

"Someone with refined interpersonal skills — and that means you, ladies and gentlemen: we chose you on that basis — can tell whether someone is upset, almost instantly, by glancing at them. We decided we could use that. We built a user interface where those 800 parameter read-outs are translated into the facial expressions, and the postures, of mannequins in a virtual world."

An array of computer-generated faces appeared on the screen behind him — the same face each time, but showing different expressions. Happy, bored, sad, angry, frightened, disgusted, amazed, and several others. All except the first were annotated with a specific engineering malfunction.

The lecturer gave the class a few moments to look from face to face, and to read the captions. Then he went on, "For the more subtle malfunctions, we needed something different. Sensitive humans are also adept at noticing deliberate rudeness. So we have another set of mannequins with repertoires of behaviour. Their level of politeness accurately corresponds to how well the underlying process is doing its job."

On the screen behind him appeared a picture of a sunlit village.

* * * * *

Joseph reached the village teashop, opened the door, and strode in. The waitress glanced at him, and said, "We don't serve your sort here. Piss off."

He turned on his heel, out of the shop, and started to cross the road. A car roared towards him and, as it drew level, the driver shouted "Get out of the road, wanker!"

The measure of all things

On the far side of the road, he approached the bakery door. A woman barred his way.

"Please let me past," he said.

She sneered. "Why should I, gay boy?"

He raised his head and spoke into an unseen microphone. "Emergency. Code sixteen".

Half a mile away from Engineering Control Centre, the emergency shutdown system began its struggle with the demonic forces of a fusion reactor running out of control.

Two gentlemen of Tushkek

It wasn't the first corpse I'd seen, but it was almost certainly the richest.

Zamira Cherimova lay on her bed, in her large, elegantly decorated bedroom. She'd been carried there, by the servants, when she suddenly collapsed while reading a fashion magazine in the family sitting room. The family's doctor had pronounced her dead – probably poisoned. She was wearing what I judged to be very expensive designer clothes, and a diamond necklace. That looked wrong. What kind of eighteen-year-old wears designer clothes and jewellery, if all she intends to do is sit around reading a magazine?

It was a cool spring day in 2030, in a secluded Geneva suburb. Not that you could see much of it from here. The house was built like a fortress. The master of the house – Utkirbek Cherimov – seldom went out, and neither he nor his daughters ever went out without bodyguards.

Mr Cherimov was distraught. White faced and shaking, he kept muttering to himself. His younger daughter Nilufar stood silently beside him, wide-eyed and fearful. His interpreter translated the mutterings when I asked him to – "My beloved Zamira – who would do this to me?" – but, mostly, he kept quiet. The fact that there *was* an interpreter was significant.

The measure of all things

Utkirbek Cherimov had always been rich – so rich that he didn't have to bother about learning English, or any other major world language. Nor did he have to make do with machine translation, like the rest of us: he could afford to employ a multilingual human translator, and a personal doctor.

I turned to Dr Isabekov. "So, doctor, your opinion: what killed her?"

He hesitated. "Chief Inspector Niveau, surely your own experts will be better able –"

I interrupted. "You saw the body first. You called the police. Tell me what you think killed her."

He sighed. "Cyanide poisoning. Because of the sudden collapse, and the smell of bitter almonds on her breath."

"Dr Durian?" Durian is the pathologist, permanently attached to my team. He'd taken a blood sample when we arrived, and his portable analyser had masses of data scrolling across its little screen.

"I agree. Enough cyanide in her bloodstream to kill her several times over."

"Tell me more."

"Well, it's a fast-acting poison. So, assuming nobody sprayed prussic acid into her face, or shot her with a poison dart, it must have been something she ate just a little before she collapsed."

I summoned the housekeeper. All the servants were Asbaks, like the Cherimovs themselves, but at least they all spoke English. The housekeeper – Raya Agalarovna – was a tall, dignified woman.

Two gentlemen of Tushkek

"Ms Agalarovna, tell me what Zamira Cherimova ate, during the hour before she collapsed."

"She had kartoshka manti for lunch – her favourite – and she drank some orange juice with them. Then she tried some cakes she'd been given."

"What cakes?"

"Some delicacies – her gentleman admirers gave them to her. I'm afraid I don't know which."

"I see. Quite a substantial midday meal."

"I've told her, more than once, that she should watch what she eats, if she wants to keep her figure, but you know what young girls are like – they never listen."

It struck me that eighteen years old hardly qualified as 'a young girl', but no doubt the Asbaks saw things differently. Also, that the housekeeper was talking about the unfortunate Zamira as if she was still alive. I said, "Fehrmann, go with Ms Agalarovna to the kitchen. If there's any of that midday meal still around, I want all of it packaged up and back at the lab straight away. The orange juice, the kartoshka manti – whatever that is – the cakes. I dare say some of it's back in the fridge. But search the waste bins too. Goehner, find out who these gentleman admirers are, and when they last came to the house."

* * * * *

Later that day, I called the team together to review the case.

"So," I said, "We have quite a few suspects. The housekeeper, the cook, and the kitchen maid all had access to her meal before she ate it. Maybe other people too. Either of the two potential boyfriends

The measure of all things

could have given her spiked cake. But nobody seems to have a convincing motive. Germond, tell me about the servants."

"Well, Chief, I'd say they all regarded her as a spoilt brat. But they didn't dislike her enough to kill her. Anyway, she was their meal ticket. They're paid well – if the master sells up and moves back to Asbakistan, they're liable to lose their jobs"

"Frick, what about the master? Utkirbek Cherimov?"

"The wealthiest man ever to come out of Asbakistan. Moved to Geneva for the sake of his daughters' education. His wife died ten years ago, and Zamira and Nilufar were the only children. He seems to have doted on Zamira."

"I got that impression too. How did he make his money?"

"Inherited it, mostly. His father was a politician, just after the Soviet Empire broke up. It's generally assumed that he feathered his nest, at the expense of the state Treasury. He invested the money more carefully than some of the other politicos, which meant that his son is sitting on a fortune. So was Zamira, God rest her soul."

"Goehner, what about these two mysterious gentleman admirers?"

"The first is Akrom Temirov. The second is Maqsud Karayev. They're both sons of fine old Asbak families, living in Tushkek. Invited here by Utkirbek himself, so that he could decide whether either of them was a suitable match for his daughter. Seems hopelessly old-fashioned to me, but then I'm not an Asbak."

Two gentlemen of Tushkek

"Or a billionaire," I said. "What's this business with the cakes?"

"Well, you or I might take a woman a box of chocolates. In Asbakistan, they say it with cake. Temirov brought Zamira a napaleon torti. Karayev brought her a ptichye moloko. Rather upmarket confectionary."

"I imagine they are. OK, both of them are suspects, because of the gifts, though I really can't see what their motive would be. The key question is, what part of what Zamira ate was poisoned? Dr Durian?"

Durian fidgeted, looking deeply embarrassed. "I can't find it," he said.

"What?"

"I really can't find it. The orange juice – the coffee – the kartoshka manti – the napaleon torti – the ptichye moloko – we recovered them all, and I can't find inorganic cyanides in any of them. I looked at other things too, like the salt and the pepper, and the sugar, and they're all clean. I thought she might have taken a pill – an indigestion tablet, maybe, or a headache tablet, but we'd have found traces in her stomach, and they aren't there."

"Well, keep looking. She finished up with cyanide in her blood-stream, and it seems pretty obvious that someone found a way to feed it to her." I sighed. "OK, that's one promising line of enquiry closed off, for now." I paused. "As I said before, lots of suspects, and none of them has much of a motive."

"Well, apart from the younger daughter, Chief," said Germond. "Now her sister's out of the way, I imagine she stands to inherit the family fortune."

The measure of all things

"Oh yes. Nilufar. I dare say there are cases on record of fifteen-year-olds poisoning their elder sisters, but I suspect they're very rare indeed. Still, we shouldn't rule anything out."

* * * * *

I detailed members of the team to investigate the people in the house on the day of the murder. Plus the two suitors.

As an afterthought, I had DNA samples taken from all the suspects, and sent off to be checked against Asbakistan state records. It struck me that one of Cherimov's business rivals might have planted an agent in the household, under an assumed name. Supposing that Cherimov had any business rivals. And supposing that Asbak business practices included assassinating your rivals' daughters.

I thought about what Germond had said about Nilufar. And it suddenly occurred to me that the two sisters might just have had lunch together.

* * * * *

Nilufar sat on the couch, in the sitting room where her sister had died, looking small and scared. Raya Agalarovna sat with her, acting as a chaperone.

"Tell me about that last lunch you and your sister had together," I said. I hoped my voice didn't sound too threatening.

"Cook made us her own special manti," she said. "We always liked it."

"And what did you drink with the meal?"

"Orange juice with the meal, and coffee afterwards."

Two gentlemen of Tushkek

"You both had orange juice and coffee?"

"Yes – there was a jug of orange juice on the table, and cook made a cafetière of coffee afterwards."

"What else did you eat?"

"Zamira had been given a couple of cakes. So we had them as pudding."

"You both had them?"

"Well ...we both had some of the napaleon torti. I didn't have any of the ptichye moloko."

"Why not?"

"It's got marshmallow in it. I don't like marshmallow."

"Tell me, what was Zamira wearing?"

"That special cream-coloured dress of hers. You must have seen it when ... when ..."

"I know. I did see it. Why was she dressed up in something special?"

"Akrom – that's Akrom Temirov – was coming round to see her in the afternoon. She wanted to impress him ..."

Nilufar suddenly dissolved into tears. If she was part of the murder plot, she was a bloody good actress.

* * * * *

I was back in my office, brooding about suspects with no motives, and poisoned food that didn't seem to contain any poison, when Frick called.

"Chief, something weird has happened."

The measure of all things

"Tell me."

"The Asbakistan Record Bureau came back, with the DNA results. All the servants are who they say they are, including the doctor and interpreter. But the two boyfriends – Temirov and Karayev – don't match at all. And Asbak Police HQ says neither of them ever left Tushkek."

"Right. Arrest both of them. For travelling on false papers."

"Can't, chief, they've both done a runner."

* * * * *

We caught them, though. They'd had their retinas scanned when they entered Switzerland, and they couldn't leave without having them scanned again. There's not much you can do to disguise your retinas.

It turned out that they were the Atallahanov brothers – Fuad and Tulkin – and they both belonged to the Thirteenth of February Group. Somehow, the Group had intercepted Utkirbek Cherimov's invitations to the Temirov and Karayev families, and dispatched a couple of imposters.

"What's the Thirteenth of February Group all about?" Frick asked. I was giving the team a final debriefing.

"On the thirteenth of February 2004, Asbak troops shot a crowd of protesters in Namanzan. Killed one and a half thousand people. Utkirbek Cherimov's father organised the massacre, and gave the order to fire. The Thirteenth of February Group have been looking for a way to get their revenge on him, or his family, ever since. I know, it's a generation ago, but they hold grudges a long time in Asbakistan."

"Poisoning the daughter seems pretty heartless."

"That was just the plan's first phase. At Zamira's funeral, they were going to shoot Utkirbek and Nilufar. Wipe out the whole family. But when we started taking DNA swabs, they knew the game was up."

"So which of the brothers murdered Zamira?"

"They both did."

"What? I don't understand."

"Dr Durian: please explain."

Durian beamed. "When we knew that *both* suitors were involved in the murder, it all became clear. The napaleon torti was laced with a cyanogenic glycoside called lotaustralin; it's quite harmless on its own. The ptichye moloko contained a special enzyme – linamarase – also quite harmless. When the two of them were mixed, in Zamira's stomach, the lotaustralin was converted to hydrogen cyanide. Zamira didn't stand a chance."

Suddenly, I wanted the briefing over with. "OK", I said "That's all for now. Thanks for all your hard work. Good result." And, as an afterthought, "It's time we knocked off for the day. Goehner, take the team out to the bar. Set up a tab – I'll pay for it. I'll be along later."

I needed to get out and walk. Outside, it was a glorious spring evening. But I hardly saw it. I was thinking of a pretty eighteen-year-old girl, wearing her best clothes and jewellery, waiting for the lover who would never arrive, because he and his brother had already contrived to murder her.

Witch in the closet

The edge of the sword glinted in the light of thirteen black candles: razor sharp, wicked. Nimue held it rock-steady, its point two inches from Lilura's heart. It was a thrusting sword, its point as fine as a needle, and it could easily cleave her flesh.

"Morire, o proditrix" Nimue said, quietly but intensely.

"Interficis!" said eleven voices in unison, all around her. The voices were soft, but passionate.

"Tunc me interficiam, si voles. Rideo mortem" said Lilura in a whisper.

Nimue raised the sword and, in a single smooth movement, thrust it into the scabbard hanging from her belt. Lilura lithely jumped off the altar. The candles flickered, in their heavy brass candlesticks.

"All join hands!" commanded Nimue. Everyone immediately held hands, forming a circle around the altar. And, simultaneously, all the candles went out.

A great silence descended on the room. Afterwards, no one could say how long it lasted.

But in the warm darkness, and the quiet, there was power, waiting to be used. And they used it.

Eventually, the ceiling lights came on, of their own accord. The thirteen women let go of each other's hands and gazed at the floor, not wanting to look at each other's faces.

It was Nimue who broke the spell. She clapped her hands. "OK, that's enough," she said. "Maeva and Fatin, will you do the honours?" Maeva and Fatin went to the corner of the room, where thirteen glasses and three bottles of medium-priced red wine were laid out. They poured out the wine. The others made their way over and each took a glass.

"That was amazing," murmured Maeva, standing behind the table. "Stunning. Did you feel that we were going to lose our grip … that it was going to get … mastery … over us?"

Morrigan gave a slight shake of her head. "Not a chance. We were in complete control, all the time."

There was a little more desultory conversation, but really, the women were too shaken to talk much.

Nimue clapped her hands again. "Lilura, have you got the crib sheets?" Lilura held up a bundle of pink A4 pages. "Bless you, Lilura. Everyone take one, and make sure you read it before you get home. And now, everyone get changed." They shed their robes, and put on their everyday clothes. Nimue spoke again. "Good work, all of you. And keep well, until we meet again. Remember: we have a strict rule. It's a law, really. You *never* discuss what happened here with anyone."

As she drove through the dark streets, Nimue glanced at the passenger seat, making sure the pink sheet was there. It was time to stop being Nimue, and revert to being Dr Mary Paulsen.

The measure of all things

She stopped at the service station under the A3, not for petrol but because it housed a small coffee bar. She bought a coffee, and sat reading the notes on the pink sheet. The group, it would seem, had spent the evening discussing Mary Karr's 'The Liar's Club'. This turned out to be 'a dark and witty account of Mary Karr's upbringing in an East Texas oil town'. By the time she'd read the page, she knew as much about the book as she ever intended to find out.

Back home, she shouted a cheery greeting to Steve, who was making supper in the kitchen. She could smell a faint whiff of garlic. It would be Steve's special spaghetti carbonara tonight. Good comforting food, and tasty, too, but full of calories – privately, she was glad they didn't have it more than once a fortnight.

"How was the group, darling?" he called back.

She went into the kitchen and kissed him on the cheek.

"Quite interesting. We're reading an autobiography by a Texan woman. I think you'd probably call it jaw-droppingly honest. She writes well, though."

He laughed. "Mary, you're amazing. You're the most intelligent woman I've ever met. And you spend your time discussing trashy misery memoirs."

"Indulge me," she said. "It's my one relaxation in the week. Apart from the time I spend with you, of course."

* * * *

The following day, driving back from the Institute, she was preoccupied with funding problems; otherwise she might have sensed that something was wrong at home. Really, the application for the next research grant *had* to succeed, or she'd have to shed staff. If the Institute was to retain its position as an international centre of excellence, she should hire more researchers, not sack them. But she wasn't 100% certain that Neville was up to writing the grant application documents. She'd have to keep him on a tight rein.

She arrived home, hung her coat up, and walked into the sitting room. She was about to greet Steve, who was sitting by the fireplace, when she realised that there was another person in the room. A young woman was in the spare armchair, hunched over a mug of tea. Mohana.

It took a moment to remember Mohana's real-life name.

"Well, that's a surprise," she said. "Katie, what can we do for you?"

Katie looked miserable. "I'd better go," she said. "I've said too much."

Mary looked at Steve's face, and decided that that was *exactly* what Katie had done.

"Steve," she said, "Fill me in on the details."

"Katie's had a bust up with her boyfriend," said Steve.

"He shouted at me ... he *hit* me," said Katie. "I couldn't stay in the flat. I couldn't think of anywhere else to go. So I came to you." She sipped at her tea. She looked at Mary with the eyes of a frightened little girl. "I ... I may have said something about our group."

"Your coven," corrected Steve.

The measure of all things

Well now, thought Mary. You didn't plan this, but you have to cope with it. This is where you find out whether you're a real enchantress or not.

"Poor Katie," she said, in her most motherly voice. She walked over and sat on the arm of her chair. She tenderly stroked Katie's hair. "You've had a horrible day ... you need to sleep ... you can sleep here ... you'll be safe with us ... things will look better in the morning ... sleeping will do you good. You'd better not drink anymore whisky." She gently took the mug from Katie's hands and put it on a side table. Katie looked at her with deep gratitude. "You *do* need to sleep," Mary repeated. Katie's eyelids drooped, and she fell asleep.

"Whisky?" said Steve. "That was just tea."

"In the morning, she'll remember drinking whisky," said Mary. "Look, we have to shift her to the spare room. Then we can talk. You take her legs, I'll take her shoulders."

She didn't weigh much – getting her to the bed in the spare room wasn't too difficult. Steve went back to the sitting room. Mary stripped her down to her underwear, laying out her clothes on a chair beside the bed, and tucked her up under the bedclothes. During all this, she remained fast asleep.

Back in the sitting room, Steve had already poured himself a whisky. Mary did the same. Then she sat down and waited.

Steve would have to start this conversation.

After a while, he said, "Are you really a witch?"

"Yes, I am. In fact, you could call me a chief witch. I formed the coven, and I lead it."

Witch in the closet

"How many people ... women ... are there in it?"

"Well, thirteen, obviously. What did you expect? Although we're going to have to lose Katie. We'll have to replace her. It has to be thirteen."

"I never guessed. Never for a moment thought ... how did it start?"

She sighed. "Do you want the whole history?"

"Yes, I think I do."

She cast her mind back. "I remember reading a book of spells when I was at school. Albertus Magnus's *Booke of Secretes*."

"And you were impressed?"

"No, I wasn't. I thought ... this is a book of advice for silly country girls. Obsessed with broken hearts. And getting their own back on people who've hurt their feelings. And underneath it all, there was this deep, deep *ignorance* about science. The way the world *really* works. No, I wasn't impressed." She sipped her whisky. "I loved science. I still do. You must realise that."

He nodded.

"So I returned it to the public library and concentrated on passing my A-levels." She cradled her whisky in her hands.

"I passed them all, of course. And I got a scholarship to Cambridge, and I was away. I got first class honours, because I *deserved* to. I worked *bloody* hard for that degree." She took another sip. "Afterwards, when I was a post-grad, I fell in with a group who were researching parapsychology. It wasn't my field,

The measure of all things

but I tagged along with them. Do you know what a Schmidt machine is?"

"No."

"It's got a circle of bulbs on the front. They light up in turn. Whether the sequence runs clockwise or anticlockwise is driven by a chunk of radioactive material inside the machine. It's said to be an absolute, physical impossibility for anyone to change the sequence by the power of their mind. *I* could do it quite easily."

"Christ."

"I could do other things too. Card guessing, forcing dice throws and roulette wheels. Whatever the experimenters wanted me to do, I scored well above chance."

"Maybe they didn't design the experiments properly?"

"For crying out loud, Steve, this was Cambridge University! Do you really think they don't know how to design an experiment, or analyse the results?"

"So you moved into parapsychology."

"No, I didn't. I had a career lined up in cognitive science, just as soon as I had my doctorate. This was just a hobby." She sipped the whisky. "Then I discovered something interesting. I was trying my hand at remote viewing. You know? They pick some photos at random, from a heap of a thousand or so, all different. You're not even in the room when they do the picking. They seal them up in black envelopes and take them to the other side of town. You stay back at the lab, and you have to *see* them, in your mind's eye, and say what they are. It started well. Two clear hits. I can still remember them: the first one was

Witch in the closet

a boat in the middle of a large lake, with two men fishing; the second was a soldier, in a minefield, with a mine detector. Then, on the third picture, I suddenly realised that nobody could possible do it. You know what I'm saying? You ask yourself, 'Given the mental equipment we've got, and the sensory apparatus, how could someone fulfil this task?' And the answer comes back, 'No *way* could anyone do it.' And then my hit rate dropped to zero. You see what was happening?"

"I think so ..."

"All that science, or rather all those years studying science, had sharpened up my sceptical faculties. And, as long as there was a voice in my head saying 'you can't do this, because it's impossible', I actually couldn't do it. I'd hit a brick wall. So I gave up."

"What happened next?"

"After a while, I found I missed it. There's pleasure in exercising a talent. You know that – you play the guitar."

"Go on."

"I experimented. I looked for some way to get round the barrier. To suspend my disbelief, I suppose. Most of the things I tried didn't work – self-hypnosis, deep meditation, smoking pot. Then I found something that did. Rituals."

"You mean ... like ... silly costumes, silly chanting ..."

"Yeah, and silly props. Altars, chalices, coloured candles ... That's exactly what I mean. Robes, sonorous Latin incantations, elaborate theatrical gestures. They work like a charm. Or rather, they

The measure of all things

work better than a charm. I've no idea why. They seem to trigger my subconscious mind." She took another sip. "Involving other people in the ritual made it much stronger. Thirteen's the optimum number. I found that, by trial and error. It's got nothing to do with worshiping the Devil. I don't personally think the Devil exists."

She took a long sip from her glass. Then she looked directly at him. "And so, my darling Steve, you're married to a witch. I wonder whether you can cope with that?"

He was silent for a while. Then he said, "What do you do at your ... Sabbats? ... Is that the right word?"

"Yeah, good word. Yesterday we raised a storm. On the Monach Islands. Lashing rain, gale force winds – it felt *really* good. And the Monach Islands are uninhabited, so we weren't harming anyone. A bit rough on the seabirds, but they coped."

Steve put his glass down. "How, Mary? How can you do that?"

"You've heard of the butterfly effect, haven't you? The weather's a chaotic system. It only takes a tiny amount of mental energy, at just the right time and place, to nudge it in the right direction. One chaotic system talking to another."

"What else do you do?"

"We don't know what we *can* do, yet. We're experimenting. Some things work, some don't. One time, we found a piece of waste ground, with a lot of spiders living on it. We made them all weave square webs. It was kind of funny."

She laughed. Steve waited for her to go on.

Witch in the closet

"We'll probably try crop circles, before too long. Find a cornfield, somewhere, and persuade a sheep to stray into it. Make it eat just some of the corn, so the bare patches form a tudor rose, or something like that." She sighed. "The difficult part is opening the gate, when we're not actually there. Telekinesis. Sometimes it works, sometimes it doesn't."

She looked thoughtful.

"Changing physical systems is hard; animals' minds are easy. People's minds are pretty easy too. Last week, we picked on a stand-up comedian, in Wimbledon. He was pretty hopeless – wasn't really up to the job. By the time we'd finished with the audience, though, they were falling about. They went home saying they'd never laughed so much. We weren't there, of course. We do everything by remote control." She paused. "The week before, we picked on a politician. Made him change his mind about a very minor policy. It isn't too difficult, when the arguments are finely balanced."

"What will you do next?"

"Work on Katie, obviously. Wipe her memories. Find her a new man…" She stopped abruptly. "Look, Steve, this isn't what's important. I need to know about you and me. Are we still a couple? Can you live with this?"

"I … I don't know. Will you wipe *my* memories?"

"No, silly. You're my man. I don't mess with your mind. It wouldn't be … respectful."

"I suppose … I suppose I'd be lonely without you …"

The measure of all things

She put her glass down, crossed the room, knelt down and wrapped her arms around him. She kissed him, full on the mouth. And soon, she knew, deep down, that he wanted her, and that he'd remain loyal to her, whatever happened.

There's one kind of magic, she thought, that always works.

The make-believe planet

I have to start with a warning. Wherever you are on the planet, you *must not* let your disguise slip. It's quite unnerving to have half a dozen Earthmen staring at you and screaming "My God, it's horrible!" More important, the Galactic Tourist Authority will then step in and wipe all their memories. The cost will be substantial, they'll charge it all to you, and your travel insurance won't cover it. So, masks firmly locked in place at all times. If any Earthman tells you you're acting like an alien, say "Sure, I'm a little green man from planet Tharg", and laugh. For some reason, this always convinces them that you aren't. (You'll find instructions on how to laugh in appendix 1).

There are no very interesting buildings on the planet. The tallest is a mere 830 metres high – if you want to see a ten-mile-high building, go to Arcturus-6. None of them are mobile (apart from some small structures called "airliners" and "ocean liners") – if you want to see a flying palace, or a wandering city, go to Achernar-4. They tend to be made of rather boring materials (brick, marble, concrete, steel, wood, mud, wattle-and-daub) – if you want to see fortresses carved from ruby or emerald, go to Vega-7.

The wildlife on Earth is quite varied, and contains some unusual species. The blue whale is impressive

The measure of all things

because of its size – very few worlds can boast a larger beast. The giraffe is one of the most ridiculous creatures you'll ever see; if you haven't come across it, it has a ludicrously long neck. The sloth is also pretty absurd; it is covered in green mould, and spends most of its time hanging upside down. But really, most civilised star-systems have zoos containing Earth flora and fauna, and there is little point in going to the source-world in the hope of seeing better specimens, since the best have already been collected and shipped out.

What sets Earth apart, and what really explains the Earth-visiting tourist industry, is the Earthmen's ability to daydream. We all like to daydream, and most of us believe that we have some talent for it, but the Earthmen have made it the centrepiece of their artistic endeavours. An Arcturan might imagine itself doing something bizarre and amusing, and share this idea with its fellows, and become something of a celebrity as a result. An Earthman, in contrast, can easily imagine a long sequence of events in which a large number of Earthmen do all manner of strange things, and experience all manner of unlikely occurrences. There may be ten or more imaginary participants in this daydream, and the episodes may run to over a hundred. Having perfected the daydream, the Earthman will make a record of it, and she or he – Earthmen have two genders – will then sell it to other Earthmen who haven't the time to produce their own. The record may be called "a novel", "a play", "a strip cartoon" or "a filmscript". If it's particularly short, it will be called "a poem" or "a joke".

Once the daydream-record has been shared, it will, as often as not, be *performed*. This is a strange business,

The make-believe planet

and it's hard to think of anything similar that takes place on any other inhabited world. A group of Earthmen – specialists in this activity – put on clothes which make them look as if they are the people in the daydream. They arrange furniture, masonry and so forth, so that it looks like places in the daydream. They speak and act as if they were in the daydream. It's important to realise that they are *not* in disguise, as *you* will be when you watch them do this. They are simply participating in someone else's daydream.

At this point, you might wonder whether they are hallucinating. Earthmen are as susceptible to delusions, brought about by brain malfunction, as any other intelligent species. But I should make it clear that the performers are **not** under a delusion. If you say to one of them "Surely you don't really believe that you're Julius Caesar?", he'll say "Of course I don't, you fool, I'm an actor." (N.B.1: Don't ask him this while the performance is taking place, or all the Earthmen present will get very annoyed. N.B.2: Sometimes he'll say "Of course I don't, you fool, I'm an actress." There must be some reason why two different words are used, but I haven't tracked it down yet.)

So, when you reach planet Earth, make your way to a "theatre" where you can watch the strange behaviour of this strangest of intelligent species. Appendix 2 provides instructions for finding the "theatre districts" of the various cities that your tour operator is likely to take you to. Watch the whole of a performance: watch the Earthmen who are performing, and watch the ones who are watching – etiquette requires that they should not speak, but should laugh, cry, cough or beat their hands together at certain specified moments in the performance. The

The measure of all things

theatre provides them with "ice creams" and "glasses of wine" as a reward for doing this.

I should mention that there are some even stranger variations on "the performance". One of these is called "opera", in which the performers use a highly distorted form of speech. Even the Earthmen find it almost incomprehensible, which explains why the words are repeated again and again. Another variation is called "musical", in which this distorted form of speech only happens for some of the time. Another variation is called "ballet": this time, the performers have given up on speech altogether, and convey the daydream by means of gestures. Earthmen have four limbs, and the elaborate gesturing is done using all of them simultaneously. How they avoid falling over is a great mystery.

I should conclude with another warning. Some of the Earthmen's daydreams are concerned with other planets and other star-systems. They call this "science fiction" (though it isn't a branch of science) or "space opera" (though it isn't a type of opera). If an Earthman – a performer, perhaps, or a "writer" – shares with you an account of extraterrestrial life, it is always a daydream. Do not, on any account, correct his mistakes. The Galactic authorities have gone to considerable lengths to keep the Earthmen in ignorance of the galactic civilisation beyond their doorstop. As I have already indicated, the cost to you, personally, of shattering that illusion, even temporarily, will be steep.

Exeat

Dear son,

I was so sorry to hear that you're unhappy at school. I wish I could come and see you, to talk about it, but as you know, that's impossible right now.

I remember being bullied at school. My father told me to stand up to them: show them I wasn't afraid, and then they'd back down. I have to say that it never worked for me. But recently I've found something that <u>would</u> have worked, if I'd had it at your age. I've decided that you should have it now. I've asked your Uncle Jim to give it to you in person. You know the coffee bar in the village? Meet him there, on Tuesday, at 12:30 in the afternoon.

Your affectionate father.

Paul read the letter twice, sitting in the corner of the common-room. He waited till all the other boys had left, on their way to their various classes, and then sobbed quietly. He'd really, really wanted his father to come and take him away. Away from this horrible school, where he had no friends, and where the boys in his common-room took pleasure in hurting and humiliating him.

It might have been different if his mother had come to see him once in a while. But she never

The measure of all things

did. In fact, she hardly ever bothered to reply to his letters.

All the other boys had exeats, at least once a term. Paul never had any.

'Exeat' – that was a distinctively Public School word. It meant a chance to go out, or maybe go home, and spend time with your family. A whole day away from this place. It was always a Sunday – nothing must be allowed to interfere with the school work, or the sports programme.

Mr Shuttleworth had explained what it meant, in the Latin class. He was a wiry little man, who wore a tweed jacket, with leather patches on the elbows.

"Exeat – third person present subjunctive of Exo, to go out. It means 'He may go out'. You see, boys, what a marvellously compact language Latin is. English needs four words to say it. Latin can do it in one."

After a while, he pulled himself together. He dabbed his eyes with his handkerchief, and combed his hair. His eyes were a little red and puffy, but it probably didn't matter. The boys in the class wouldn't care, and the masters never seemed to notice.

He was late for the Latin lesson, but he got away with it, because Mr Shuttleworth was even later. And he had a piece of prep to hand in – the translation they'd all been given. He was pretty sure he'd got it all right – he was good at languages – but when Mr Shuttleworth looked at it, he shook his head.

"Your translation's good, Schofield, but your work's always so *scruffy*. I'm taking ten marks off simply for that."

He was crestfallen. He couldn't tell Mr Shuttleworth what Purvis had done. Namely snatching the translation away from him just as he was finishing it, and crossing out every fifth word.

"Why did you do that?" he'd said.

"Did you think we were going to let you show the rest of us up, you nasty little swat?" Purvis had jeered. And he'd punched him, to make the point. Hard enough to hurt, but not hard enough to leave much of a bruise. The other boys – Reid, McCrevan, Luckman – had laughed.

He hadn't had time to rewrite it all from scratch, and, anyway, Purvis would simply have done it again. He *had* had time to correct all the crossings out, but Mr Shuttleworth was right, it looked a total mess. He deserved to lose marks.

* * * * *

At 12:20 every day, they were allowed half an hour out of School to visit the shops in the village. He had to run to get to the coffee bar in time. It had once been a country pub, built with fake Tudor half-timbering in the nineteen thirties, but for years now it had sold only hot drinks, soft drinks and snacks. He pushed open the door and went in. There was one customer, sitting in the corner.

"Hello, Paul. Sit down. Get your breath back, and I'll buy you something to drink."

The measure of all things

"Hello, Uncle Jim. I can't stay long. I've got to be back at school by ten to one, ready for lunch."

Uncle Jim was Paul's father's twin, and looked a lot like him. Somehow, that made Paul feel even sadder. He bought Paul a lemonade. He indicated a long package, like a roll of wallpaper, only twice as wide, lying on the bench seat beside him.

"Your father said I was to give you this. D'you think you can carry it back to school, and put it somewhere safe?"

Paul tried lifting it. He nodded. "I've got a locker to keep my rugby kit in. It'll fit in there. But what is it?"

"Don't rightly know. Your father says it's a portal, but I've no idea what that is. Oh, and apparently there's a password. He says treat your birthday as eight digits, with no dashes or anything, and that'll work."

* * * *

Eight thirty was bedtime for his year. You got undressed, washed, put your pyjamas on, and were in bed by nine o'clock; a prefect checked you were all there and turned the light out. Then you and the other five boys in your dormitory were allowed twenty minutes' talking, in the dark. It was a time he dreaded. Purvis was in his dorm, and never tired of telling him what a pathetic, useless, puny creature he was. The other boys seemed to enjoy it, and joined in. Last night he'd tried to answer back, and Purvis had announced his intention to break his arm the next time they were on the rugby field.

Exeat

"Don't think I wouldn't get away with it," he'd said, "I wait till the ref's looking at his watch, make sure there's a couple of lads between him and me, and crunch! These three will be there, and they'll swear it was an accident. Won't you, lads?"

There was a murmur of assent. No one wanted to make an enemy of Purvis.

Paul had lain in the dark, clutching the iron rail that formed the bed-head, as if it could give him some sort of protection.

But that was last night. Now, lights-out was an hour away. It was just after eight, and no one cared if he slipped down to the changing-room, where he'd concealed the strange package in his locker. He got it out. It was a roll of something like neutral-grey coloured plastic, and there was a thick elastic tie around it, which he removed with difficulty. He unrolled it. There was a large, featureless, intensely black, patch on one side – about two and a half feet wide, and five and a half feet long. There seemed to be a couple of hooks at the end of the roll, so he hung it on the top of the locker door. It unrolled very neatly, forming a flat, vertical sheet: the top edge didn't sag, and the bottom didn't curl up. He wondered what it could be made of. And he gazed in puzzlement at that strange, black rectangle – as tall as he was, and as wide. There was a pad with number keys on it to the right hand side, at about chest height. He wondered what one was meant to do with it. Then he realised that he knew. He typed his birth-date into it: two digits for the day, two for the month, and four for the year.

The measure of all things

Suddenly, the black patch wasn't black anymore. A swirling pattern appeared, and, as quickly, disappeared. Then he was looking through an opening, into a different room.

It looked like a cabin in a warship. Grey walls, seemingly of metal, metal doors fitting into metal flanges, complex charts clipped to the walls. And there was a man sitting in front of some sort of machine, wearing a black coverall. He looked up, and saw Paul. He looked puzzled. Then he smiled, and beckoned him.

Paul was transfixed. He could have screamed, but he didn't. He could have turned and run, but he didn't.

The man said something incomprehensible, and beckoned again. Hardly knowing why he did it, Paul stepped through the portal, into the other room. There was a strange, unidentifiable smell, something like ripe apples.

The man came towards him, still smiling, and reached behind him. Paul turned, and saw the changing-room, through the portal. This side of the frame of the portal was studded with buttons and knobs, illuminated digits and coloured lights. The man touched one of the buttons, and the changing-room vanished, to be replaced by a featureless black rectangle.

Paul found his voice. "Please sir, where am I?"

The man put a finger to his lips. He took Paul by the arm, led him across the cabin, and sat him down in a seat. Above the seat, supported by a cantilever arrangement, was an elaborate metal helmet, with a thick bundle of cables leading away

Exeat

to some sort of control panel on the wall. The man pushed the helmet down so that it fitted over Paul's head. Paul saw him touch another button, on the control panel, and immediately there was an intense, dizzy, swirling sensation inside his head. After a while it subsided.

"Good," said the man, "now we can talk. You've just learned another language, namely the one we speak round here. May I ask your name?"

"My name's Paul Schofield, sir."

"Pleased to meet you, Paul-Schofield. My name's Sergeant Becsulet."

Paul expected the man to shake hands, but he didn't – instead, he held his hand vertically, his palm outstretched. Paul wasn't sure whether to copy him, so he didn't. Instead, he said, "Would you tell me where I am?"

"Where do you think?"

"I ... I don't know. In a spaceship?"

"No. In a fortress. Fort Grax."

"On some other world?"

"No. On Planet Earth, roughly where you were a few minutes ago. The difference is that you're one hundred and eighty thousand years in the future."

"Oh." For a while, he couldn't think of anything to say. Then, "Excuse me sir, is it possible to go back? If it is, I should go back now. I'm supposed to be in the dorm in ten minutes."

The man smiled again. "You can go back now, if you want to. Or you can stay for up to five days.

The measure of all things

However long you stay, when you go back, you'll arrive 6.8 seconds after you left."

Paul thought, and decided he really didn't want to go back, just yet.

Sergeant Becsulet lead him through narrow, grey-metal-lined corridors to the Commanding Officer's cabin. He knocked, and waited until a voice shouted "Enter!" through an intercom over the door. He opened the door, and they both went in.

"Beg pardon, ma'am," said the sergeant, "But this boy just wandered through the portal. His name's Paul-Schofield. "Can he stay a while?"

The Commanding Officer was a blonde woman in her fifties. She gazed thoughtfully at Paul. "How old are you, boy?" she asked.

"Thirteen, ma'am."

"And from the mid-twentieth century?"

"Yes, ma'am. Nineteen sixty one."

"Yes, OK – why not? I doubt we'll find ourselves at war in the next five days. And we're not short of rations. You can be a powder monkey. Sergeant, find the boy a spare cabin, get him some bedding, and show him where the Mess Hall is."

"Yes, ma'am," said the Sergeant, and pointed at the ceiling. The woman did the same, and Paul guessed that this was how saluting was done among these people.

"Two or three rules, Paul-Schofield. One, you don't touch any of the weapon systems. Two, you don't interfere with any of my men when they are

Exeat

operating or maintaining the weapon systems. Three, when you go back, which will be in five days, or less if you ask us, you don't say anything about what you've seen and done here. Or even about coming here. Understood?"

"Understood, ma'am."

"You won't be believed, even if you do. That's all."

They left the cabin. "That's our CO," said the Sergeant. "She's not a bad type. I've served under worse. You'll address her as 'Major'. Her full name is 'Major Izlemibu'. Come on, I'll find you a cabin."

"Thank you, Sir. Er ... can you tell me what a powder monkey is?"

"No idea – it sounds like something from your age. We don't have monkeys anymore; or any other wild creatures. But the Major's been reading up on your times. It's probably some idea she picked up."

* * * * *

Over the next five days, he learnt a lot about the men and women who lived in Fort Grax. There were fifteen of them, and they were a contingent of an army called the Human Defence Force. Planet Earth had been ravaged by an interstellar war with an alien race called the Marauders. The war had moved on – there had been no fighting on the planet for thirty-eight years – but, throughout that time, the little garrison – the only garrison on the entire planet – had remained on alert. The war could resume at any time, and the

The measure of all things

Human Federation wasn't prepared to give up their beloved (but currently almost uninhabitable) mother planet without a fight.

The soldiers made regular survey flights over the landscape. Paul persuaded one of them – Corporal Vernost – to take him along. They flew for hours over tumbled masonry, the ruins of some enormous city. "At one stage," explained the Corporal, "About thirty thousand years ago, practically the whole of Earth's landmass was one big urban area, with big bridges between the continents. Then things changed – large areas became countryside".

They flew over some of this countryside. But it was completely blackened; cinder fields, with drifts of grey ash, and no living thing anywhere. "What happened?" asked Paul. "All burnt out, during the last war," said the Corporal, grimly.

They flew over an enormous crater, covering many square miles. Again, the ground within it was black, sterile. "The last war?" asked Paul. "Right," said the Corporal. "Bomb blast. A big one".

And finally, they flew over some green country. Grasslands, clothing low hills, and river valleys. There were some clumps of small trees. By contrast with everything else he'd seen, it was quite beautiful.

"We're terraforming the planet," explained the Corporal. "We've done it to other worlds. Now we're doing to Earth. We lay down topsoil, plant grass, trees … it's slow work, takes centuries, but in the end, we'll have replanted the whole world.

Exeat

In due course, we'll introduce grazing animals. Birds. Predators, to control the numbers."

Back at Fort Grax, he learnt more about how the fortress operated. It could support itself by mining and manufacturing and growing the material resources it needed. But it had a huge problem with personnel. Every now and then, a member of the garrison would die in an accident, or, more likely, be posted out, and they were expected to fill the gap in the ranks.

"Are there no people living on Earth? I mean, outside the fort?" Paul asked.

The adjutant, Captain Kitartas, who had taken it upon himself to answer Paul's many questions, smiled sadly.

"There's a small community of farmers, living under the Pacific. But they're no use to us, as soldiers. It's the same for most of the race – all the aggression was bred out of them a couple of hundred generations ago."

"How did that happen?"

"There was a civil war. Rather devastating. The rulers, on the winning side, decided that it would be better if the traits that made people aggressive were edited out of the human genotype. So they were. Eventually, of course, there were mutants, who had the old traits. Everyone in the army is bred from that mutant stock."

"But there aren't enough of you?"

"No, there aren't enough of us."

"So where do you get your soldiers from?"

The measure of all things

"We have to recruit fighting men and women from the remote past. From your era. Your father's one of our recruiting officers."

"Oh." Something occurred to him. "That's why he had a portal to give me."

"Mmm. He shouldn't have done that, really. But I think we'll let him off with a reprimand. You've been good company."

Paul considered that. They *had* seemed to enjoy his company. He'd recited poems for them, and sung hymns, and told them stories from English history they'd never heard before. They'd treated him something like the regimental mascot.

* * * * *

And then his five days were up. Major Izlemibu put a hand on his shoulder.

"Paul, I'm afraid it's time to make a choice. The time-thread will snap if you don't use it in the next six hours. You can go back to your school, in the twentieth century, and resume the life you had. Or you can stay here, and we'll train you to be a soldier."

"Why shouldn't I stay here?"

"Your friends and family would miss you. And we haven't much to offer you. This is an old planet, almost dead, and we're just a bunch of rough soldiers, living in an outpost."

Paul thought for a while, and then he made his decision. You already know what it was.

The Sylvani

Five miles into Deiliog Forest, I came to a crossroads, and stopped to check the map. It was there that I saw a green man.

I had the map on the car seat beside me. I had found my rough position, or so I thought, and glanced up to see whether there was some sort of signpost. There, standing at the roadside, was a small man, with his arms folded, looking straight at me. He was about five feet tall, and he had a malevolent grin. His skin seemed to be pale green, and he seemed to be wearing clothes made from leaves.

I reached for the button that controlled the window – I intended to open it, and ask him for directions. But that meant that I took my eyes off the man momentarily and, when I looked back, he was gone.

I drove on, and eventually I came to the cottage – it was called Tŷ Gwydion – where Dr Ceridwen Reece lived. I hadn't seen any other dwellings, or any buildings of any description, since I left the main road, miles back.

The cottage was in a small clearing, fenced off from the forest. Dr Reece was in the garden when I arrived, singing softly to herself as she deadheaded the roses. A tall, dark-haired woman, wearing a garden jacket and a woollen skirt, who I judged to be in her late fifties. She saw me and greeted me.

The measure of all things

"You must be John Miller," she said. "I was expecting you."

We shook hands, and she invited me in and sat me down in her small sitting room. There were a lot of bookshelves, but I noticed that she seemed to be taking the books off them and packing them in crates.

She made a pot of tea, and, as she did so, I could hear her singing. It was the same song that she'd been singing in the garden: an old folk-song, perhaps.

"Seven hundred elves from out the wood, foul and grim they were."

She saw me looking at her, and stopped, smiling.

"Sorry. That song's been on my mind. Steeleye Span had a minor hit with it, a few years back. They cleaned it up quite a bit, though – the original is *way* too bloody for modern taste."

"Do you have hippies, living in the forest? I asked.

"Used to," she said. "They would make an encampment, well off the main tracks, clear away the young saplings, and grow marijuana. They're not around anymore."

"Only I saw someone by the roadside, on the way here. He seemed to have tinted his face green, and he was wearing clothes that looked as though they were leaves."

"Where did you see him?"

"At the crossroads, back along the forest road."

"I'd say you were lucky. If you see him again, when you're driving back, I'd advise you not to stop."

"Why?"

The Sylvani

She smiled. "Look, Mr Miller, we're just making conversation. Why don't you say what you've come to say?"

I sighed. "You know it's bad news?"

"If it's what I think ... you could call it that."

"You've been the Forest Manager here for fifteen years. I have to tell you that, in view of the government cuts, Natural Resources Wales can't afford Forest Managers any more. I have to tell you that you've been made redundant.

She smiled again, a sad smile, or so I thought. "I can't say it's a surprise. Look around you, Mr Miller. I'm half packed up and ready to go."

"Of course," I went on, "there's a redundancy package. You'll be paid a lump sum, on the basis of the years you've worked for us. As to this house, NRW would be prepared to sell it to you at an advantageous price."

"No, Mr Miller, I don't want the cottage. NRW can sell it to whoever they like. But I somehow don't think there'll be many takers." She got up, and took my teacup, which was empty. She said "Now, to business. Are there any papers for me to sign? I'll happily sign them. And then I'll finish my packing. I'm hoping to be out of here by the end of tomorrow. I'll post you the keys, if that's OK."

"You really don't have to rush ... we wouldn't want to put pressure on you ... we know it can be a difficult time ..."

"No, I don't think you understand." She stood by the fireplace. There was a long pause. She was apparently making up her mind what she should say. Eventually,

The measure of all things

she went on "I suppose I should tell you why I want to leave here. I suppose it's my duty ... although there's really nothing you can do about it."

She walked out of the room, and came back carrying two glasses and a bottle.

"A glass of wine?" she said. "I'm going to have one." With that, she unscrewed the bottle top and poured two glasses of Chianti, one of which she handed to me.

"You know I've got 'doctor' in front of my name? What do you think I'm a doctor of?"

I was thrown a little off-balance. "Horticulture?" I said.

"No, I retrained as an arboriculturalist before taking this job. But originally, I was a preternaturalist."

"What's that?"

"I studied the history of magic."

"Oh."

"In my thesis, I explored the reasons why magic stopped working. Particularly forest magic. It *did* work once, you know. In early medieval times, town dwellers and country dwellers were terrified of the forests, because of the dark magic you found there. If you look at the carvings in medieval churches, you'll always find a carving of a green man somewhere. A face, with leaves and branches sprouting from it. Why? Because it was really important that you didn't cross the men in the forest."

"What's a green man?" I said.

"You saw one, on the way here."

The Sylvani

"Oh." I thought about that. "What happened if you did cross one of them?"

"If you even met one, he was liable to strike you dead with a spell. Especially if you met him at night. I think I know what sort of magic they were using, but I don't know any effective counter-spells."

"And ... you said the magic stopped working. Did it?"

"It certainly did. Shakespeare realised it – all the educated men in Elizabethan times did. Prospero's last speech in *The Tempest* is all about the magic going away. It paved the way for the invention of science. And major forest clearances."

"So ... why did the magic stop?"

"I didn't really come up with a convincing answer. But now I think I know." She glanced at the clock. "Christ, it'll get dark in about two hours. You'd better go now - you can *not* drive through this forest in the dark. They'll find you and kill you, like they killed all the hippies."

"What?" I was starting to feel scared. Partly, it was being alone with this mad woman. And partly, I was remembering that malevolent, grinning face.

"I've tried to reason with them ... but you can't. They don't think like humans."

She looked as though she was going to refill my glass, then thought better of it.

"Look, I'll tell you why the magic went away. It'll help you understand what's going to happen in the future. Then you have to go. Right?"

I nodded.

The measure of all things

She swirled the wine in her glass, and gazed into it.

"I had all kinds of ideas," she said. "Magic as a natural resource, that got used up. That's the Larry Niven theory; but it doesn't really work. Then I thought maybe that magic stops working, for reasons of hysteresis, when a country produces large amounts of steel. Or, if a country burns large amounts of fossil fuels, it disrupts the energy flows that magic depends on. Great ideas, both of them, but they don't really work either."

She looked up at me. "You realise, of course, that in prehistoric times, the whole of Britain was covered in forests? Apart from the mountain tops, and the rivers? Then humans colonised the British Isles, and started to clear the woodland. They did vast amounts of tree felling. You see what that means, don't you? From the point of view of the trees, humans are predators."

"Yes, I suppose so …"

"Evolution working the way it does, the trees evolved a defence."

"Oh. What defence?"

"Isn't it obvious? The green men. A green man is like … like a limb of the tree. A weapon to defend it against its worst predator. Its purpose is to kill human beings. It may make a distinction between a harmless traveller and a woodman, but then again it may not."

I sipped my wine. "You haven't told me why the magic stopped working."

Once more, she gazed into her wine glass. "It's an epigenetic effect."

"I'm sorry, I don't understand."

"In the end, every characteristic of a living creature is determined by its genes. You've got two eyes because your genes *dictate* that you should have two eyes. An oak tree produces a green man because its genes tell it to. But a change in the environment can switch genes off. The genes are still there, but they're … ineffective. Inactive. There's masses of research on it." She gestured to a pile of papers, which turned out to be off-prints from a journal on genetics.

She continued. "Something happened to the trees, at the end of the medieval period, that switched this particular set of genes off. They stopped producing green men."

"What was it?"

"It got colder."

"You're kidding!"

"No, really. The centuries from 950 to 1250 are known as the Medieval Warm Period. The centuries from 1550 to 1850 are known as the Little Ice Age. It's historical fact."

"And you're saying that things are going back to the way they were?"

"It's not just a theory, Mr Miller. I've been counting the number of green men in this forest. When I got here, it was almost none. Now, it's going up all the time. Average temperatures are the same now as they were in the eleven hundreds. Because of global warming."

She looked at the clock again. "Time you went. Don't drink any more wine. If you set out now, you'll get to

The measure of all things

the edge of the forest well before dark. They won't follow you beyond the boundary."

"But what about you?"

"I'll be all right. I have ways of convincing them that I'm not a threat. They work, at the moment. Though they won't for much longer. You see why I want out?"

She got up, and took my wine glass away from me.

"Oh, and where's that form I had to sign?"

I got it out of my briefcase, and she signed it. I promised to send her a copy.

"Now get going."

We went out to my car. In the shadows under the trees, beyond the fence, I could see several faces watching us. Green faces. I counted six, but there could have been more.

She gestured towards the cottage. "The removal men will come here tomorrow. As I said, I'll post you the keys. Then I'm emigrating. To Iceland."

"What? Why do you need to ..."

"And if they start a programme of forestation in Iceland, I'll move to Greenland. You see, Mr Miller, I think Britain is going to have real problems in the near future. Global warming isn't going to stop."

Along the road, I could see several figures on the grass verge. They didn't look human. They did look, somehow ... insolent.

"If there's going to be a war between the green men and the humans, I'm not at all sure that the humans can win. We don't have the right weapons. We've forgotten everything we ever knew about magic."

"But ... there aren't many forests left ..."

"Oh, it doesn't have to be forests. You know what an English city is like. All those leafy suburbs. Tree-lined streets. All those municipal parks. Millions of trees."

Unexpectedly, she gave me a hug, and kissed me on the cheek. She said, "Nice to meet you, Mr Miller. Have a safe journey home."

Surprise ingredient

'Wizard's Apprentice Co. Authentic occult supplies. We may not be the cheapest, but we're the best!'

Dawn read the webpage twice. "Right," she murmured, "That should do nicely." She highlighted the site's web address, and copied and pasted it into the document she was writing. Then she captured some screen shots, and pasted them into her PowerPoint presentation.

Downstairs, the front door clicked shut. She glanced at the clock in the corner of her screen: nine minutes past midnight. She had to fight down a sudden, irrational anger. *Damn* him! He spends the evening with a woman. They go to her place and make love. When they're through with each other, he comes home. And I'm supposed not to notice? Not to care? I wonder who it was? A student? A work colleague? A casual pick-up in a singles bar? Whoever she was, she was younger and prettier than me, that's for sure.

By an effort of will, she fought down her feelings. When Paul had married her, he'd told her it would be an open marriage. So it had turned out, at least from his point of view.

With as pleasant a tone as she could manage, she called downstairs, "Hello dear. Had a nice evening?"

* * * * *

Surprise ingredient

The class – all eight of them – faced her as she stood beside the large screen, and showed them the pages she'd downloaded.

"I think we'll scrub round the cupro-magnetic healing bangle ... the triple-goddess candlestick ... the astral projection incense. But this looks interesting." She clicked the mouse on the rostrum, and a page appeared headed *'Spell ingredients – non-herbal'*.

"You can ignore the one called 'dragon's blood'", she said. "It's a tree resin – they use it in the printing industry. As to the others ... Cocatrice skin? Griffin's claws? Phoenix feathers? Pegasus hide? Harpy hair? Wyvern talons? Mermaid scales? Unicorn horn? Notice the message at the bottom – 'all our spell ingredients are carefully sourced and we go to great lengths to ensure that they are genuine' – I think we can safely discount that, since none of these creatures exist, or ever did." The class chuckled dutifully.

She continued. "As you know, the Diploma course requires you to do a final project. This will be it. Each of you will choose one of these supposedly occult substances" – she gestured towards the screen – "and buy a sample, from this website. Then you will use the DNA analysis techniques that you've learned, here, to find out what it really is. Some of the marks will depend on how precise your identification is. Then you will write up your findings in a report, using the standard CITES format." She touched the mouse again, and a web page headed 'CITES – Convention on International Trade in Endangered Species of Wild Fauna and Flora' appeared on screen. "You'll find the details here."

The class duly wrote down the web address.

283

The measure of all things

"Now," she said brightly, "Who wants to take the Cocatrice skin?"

* * * * *

She found Professor Fabella sitting in the campus coffee bar, sipping an expresso, and reading *Renaissance Historical Review*. She and the professor had served on the library committee together, and they'd become close friends.

"Jaques, I've got a question for you. What do you know about alicorn?"

"Sounds like a secret government scheme. I can see the headlines: 'Project Alicorn – we reveal the truth'. No? Maybe it's a piece of software? 'Read our exclusive review of Alicorn v.3.0'?"

"Jaques, be serious. It's what the alchemists called unicorn horn, as you know very well."

"And so it is. Why do you want to know about it?"

"Something weird has happened." She told him about the project she'd set her forensic genetics class. "Most of the substances turned out to be the sort of fakes I would have expected. The cocatrice skin came from an adder. The griffin's claws, and the wyvern talons, both came from a vulture. The phoenix feathers came from a jackdaw. The pegasus hide came from a mule. The harpy hair came from an African woman. The mermaid scales came from a golden carp. But the unicorn horn ... the student couldn't identify it. Neither could I. Genetically, it's a species related to the horse, but it's an unknown species."

"And horses don't have horns, do they? This is very interesting. Look, if you want to read up on unicorns, there are a few books on cryptozoology in the library

Surprise ingredient

– have a read of Peter Costello's *The Magic Zoo*. But as to the material itself, might I have a look at it? And, I know I'm not a proper scientist, but I'd like to do a little experiment, if you don't mind."

* * * * *

The materials lay on a white glass sheet on a workbench in a corner of one of the labs. A section cut from some slender animal horn, two centimeters long, with a spiral ridge round its outer surface. Some fine off-white powder, which was actually ground shavings taken from the horn.

Jaques examined them with a magnifying glass, taking care not to touch them. Then he took out of his briefcase a plastic box that might perhaps have been designed to hold a round of sandwiches. He placed it on the bench, and took the lid off: inside was a moist sugar cube. He produced a spatula, scooped up some of the off-white powder, and sprinkled it on the cube. Then he took out another box: this one turned out to contain a live cockroach. He tipped it into the other box. It explored its new surroundings, found the sugar lump, and started to eat it.

The professor watched it for some time. Then he said "Amazing!" And beamed.

"What? I don't understand," said Dawn.

"I soaked the sugar cube in fast-acting insecticide. The roach should be dead by now. But it seems quite happy."

"So? It's obviously resistant to the insecticide."

"I don't think so. Not *this* insecticide. You haven't read that book yet, have you? All the sources, right

The measure of all things

back to Ctesias in Ancient Greece, say this about unicorn horn: it has the power to destroy all poisons."

* * * * *

Paul looked at her with something close to adoration. She smiled back at him, and kissed him. They hugged and kissed a lot more these days.

"Shall we go out for a drink?" he said.

"No ... no, I have to stay in and write an exam paper. But you go, if you like." In fact, she'd written the paper a week ago, but she'd decided it was time to test him.

"If you can't come, I don't want to go out. I'll stay here. I really only want to be with you."

She smiled contentedly. Another thing that all the sources say is that alicorn is an infallible aphrodisiac.

Riding on a smile and a shoeshine

Peter had been a travelling salesman almost all his adult life. When he had started, as a young man, people called him a "traveller". Nowadays, that meant something different – a gypsy, a tramp or an itinerant drop-out. You still heard the phrase "commercial traveller" occasionally, but not all that often in these times. The truth was, the profession was on the way out. His customers were becoming accustomed to picking their own goods from the Internet, and neither they nor the producers and wholesalers whom he represented felt much need of a visitor bearing samples and a sales pitch. Nevertheless, he was good at his job, and still found work. Like many another salesman, he had an easy smile, and kept his shoes well shined.

The firms he represented had changed over the years, and, consequently, so had the products. At one time, he had been selling envelopes to offices, at another he had been selling fan-heaters to electrical shops, at another TV sets to the same shops. There had even been a miserable period when he was reduced to selling asphalt, door to door – "Good morning, madam, we can resurface your drive at a very reasonable rate" – and frequently had the door slammed in his face. Generally, selling to shops and commercial firms was a much happier experience.

The measure of all things

The manager of a medium-sized shop, without too many customers, quite liked to see his friendly face, and to spend half an hour chatting, after which he or she would probably place an order large enough to convince both of them that the time had been well spent. Currently, he was selling memory-sticks and similar electronic gadgets to small stationers.

This evening, he was driving down the A171 from Whitby to Scarborough. On the passenger seat of his Ford Focus was a road map of Yorkshire, and on the back seat was a bag containing three changes of clothes, a cheap novel, and a toothbrush. And, of course, a briefcase containing his all-important samples.

The sky had been heavily overcast all afternoon – in fact, he hadn't seen the sun for days. And now it was starting to rain. It was going to be a foul night. He flicked the switch, and his windscreen wipers sprang to life.

Still, Whitby and Scarborough are only seventeen miles apart, and he reckoned he'd done about half of that. He had a room booked in Scarborough, in a B & B. No sense in wasting money on a hotel. Just at the moment, he'd be glad of a bed, and a meal in a local pub. A road sign told him that he was entering the Harwood Dale Forest. It was getting dark, and he turned on his headlights.

The rain was getting harder. There were no houses or farms in sight, and no other traffic on the road – in fact, the only signs of anything built by man was the road itself. There was thick woodland to the left of the road, and dense undergrowth on the right. Briefly, he could make out the moors, in the distance, through the driving rain. Then it was more closely-planted

Riding on a smile and a shoeshine

woods to the right, and the scenery on the left became shrubs and wet bracken.

He had just decided to turn on the radio – get some entertainment, preferably music – when he spotted something strange. As he negotiated a bend, his headlights picked out something very large, round and metallic ahead of him, some way from the road. It was just a glimpse, but the vegetation around it appeared to be smouldering. And – was that a burning tree?

He carried on driving for about a minute, then braked. This actually was something inexplicable, wasn't it? Smouldering vegetation, during a rainstorm? Had he stumbled on the site of a plane crash? Since he wasn't in a hurry to get anywhere, it wouldn't do any harm to take a look, would it?

He turned the car around and drove back. When he got to the bend, he slowed, and drove the car onto the grass verge, with his headlights pointing towards the open ground. There certainly was a huge metal object there, but it didn't look like a plane. It seemed to have pushed over small trees, and something had made the trees and the bracken catch fire, though the flames were guttering out now.

He narrowed his eyes. It didn't look like an airliner ... it looked more like ...

"Oh my God," he said, under his breath, "it's a flying saucer."

Peter wasn't a courageous man. He sat in his car and shivered. Then he got out his mobile phone and turned it on. No signal – not too surprising on the North York Moors.

The measure of all things

But perhaps Peter had more courage than he knew – perhaps he had hidden reserves that he had never needed in his life till now. He considered driving away as fast as his trusty Ford Focus would carry him – and rejected the idea. I found this, he thought, no one else. If there's an opportunity here, it's mine.

The sky was now quite dark. Beyond the patches of light cast by his headlights, and the flickering red flames, there was intense darkness. He searched around and found his plastic mac and, after a struggle, got it on. He also found his torch, and clicked it alight. He opened the car door, and stepped out. His foot landed in a puddle, with an audible splash. He crossed the road, and then climbed the grass embankment on the other side. There was a low hedge between him and the ground where the saucer had landed. Or crashed, perhaps? He walked along the hedge, and found a gap, which he pushed through. Then he made his way across some rough ground, the beam of his torch making a pool of light in front of his feet. There was a fence – he could have climbed over it, but instead he walked along it and found a gate, which he was able to push open. He paused to look at the huge metal craft, as large as a storage tank in an oil refinery. Again, he wondered if it had crashed. He couldn't see any torn or crumpled metal, but really it was too dark to be sure. The shape was like an upturned soup plate. He couldn't see any ports, or openings of any kind. But he could hear a faint humming.

He moved forward. The ground was uneven. He had to concentrate on the patch of light in front of his feet to avoid walking into bushes. Sometimes, a brittle twig would snap under his foot.

Riding on a smile and a shoeshine

Halfway between the gate and the craft, an enormous voice spoke to him. He halted, in total confusion. It took him a moment to realise that the voice was inside his head – no sound had passed through his ears at all.

Please don't be alarmed, said the voice. *I know that you haven't conversed in this way before, but, believe me, it is the only easy way for me to communicate with you.*

Peter wondered whether he was meant to reply and, if so, how. Perhaps if he just spoke, the creature could read the thoughts? You can't speak without first organising your thoughts, can you? He said aloud "Hello. My name is Peter."

Hello, Peter said the voice in his head. *I am the Captain of this ship. I am the Colonel-in-chief of this project ... no, sorry, that was the wrong concept. I am in charge.*

"Do you have a name?"

The voice seemed to hesitate. There was a fragment of thought, immediately suppressed. Then it said *That is a hard question. Of course I have an identifier, used among my people. But ... a version of it that you could understand? No, that is too difficult. You may call me ... Mary.*

"Mary?"

Yes. I see in your memories that you once knew a human called Mary, and liked her. She was of the female gender – the gender that produces live young – as am I. I would be pleased if you were to call me Mary.

For a moment he remembered his Mary. They'd been engaged. But it hadn't lasted long, and it had been quite a few years ago.

Not a good time to remember it.

291

The measure of all things

He said, "What are you here for, Mary? Have you come to conquer us? To enslave us?" He immediately wondered whether he should have asked these questions. But, since the alien could read his thoughts, there didn't seem much point in trying to conceal his fears.

No, that is not our way. We have come to exchange things with you ... humans. We have much that you would like. You have things that we would like.

"Have we?" he asked, in mystification.

Yes ... yes, I'm sure you have.

"Mmmm. Yes ... maybe we do. Mary, can ... can I interest you in a sixteen gigabyte memory stick?"

It was the start of a beautiful, and very profitable, friendship.

Exploring history

"I didn't realise that time travel would be so *slow*", said Glenys, gazing out of the window.

Julian smiled at her. "Take it from me," he said, "If the chrono-technologists could find a way to speed it up, they would. Short-haul time flights are much less trouble than the long-haul ones".

They were sitting facing each other, separated by a small table, with a large, round-cornered window between them. Anyone familiar with a twentieth or twenty-first century railway carriage would have recognised the arrangement.

The scene outside the window was a valley, leading down to a lake – but, unlike the view from a railway carriage, the viewpoint didn't change. It appeared to be a summer morning. In fact, what they were seeing was a sample of moments, chosen from a succession of mornings, as the timeship slipped easily from one day to the day before, and then to the day before that. It didn't look *quite* right: there were no clouds in the sky (just a general bright haziness), and no animals in the scene. Clouds, and birds, and sheep, and farm-workers, moved far too fast to remain in vision from one sampled-instant to the next. But the vegetation stayed in place. If you watched carefully, you could see the season changing, from summer, to spring, to winter, to autumn. The optical filtering ensured that each day had roughly the same level of illumination as the one next to it. But still, summer was noticeably

The measure of all things

brighter than winter, and the grass was greenest in spring.

The intercom pinged, and the stewardess's voice spoke: "Ladies and gentlemen, we will shortly be arriving at 1914. Would all passengers for this year please assemble, with their luggage, in the disembarkation port? And please make sure that you have all your belongings with you when you leave." It pinged again.

Further down the compartment, people started getting up and taking their luggage off the overhead rack. Glenys looked puzzled. "There seem to be quite a lot of them," she said. "Why would 1914 be so popular?"

Julian said airily, "Oh, you know, the last golden summer before the First World War. The world's about to change forever, and nobody knows. It's supposed to be a great place for a honeymoon."

Glenys said "Yes ... yes, I can see that ..."

The intercom pinged again, and the stewardess said: "Last call for 1914. Trans-century Timeways would like to take this opportunity to thank you for travelling with us, and to wish you a pleasant stay." And it pinged once more.

"... But I'd worry about staying too long," Glenys continued, "And getting caught up in the war. I mean, if you're a man, you might get called up, and sent to the front ..."

Julian shook his head. "No, it didn't happen for quite a while. It was all volunteers to begin with."

Suddenly, the view through the window changed to an indoor scene. There was a platform right beside

Exploring history

the timeliner, a wall beyond that, and a roof overhead. A large sign said '1918'. Quite soon, people were bustling into the timeliner's entry port at the right end of the platform, and bustling out of the one at the left. All carrying suitcases.

Glenys said "They're not hanging about, are they?"

"We're only here for three minutes. Everyone has to get on or off in that time."

"What happens if you're struggling with your suitcase?"

"They have porters to help you. They can't hold the ship up."

"Why just three minutes?"

"The station's only here for twenty-four hours. That's ... just a moment ..." – he tapped the keys on the computer built into his wrist-watch – "One four four oh minutes, which is four hundred and eighty three-minute slots. Once they've used the station 480 times, they have to demolish it and build another one somewhere else, which is expensive."

"Oh. So they build the station, and just use it for one day, then knock it down? Why?"

"The locals aren't supposed to notice that it's here, and the company fixes it so they don't. The local farmer and his wife get called away to a family wedding. The shepherd finds himself sick in bed all day. That sort of thing. Doing it for more than 24 hours is just too difficult."

There was another ping, and the stewardess's voice said: "Ladies and gentlemen, the doors are now closing. The next stop will be 1870." She paused.

The measure of all things

"The restaurant car will be opening shortly, for afternoon tea." A moment later, the view of the station was replaced by the valley and the lake.

"Shall we go and have some tea and cakes?" asked Julian.

"You go if you like. I'm happy just to sit here and watch the countryside change. ... That lake, down the valley, is it getting smaller?"

"Yes, it is. They flooded the valley to make a reservoir. You're watching it fill up; only you're watching it in reverse."

"Oh. It's funny the way we can see the world, but the world can't see us. That's right, isn't it? The locals don't know we're here?"

"Mm, that's right. We're only here for a tiny fraction of each second – much too short for anyone to actually see us." He paused. "Right, I'll go off and get some tea. Can I bring you back a cup? And a cake?"

"Yes, that would be nice. Thanks."

Glenys watched the lake slowly shrinking. It was funny the way it left verdant grass behind it, rather than the mud flats you'd expect. And every now and then you'd catch a fleeting glimpse of a boat, which someone must have left there for several days, by the lakeside.

"Is this seat taken? Can I join you?" She turned. A young man was gesturing at the seat beside her. He was in his twenties, dark-haired and sun-tanned – unusual, in the mega-city that Glenys and Julian came from. She smiled at him, and said "Yes, why not? My name's Glenys".

Exploring history

He smiled back. "Glad to meet you. My name's Max." He sat down.

"Where are you headed for?"

"Seventeen twelve."

"Further than us. We're only going to eighteen fifteen. All that excitement at the end of the Napoleonic Wars. Some terrific parties."

"Make sure you don't stay too long. Eighteen sixteen was horrible."

"Really? I don't remember reading …"

"The weather was horrible, all over the Northern Hemisphere. It was the year without a summer. Lord Byron and the Shelleys went on holiday to Lake Geneva, but none of them felt like going out, so they just sat around and invented horror stories. That's how *Frankenstein* got written, and *The Vampyre*."

"Ah, here's Julian! Darling, this is Max."

Julian had appeared from down the aisle, carrying a small tray. He said, "Hi Max – sorry, can't shake hands. Tea for you, darling, and black forest gateaux. Sorry it took so long. There were a lot of grim-faced men in grey uniforms in the corridor. Time Police, I think."

Max frowned. "That doesn't sound good. The TP usually keep a very low profile. I wonder what's up?"

The intercom pinged. But this time it wasn't the stewardess's voice; it was a man, and he sounded agitated. "Ladies and Gentlemen, I'm sorry to have to report that we're experiencing some operating difficulties. Please remain calm –"

The measure of all things

Another voice cut in. Calmer; more controlling. "That's enough from you, Captain. Ladies and Gentlemen, we're in charge of this vessel now. And we're the Black Hand Gang. I'm afraid we won't be stopping at 1870, or anywhere else until 1812. To all you millionaire fun-lovers, with your elaborate holiday plans, I would say **tough**. In the end, your needs and desires don't matter. You've never known what it is to fight for a cause. That's all for now."

The intercom pinged, and, after a short pause, pinged again. This time it was the stewardess's voice, and there was a note of desperation in her voice. "Ladies and Gentlemen, *please* remain calm. We are doing all we can to ensure that normal services are restored as soon as possible." The intercom cut off.

After a while, Max said "The idiots".

Julian said "Who? The timeliner crew?"

"Well, them, certainly, for letting it happen. But I meant the hijackers. They don't know how to fly this thing. If they insist on elbowing the pilot, and the co-pilot aside ... this could be a disaster."

Glenys said "Oh my God."

Julian looked pale, and there was a tremor in his voice. He said "Who are the Black Hand Gang? Do you know anything about them?"

"I'm afraid so," said Max. "Arguably, they started the First World War, by assassinating Archduke Franz Ferdinand in Sarajevo. The history books say they were Serbian nationalists, but really they were something much bigger. They've got a grand scheme to reshape European history."

"And 1815's important to them?" said Julian.

Exploring history

Max said "I suspect they want to fix it so that Napoleon wins the battle of Waterloo."

"But ... I don't understand ... " said Glenys. "We were going to 1815 anyway – why do they need to hijack the timeliner?"

Max shook his head. "We were going to the time node that the company's set up in June 1815. Just in time for the Battle of Waterloo. This lot are going to want to go to the beginning of the year so they can ... well, start changing things. In good time. That means they'll attempt an emergency landing. And an emergency landing *that* close to an established node is never going to work."

"What will happen?" said Julian.

Max looked grim. "Do you really want to hear this?"

Glenys spoke, in a small voice. "Yes, I think we'd better."

"There'll be a big time eddy. Space-time treats that as a high vacuum, so it collapses straight away. The history books will say that there was a really massive explosion, cause unknown."

"Is there anything we can do?" said Glenys.

"Say a prayer, maybe? Are you two religious?"

Julian looked at her, and said, softly, "Darling?"

Glenys said "No, I can't think of any prayers."

There was a long pause. Then Glenys said "This is awful ... just waiting like this ..."

The door at the end of the compartment opened, and a man came in. He was young, and looked fit. He was wearing nondescript clothes and carrying a handgun.

The measure of all things

He satisfied himself that there was no one further down the compartment, then sat down in the seat next to Julian. He said "Don't move, any of you." His gun was resting on his left forearm, pointing at Glenys, and his right forefinger was on the trigger.

Julian said "Christ almighty. Who are you?"

The young man said "My name's Gustavo, not that it matters. I will shoot you if I have to. I'm going to sit here quiet with you, and when the Time Cops come in, you'll say we're all a party travelling together. I'll keep the gun out of sight, but I *will* shoot you if you betray me."

He moved the gun under the table. Out of sight. Glenys was pretty sure it was still pointing at her.

But, simultaneously, she became aware that there was a man standing in the next bay, behind the seat where Julian and this man called Gustavo were sitting. A man in a grey uniform. She hadn't any idea how he had got into the compartment. He, too, was carrying a handgun. Smoothly he moved round, so that he was standing beside Gustavo and pointing the gun at his head.

He said, "No you won't, Gustavo. It's over. We've got all the others. Give yourself up now. You've got nowhere left to run."

Gustavo didn't flinch. He didn't turn to look at the cop; his hands remained out of sight under the table. He sighed, and said "So? So why should I? I could shoot these people now, so you won't forget the Black Hand Gang. You would know we mean what we say, do what we must do."

Exploring history

The Time Cop said, "No, Gustavo. No need to act crazy. It's over. And, believe it or not, your mission was a success."

"*What?* How can that be?" said Gustavo.

The Time Cop said, "You wanted to stop Napoleon winning the Battle of Waterloo? He didn't. You've strayed into a timestream where he *lost* the battle.

Gustavo swore: "Numele lui Dumnezeu!"

The Time Cop continued, "So, just give me the gun and come along with me. There's a good fellow." And, after a brief pause, Gustavo put both hands on the table, and then handed his gun to the cop. For a moment it looked as though he was going to say something. But he thought better of it, and the two of them left.

Julian reached out and took Glenys's hand, and stroked it. He said something soothing.

But Glenys was thinking about what the cop had just said. Everything we've been told about time is wrong, she thought. There's only one timestream? No, there's world after world after world, all running parallel to each other. Worlds where all the bad things in history that might have happened actually did happen, and worlds where all the good things didn't. The authorities know about it, but they chose not to tell us. She said, "You know, I think I've just learnt something about time that I'd really rather not have known."

The intercom pinged, and the stewardess said: "Trans-century Timeways would like to apologise for the recent untoward events, and assure you that everything is now under control. We would like to

The measure of all things

thank you for travelling with us, and hope that you find the rest of your journey pleasant. We will shortly be arriving at 1870. Thank you."

The intercom pinged again.

Taking the train up to London

As I reached the steps into Motspur Park Station, I heard the loudspeaker on the platform making a familiar announcement.

"The train now arriving at platform one, is the two forty five to London Waterloo, calling at Raynes Park, Wimbledon, Earlsfield, Clapham Junction, Vauxhall, and London Waterloo. This train is formed of eight carriages."

I would normally have run up the steps, along the bridge, and down onto the platform where the train was waiting. I'd often done it before. Through the fence, I could see train doors opening, and people getting on and off.

On this occasion, I decided not to. It really didn't matter whether I caught the train: no one was waiting for me at the far end. There'd be another one in five minutes. No, for once I wouldn't waste my energy running up and down stairs. I'd saunter onto the platform in good time for the next train.

As I climbed up the steps, I thought about the recorded announcement. Pointless, really. Everyone knew where the train was going: trains to London always stopped at the same six stations. There wasn't a choice; going north, the line didn't branch.

The measure of all things

Unsurprisingly, when I reached the platform it was empty. I didn't bother to look at the indicators. I sat on a bench and waited. Hardly worth taking my book out: I could already see the train coming down the line from Worcester Park.

The loudspeaker came to life.

"The train now arriving at platform one is the two fifty to Lambeth Marsh, calling at Cottenham Park, Worple Lane, Summerstown Graveyard, Falcon Inn, Nine Elms, and Lambeth Marsh. This train is formed of eight carriages."

I was bewildered. That was all wrong, wasn't it?

The train pulled in, looking perfectly normal. Rather wildly, I looked around for a concealed camera. Was there a TV crew, getting a laugh out of an innocent rail passenger? If so, it was well hidden. Well, they couldn't fool me: this was the two fifty to Waterloo, and I intended to catch it. I pressed the button on the carriage, the door opened, and I climbed aboard. No one else inside. The door closed, and the train started.

I looked out, at the backs of houses that I must have seen a thousand times before. All perfectly normal. Clearly, the announcement had been someone's silly joke. Not worth giving any more thought to it. I took out my book, and starting reading from where I'd left off.

After about five minutes, the train pulled in to Raynes Park, or so I thought. I hardly noticed. The doors opened; I carried on reading. Someone got in, and seated themselves a little way along the carriage. As the doors closed, I glanced through the window.

Taking the train up to London

The track at Raynes Park is on an embankment, so if you're in a carriage, you're level with the rooftops. I looked down the slope, past a few trees, to the shopping street below. And I realised it didn't look right. There should have been a charity shop, a funeral director, and a pub. The pub was there, but the rest of the row seemed to be tumbledown houses. Why was everything so shabby? Why no traffic? Why no street lights? And ... the road seemed to be *cobbled*. How could that be?

The train pulled out. We were now passing a leafy lane. Still no cars or trucks, though I did see a horse and cart. I tried to remember what should have been on the far side of the road – small blocks of flats, I thought. But instead, there were shacks, made of rough timber. They had chimneys, and some of them were smoking. Smoking chimneys? In London?

I got up, and walked to where the other passenger was sitting. His clothes were curiously old-fashioned: a dark green flannel jacket, with a high collar, and silver buttons down the front. He had a luxuriant moustache, mutton-chop sideburns, and was reading a leather-bound book. I sat down opposite him.

"Excuse me, could you tell me what the last station was?"

He looked up. "Cottenham Park," he said, then went back to reading his book.

I fidgeted. Looking through the window, I noticed the lane had gone. Instead, we were travelling through woodland.

But this line didn't pass through any woodland. Nor did any other lines I could think of in Greater London.

The measure of all things

After a while, roads appeared again. The buildings along them looked more substantial, though hardly modern. Some were stone, some brick, all were thatched. There were no cars, but a few horsemen. We pulled into what should have been Wimbledon Station.

In a way it was familiar. A lot of platforms, side by side, with stairs leading up to an overhead concourse. Each platform had its own glass-panelled roof. No electric lights or indicator boards that I could see. Signs hung from the roof, showing the station's name: they didn't say "Wimbledon", they said "Worple Lane".

A lot of people were milling around. They looked like extras from a movie, set in medieval times: a few of them were wrapped in cloaks; others wore loose jackets, long skirts and baggy trousers made of coarse cloth, in shades of grey, brown and black. Very few got on board the train.

I *had* to know what was going on.

As the doors closed, I said "I expected this to be Wimbledon."

The man opposite put his book down. He said, "No, it's Worple Lane. There's a village on a hill near here, called Wimbledon, but railway lines don't go to the top of hills."

He leaned back, and gave me a long stare. Then he said, "I think you've taken the wrong train, young man. I'm very sorry."

I was puzzled to be called 'young man' — I would have said I was older than he. But, as I tried to think

Taking the train up to London

of a reply, he said, "A word of advice. Don't get off the train."

"Why not?"

"Your world is a law-abiding place. This world isn't. If you get off, and wander around, the footpads will soon spot you as a foreigner. They'll rob you – probably murder you. Much better to stay on the train till it gets to the terminus."

"My world? I don't understand."

"Where did you get on?"

"Motspur Park."

"I thought so. It's the last stop before the train makes the jump between the worlds. They made a mistake. They shouldn't have opened the doors."

"I ... I don't understand ..."

"You don't really need to. Just stay on the train till it gets to the end of the line. And then stay on it some more. Eventually, they'll take the train out again. When it gets to Motspur Park, get off."

He looked through the window. I could see open fields, and a plough-horse pulling a plough. "It'll be Summerstown soon. I get off there. Remember what I said: stay on the train till you get to Lambeth. Then stay on it till it gets you back home."

"Lambeth? I thought the end of the line was Waterloo?"

He laughed. "Yes, I heard that in your England, the British won a battle at a place called Waterloo. Against some Frenchman. In this England, they didn't. So no cause to name a station after it."

The measure of all things

The train slowed. "Have you got gold in your pockets?" he asked.

"No ... no gold," I said weakly.

"Then you'd better pray the ticket collector doesn't get on board." He stood up, as the train halted. A large sign on the platform said 'Summerstown. Alight here for Earlsfield Necropolis.' He pressed the button to open the door, and stepped out. "Good luck," he said.

The train pulled out, passing an enormous cemetery. A number of hearses were to be seen, decorated with black plumes and drawn by black horses.

I tried to make sense of it all. I seemed to have strayed into some looking-glass world, where I was still in London, or Surrey, but everything was wrong. Except ... this was undoubtedly an electric train, and anyone who travelled by South Western trains would have been familiar with how it looked.

I pondered this, and watched the landscape passing the windows. More farmland, and the occasional village. Teams of oxen, pulling ploughs. Copses, and small ponds. Once, we passed a substantial road, with a troop of cavalry riding along it. Black uniforms, with gold piping.

We approached the next station. The tracks branched; there were many platforms, and high brick walls on either side of the cutting. Once again, it was almost recognizable: anyone who knew Clapham Junction would have found it vaguely familiar. There were large signs on each platform, announcing it as Falcon Inn.

Taking the train up to London

Now I could see other trains. The carriages looked impossibly old fashioned, and they were all pulled by steam engines. The engines were painted black, and generally filthy, as were the platform roofs.

The doors opened, and several people got on. One was a shabbily dressed young man who came and sat opposite me. There was something furtive about him.

This, I thought, was my chance to learn more. As we pulled out, I leaned forward.

"Excuse me, do you often travel on this line?"

Now he looked scared. "Never been on it before," he muttered.

"Only, it seems smarter than the other trains."

He looked at me as though I was an idiot. "Well, it's electric, isn't it? Only electric train in the country."

"How can that be?"

He shook his head, "Mister, don't you know? It comes from a place where there's lots of electric trains. Sort of, outside the country. We're not allowed to go there. But they – the people who run the place – send a train up to London, every now and then, so they can see what's going on. We're allowed to ride on it, always supposing we've got the fare. And they laid a special electric rail – it fries you if you touch it."

He glanced past me, and stiffened. "Christ," he said, "An inspector." He looked at me pleadingly. "Mister, can you lend me a gold piece? Only, only I've lost my ticket. If the inspector catches me, he'll put me in prison."

"I'm sorry," I said, "I don't have a gold piece."

The measure of all things

He obviously didn't believe me. "Please mister, they'll put me in Horsemonger Lane Gaol. People *die* there …"

He realised he wasn't getting anywhere, got up and ran towards the door at the end of the carriage. I looked at the man sitting across the gangway. He'd taken a card, the size of a DVD case, out of his pocket. It had gilded edges, script printing, and an embossed gold medallion on it. With a sick feeling, I realised that it was his ticket.

All I had was a Freedom Pass, authorised by the London Borough of Merton. Which, I strongly suspected, didn't exist in this world.

"Tickets please," said a voice behind me.

Hark the herald angels sing

There had been a great city here once. Katreana. Millions of people had dwelt in it. Had they been happy? It was long ago, and few records have survived, so no one can say for sure. Then, as the world got hotter, the river that brought water from the far-away mountains dried up. Or rather, it was a raging, uncontrollable torrent for two months of the year, and a dried mud channel for the rest. No city can live without water, and the people left, hoping that other parts of the world would treat them generously. It was a chaotic time, and there was much violence and misery. The population of the world shrank dramatically.

Now, over a thousand years later, people had returned. There was land here that could be farmed; land that could support a community, and give it space and freedom. It was true that the area around the river mouth was mainly patches of concrete and tarmac, and mounds of fallen masonry, but beyond the city limits there was soil that could be tilled. Trees could be felled for timber, and bricks and stones dug out of the rubble and used to make houses. Above all, there was a trickle of water in the ancient riverbed all the year round – enough to irrigate the fields, and to provide a little settlement with water to drink and in which its people could wash.

The measure of all things

The settlers arrived at the end of winter, and set about building homes. A very small settlement – they called it a town, but it was scarcely more than a village – grew up on the edge of the ancient ruins. They were independent-minded folk, but, nevertheless, they felt the need for some leadership in the community, so they elected a mayor. Then they set about ploughing the land, and planting crops. Of course, they had brought supplies with them, but such stocks are always limited, and they ate sparingly during the months that followed. Their relief, their joy, was immense, when, come the autumn, they gathered in their first harvest, and it was bountiful enough to feed them for the rest of the year.

Not all the colonists were farmers. Some fished the ocean, and some hunted wild game, providing the villagers with much-needed fresh fish and meat. Some mined the city, digging up ancient machines that could be smelted for their metals. They had solar furnaces that they'd brought with them from afar.

The languages of the world had evolved over the centuries, and the archaic residents of the city would not have understood the speech of the newcomers. Nevertheless, they still used the calendar that civilised folk had used for three thousand years. When the month of December arrived, no one was surprised that the land grew cold and the days grew short. The villagers wondered whether a mid-winter festival might be appropriate. The consensus was that it would, so it was agreed that there would be a modest feast, a week before the end of the year, and close to the winter solstice. A public meal, in the evening, that everyone would be invited to attend. The hunters were confident that they could shoot enough wildfowl to provide everyone with rich meat. There'd be music,

Hark the herald angels sing

and dancing. People could give each other gifts, if they liked.

It was a rather splendid occasion. Long trestle tables had been set up in the village square, with enough seats for everyone. The weather was dry, and the cold winds had dropped for once, though the sky was cloudy. Every farmer had provided produce, every household had provided a cook, and on the tables there were bowls of fruit and nuts, dishes of roasted vegetables, roast fowls dressed with delicious sauces, and flagons of wine. All the food anyone could wish for. Rows of braziers kept everyone warm. The children had taken the feathers plucked from the fowls, glued them together to make fluffy balls, and dyed them in bright colours. They'd strung them overhead, on cords strung between poles, as festive decorations.

The villagers ate and drank their fill, and amused each other with funny stories. In truth, there was little new in the anecdotes they had to tell, but the wine, and the feeling of good cheer, meant that everyone laughed uproariously.

As the eating and drinking came to an end, the Mayor rose to make a speech.

"My friends," he started, "We have much to celebrate …". He fell silent, gazing at the sky. For a moment, the villagers thought that he had forgotten his lines. Then they realised that he was staring at something remarkable. They all turned and gawked at the heavens over the ruins beyond the village boundary.

In the sky, a dozen spectral figures had appeared. They were huge, and they appeared to be human beings with great wings growing from their shoulders.

The measure of all things

Three were holding harps; three were holding long trumpets. They clearly weren't solid creatures – you could see through them, to the contours of the clouds behind – they were more like sketches, painted in silver and pink and gold. Silver robes, pale pink skin, golden hair and wings and harps and trumpets. And then, they sang.

A great peal of music seemed to roll over the landscape. The figures were singing, in four-part harmony. No one in the village could understand any of the words, but the beauty of the singing was overwhelming.

And then, after a few lines, the music faltered, in mid phrase. The figures in the sky flickered and faded.

Wisely, the Mayor didn't try to resume his speech. He signalled to the musicians, who played a cheerful dance tune. There was some dancing. Friends embraced, lovers kissed. But really, the villagers were too overawed to throw themselves into the celebrations. For the most part, they sat at the tables and asked each other, what was *that*? What *happened*?

Next day, the Mayor called on the village Schoolmaster. They knew each other well enough to call each other Jaro and Zibor. They sat together in Zibor's parlour, and Jaro asked the same questions.

"Last night – the figures in the sky – what was *that*? What *happened*?"

"I don't know," replied Zibor. "In ancient times, people followed religions. They expected miracles to happen. What we saw last night looked very much like a miracle."

Hark the herald angels sing

"Do you think it was something to do with one of the old religions?"

"Yes, I do. One of the lines in the song sounded like *Krystiz-borninn-beth-leehem*. I think there are some words there taken from the religion called Christianity. It was very widespread before the great catastrophe."

"Did this religion have gods?"

"Well, almost all the old religions had gods. I haven't made a study, but I seem to remember Christianity had five of them. The Father, the Son, the Ghost, Virgin-Mary and Santa Claus."

"Do you think one of the gods has come back to life? The Ghost, maybe? That certainly seemed like a choir of ghosts."

"I don't know. But if a god is trying to communicate with us, why do it in a language we can't understand?"

"I don't know either. And I don't know what we can do about it. I don't really want our people to be terrified by ghosts. We have enough problems without that."

"I don't think they are terrified. I've talked to a few people this morning. They don't feel threatened. They feel that the ghosts of the city-dwellers are, somehow, welcoming them. Giving them their blessing."

They talked further. In the end, they concluded that there was nothing to be done.

But the villagers didn't forget the incident. In particular, a young farm hand called Stasiak heard what Zibor had to say. He spent some time at the village's terminal, researching Christianity. Eventually, in an extremely ancient document, he found the

The measure of all things

words and music to what had once been known as a carol.

Exactly a year after the first mid-winter feast, the village held another. And, exactly as before, the figures appeared in the sky. This time, Stasiak and some of his friends joined in the song. When the celestial choir faltered, as it did at exactly the same point as the year before, they completed it. The villagers weren't sure what to do, so they applauded.

"What *is* it – this ... thing ... that appears in the sky at our mid-winter feast?" asked one of the villagers, a farmer.

"It's a miracle, of course. A Christian miracle," replied Stasiak.

"I don't know what *Christian* means," said the farmer. "Or what a miracle is."

"I know you don't," said Stasiak, smiling sympathetically. "Let me tell you. Let me teach you."

It was in November of the third year after the settlers had first arrived that one of the miners had a nasty accident with a furnace. A crucible of molten steel slipped and splashed his hand. Florian was an old man, and it was soon clear that he wasn't going to recover from his burns. Jaro, still the Mayor, was deeply grieved: apart from the fact that he was a friend, Florian was the most scientifically knowledgeable of anyone in the village. Jaro visited him to pay his respects.

"I'm glad you're here, Jaro," said Florian from his bed. "Something's been weighing on my mind."

"Has it, indeed? Then tell me about it" said Jaro.

Hark the herald angels sing

"It's about the figures in the sky, at the mid-winter feast. Every year they come back. I think I caused them." He squirmed under the bedclothes – the village doctor had given him painkillers, but he was still very uncomfortable.

"Go on," said Jaro.

"You know Stasiak's spent all that time on the terminal, researching Christianity? Well, I've done some of that too. The Christians used to have small temples called 'churches', and large ones called 'cathedrals'. There was a cathedral in the city. The remains are still there. I think they put a machine in it, to project images onto the clouds. I don't think it ever stopped working."

"After all these centuries, Florian? Surely ..."

Florian shook his head. "The ancients could build things to last, when they wanted to. And if they were building something religious, that's exactly when they *would* want it to last."

"I see. And why do you think you're involved, Florian?"

"That first autumn, the lads and I excavated this big stone building. I think it must have been the cathedral. We uncovered some large slabs of black glass. We could have smashed them, to find out what was underneath, but it seemed like too much trouble. There was other stuff which we took instead – I remember some silver crosses. And brass candlesticks."

"Go on."

"I think the glass slabs were solar panels. I think they charged up the batteries for the projection machine,

The measure of all things

and brought it back to life. There must be lasers, set up so they scan the clouds. Draw a picture. And loudspeakers. It's set up so that it does its trick on the night of December the twenty-fourth, every year. I don't know what's special about that day."

"Florian, you may be right. But what do you think I should do about it?"

"Maybe you should switch the machine off? Put the earth back – cover it up? Or at least tell everybody, so they're not fooled any more?"

Jaro smiled, and held his hand. Florian slipped into unconsciousness.

"Yes, I could do that," murmured Jaro, "but Stasiak and his Christians would never forgive me."

Florian died soon afterwards. Jaro was not the only person with whom he had shared his thoughts, and by mid-December, there were rumours about the machine in the ruined cathedral. It caused something of a division in the community, between believers and non-believers. The Christians declared that the cathedral was holy ground. They walled it off, and insisted that no one who was not ordained could enter it. "Ordained" was another word that the settlers hadn't heard before.

The third mid-winter feast was just as splendid as the first and second had been. But there was a subtle change in the character of the event. Jaro no longer felt that he was presiding. That role had passed to Stasiak, who was resplendent in his robes as the first bishop that Katreana had seen for a thousand and fifty years (the ancient records included pictures as well as text). His friends were dressed as priests, and deacons. There were a few new converts, not dressed

Hark the herald angels sing

in any special way, but they too had learnt the words of the carol and joined in the singing. An observer, knowing something of ecclesiastical history, might have thought it a rather overblown spectacle, bearing in mind how small the congregation was.

But not in subsequent times. A few years later, the congregation had swelled to enormous proportions. The Katreana Christmas celebrations – where men sang to angels, and angels sang to men – had became world famous, and nothing was going to stop them.

Bounty of the soil

Alright me ansum! Ow be on? Me darter a-went up to London, and she told I, "Vadder, they city voaks ave a proper noggerhead idea of what us do yer in Zummerzet." Cordin er, tis cuz they advertisin bauys didden tell ee what's really gwains on. Zo I thought I'd put ee straight. Twoodden do no arm, ood it?

Zmarnin, I'm standin' on the ighest point of my varm in the Quantocks, 'bout 900 veet 'bove zea level, the vust rays of zpring zunshine beatin' down on me. The vield is empty, cept vor a small vlock of turnips.

Ee city voaks probably doughun know what I be talkin' 'bout. Ee go to the supermarket, and ee buys a pack of spring lamb, vresh vrom the varm, and ee think ur's real meat. Well, so ur was, back it the start of the twenty-vust century, but thicken were a generation ago, and us country voaks do things different now. Un o' our lads worked out that sheep bissen all that good it turnin' grass into lean meat, and bred a giant turnip that did the job a whole lot better. Took a bit of gene-splicin', of course. But I allus say, if ee want to be a genleman varmer, reapin' and zowin' and ploughin' and mowin' won't do un – ee've got to get in the lab and start linin' up the gene zequences.

Leastways, them turnips is scurryin' bout the vield on their little trotters, wolfin' down the grass, and gettin' vatter as I watch um. Be ready vor slaughter soon.

Bounty of the soil

When ee get ur, ur'll be good red meat with a picture of a lamb on the wrapper.

If I turn abough, I can see the ten acre vield, planted out with underpants. Does yer eart good, to see all thik woven cotton pokin' up through the soil. Time was, a couple of centuries ago, ee din grow cotton in England, cuz there wern enough zunshine. Plenty of zunshine now. Also, so they larnt me it school, all ee got out of a cotton plant back then was a lump of cotton wool – ee ad to card ur, spin ur and weave ur in a vactory. Turbul lot of work. Solution was obvious, zims to me. Ee jis cross the cotton plant with a spider, and ee've got a thread. Cross ur again, with a weaver bird, and ee've got a piece of cloth. Do a vew more tricks that I baint tellin' ee abough, and ee've got a pair of Y-fronts.

They need a bit longer. That's a varmer's skill, judgin' ow the crop's doin', and when to arvest. If I sent in the drasher now, they'd all be smarll, or chillurn size. 'Nuther week, aaf of um will be midlen size. Week after, we'll ave zum gurt big, and zum XL.

Round the edge of the vield, I've planted zum scarves. Zame sort of idea, cotton plant crossed with a silk worm, but I stuck zum butterfly genes in too. The bushes ave jis got ankichers on um it the moment, but, when they're vull grown, they'll be silk scarves with butterfly wing designs on um.

I've got a vield over yonder where I'm growin' vruit bushes. Bet ee doughun know what's inside the berries, once the usk's vallen off. Asprins! Once they're ripe, each un is parfect round, and ur's got zackly 300 milligrams of acetylsalicylic acid in ur. What's more, ur's stamped with the logo of a well-known drugs company. The drugs agency cassen tell

The measure of all things

the difference, and neither can ee, my acker. Then I release the caterpillars, and they pluck um and put um in pill bottles, vifty it a time.

Ee might zay, "Dang I, yew woant make much dibs vrom aspirins." Core snot. I be werkin on Viagra at the momen. But I annus made it werk azyet.

I could gwon, but I woodden want to bore ee. When Cursmas is comin' along, I'll ave giant carrots scurryin' around in the bottom vield, vull of turkey meat. Bootiful!

They that take the sword

Joe Sledge's diary was read out in court.

I hate him. I really, really hate him. I will kill him. I don't know when, but I will do it.

The prosecution made much of the words, written a week before his grandfather's death. Also the fact that he was apprehended in his grandfather's bedroom with a smoking gun, his grandfather's body having been pierced by three bullets as he lay in bed. It would have been an open-and-shut case, if the defence hadn't called a pathologist who demonstrated, convincingly, that the grandfather had died at least three hours before the shooting, probably from heart failure. The jury acquitted him.

"Do you feel lucky?" shouted a reporter, as he walked out of court.

"No," he shouted back. "I wanted to kill him. I didn't get the chance."

The police drove him back to his grandfather's house and left him there. Actually, not his grandfather's house any more. It was his house: he'd inherited all his grandfather's property. Not that it gave him any pleasure. He couldn't get rid of the feeling that the old bastard had cheated him. He deserved to die at

The measure of all things

my hands, he thought, but he escaped. Damn him forever.

Outside, the reporters were camped on his doorstep. They all wanted his exclusive story. He ignored them. They rang the doorbell, so he took the batteries out of it. They rang the phone, so he took it off the hook. Eventually, though, he had to go out and buy food. He phoned for a minicab, and, when it arrived, he glowered at the reporters, and barged through.

At the supermarket, he was selecting ready meals from the chill cabinet, and wondering whether he should abandon his wire basket and find a trolley, when a stranger came up to him.

"Excuse me, Mr Sledge, can we talk?"

"No we can't," he said. "You're another bloody reporter, aren't you?"

"No, I'm not. I don't want your story. I'm here to make you an offer. I can help you achieve something you really want. I can help you kill your grandfather."

"Oh, *sure* you can. How are you going to do that, bearing in mind that he's already dead?"

"I have access to a time machine."

That brought him up short. He put down his wire basket and sized the man up. Small, dark-haired, wiry. Sun-tanned. Wearing a dark suit, white shirt and a sober tie. A reporter with a clever line in patter? How could anyone tell?

It was a large supermarket, with its own coffee bar. He found himself sitting in it, sipping a black coffee, opposite the stranger, who turned out to be a certain

They that take the sword

Dr Joshua Lewis. The man said that he worked for something called the "Temporal Research Institute", and showed him glossy brochures with TRI embossed on the cover, and pictures of elaborate machines inside. He had a card, which described him as Deputy Head of the Experimental Division. In spite of himself, Joe found that he was beginning to believe this man and his outrageous story.

Then Dr Lewis made him a proposition: he could, if he wished, become a volunteer participant in the TRI's research project. There would be no salary, but they would pay his travel expenses, to the Institute and back. If he *did* agree, they would provide him with a suitable weapon, and take him to somewhere in the past, where they could *guarantee* that he would meet his grandfather. What he did next was entirely his own affair. Then they would bring him back, to the present.

This is crazy, though Joe. Completely crazy. I should walk away. Or at least say: give me a week to think about it.

But he didn't.

He said, "If I shoot him, the police will arrest me. I've already been there. Why would I want to go through all that again?"

Dr Lewis shook his head. "The police won't arrest you. They won't have any idea who the culprit was. Believe me, it won't be an issue."

And that was that. For reasons that he hardly understood, Joe signed the contract. He became a volunteer research associate of the Temporal

The measure of all things

Research Institute. Dr Lewis shook him warmly by the hand.

He took a cab home, packed a suitcase, searched around until he found his passport, and took another cab to Heathrow. He met Lewis there, and the two of them flew to North Africa.

They landed at Marrakech, and used a small private plane to fly east. The Temporal Research Institute was a neat cluster of white-washed buildings in the Atlas Mountains.

"We're on the border between Algeria and Morocco here," said Lewis. "It's really disputed territory. It means that if anything goes disastrously wrong, both countries can disown us."

"Is anything *likely* to go disastrously wrong?" Joe asked.

"Could do. We're messing with titanic forces here, and we don't always know what's going to happen. Also, there's the ethical aspect."

"What do you mean?"

"Look, there isn't a university anywhere in the First World that would let us do this current project. We'd never get it past an ethics committee. We had an ethicist on our project team – she resigned on day one."

At the main laboratory, he met Professor Arkady Adamenko, the Project Leader.

"Young man," he said, in a thick Russian accent, "I am very anxious not to impel you towards a course of action you do not wish to take. But, at the same time,

They that take the sword

I understand that you have an entirely natural desire to punish your grandfather for what he did to you."

"He was a sadistic bastard," said Joe, with feeling.

"Quite so," said Adamenko. "And you hate him so much you want to kill him?"

"Yes, I do."

"Then we will enable you to do that." He consulted a typed report on his desk. "He grew up in Lytham St.Annes. We will send you to a spot, fifty-five years ago, where we know you will find him. Here, take this –" he handed Joe a Luger pistol "– and the best of luck."

Joe looked at the pistol, and shoved it in his pocket. This was all going much too fast.

"Just a moment – fifty-five years ago?" he said, but Lewis was already hustling him out of the room.

In the main laboratory space, an enormous machine was surrounded by technicians in white coats. The whole place was filled with humming and throbbing.

"Noisy," remarked Joe.

"Yeah," replied Lewis. "We've got bigger magnets than the Large Hadron Collider. Means a lot of liquid helium. Big refrigeration units, and lots and lots of power."

He approached a man with a clipboard, who seemed to be some sort of chief technician.

"Are we ready?" he asked.

"Yes, sir," replied the man.

The measure of all things

All the machinery seemed to be focussed on one small, metal cylinder. It had a door, secured by screw clamps. Lewis opened it, to reveal a chamber which was just about large enough to stand up in. It was lit by a single fluorescent light, and there was a padded seat attached to the wall. Lewis ushered Joe into the tight little cavity. Joe stepped in, and sat down on the seat.

"Here," said Lewis, "You'll need this." He handed him a faded black-and-white photograph. It showed a small boy, in a torn woollen pullover, sitting on a swing.

"This is what your grandfather looked like in 1959. We'll drop you at a pillar-box in St Alban's Road: you'll find him across the street, in a playground. Shoot him. Then come back to the pillar-box, and we'll scoop you up."

He noticed the bewildered look in Joe's eyes. "Look, however it works out in the playground, just make sure you're back at the same pillar-box within the next half hour. I promise we'll bring you back."

Joe had questions to ask, but Lewis closed and the door before he could say anything. There was a sound of the clamps being screwed shut.

The light dimmed, and there was a gut-wrenching sensation.

For a moment he thought he was going to be sick. Then the strangeness of his surroundings put the thought out of his mind. The metal cylinder had vanished, and he was sitting on nothing. He staggered backwards, and found himself leaning against a pillar-box.

They that take the sword

He straightened up. He was standing in a street, on a bright, sunny day. There were no people in the street, and no traffic, but a car was parked down the road, looking both very old-fashioned and fairly new. Across the street was a children's playground.

He moved the photograph to his left hand. He felt inside his pocket, and pulled the Luger out.

He crossed the street, and went through the gate: the playground contained some seesaws and a swing. They were made of wood and metal rather than plastic; painted in post-office red and steam-locomotive green.

Sitting on the swing was a small boy of about nine.

He looked sad. Alone. There were no other children, and no adults, in the playground.

Joe walked towards the child, his pulse racing. Could this *possibly* be his grandfather?

The photo matched. And there was something about his eyes, his nose, the shape of his jaw, that he recognised.

The child saw him. The look of sadness was replaced by fear.

"Is that a real gun, mister?" he said.

"Yes," said Joe, and raised it.

And then …

And then he couldn't do it.

An intense feeling of compassion crept over him. This was just a sad, lonely little boy. He deserved pity, not death.

The measure of all things

For a long moment he stood there, the gun wavering. Then he shook his head. He stuffed the gun back into his pocket, and turned and walked away. Back to the pillar-box. He didn't have to wait long. There was the same nauseating sensation, and he was in the metal-walled compartment.

The door opened, and Professor Adamenko and Dr Lewis beckoned him out. Then they took the gun away from him. A quick inspection satisfied them that it hadn't been fired.

"Tell us exactly what happened," said Lewis. He was carrying a compact voice recorder, and he held the microphone close to Joe's mouth.

"I couldn't do it," said Joe. "He was there. I walked up to him. I pointed the gun at him. Then I couldn't do it."

"Tell me what you felt. As precisely as possible," said Lewis.

"I felt ... compassion. I felt it very strongly."

They went to Adamenko's office, where there were more questions, and his answers were meticulously recorded.

"And finally," said Lewis, "How do you feel now?"

Joe considered. "I feel ... at peace with myself. As if a burden has been lifted. I had power over him, but I chose not to use it."

And that might have been the end of it. But suddenly Joe felt uneasy. It had to do with Lewis and Adamenko's expressions – a sort of studied neutrality.

They that take the sword

"There's something you're not telling me," he said. "This ... experiment, would you call it? ... has cost you a lot of money, a lot of effort. Why did you do it? What were you trying to find out? What *did* you find out?"

Adamenko said, "Lewis would probably say that you should be left with your comforting illusions of free will. Personally, I see things differently. The truth shall set you free, as the Bible says. So, if you ask me directly, I will tell you what we found."

"Professor, I *am* asking you exactly that."

"It wasn't just you," said Lewis. "We located nine men with a proven compulsion to kill their grandfathers. Or, in one case, their grandmother. In every case, it was hatred that drove them, rather than a calculated desire for material gain. But in every case, *force majeure* had prevented them from performing the killing."

"We found most of them in America, of course," said Adamenko. "People have a stronger tendency to shoot each other in the USA than anywhere else. Some we had to spring from jail. We offered all nine of you the chance to do away with the object of your hatred, when the offending person was a child."

"Why?" said Joe.

Adamenko laughed. "Mr Sledge, you've just lived through a famous paradox. You didn't realise? For a very long time, professors of physics and suchlike have been indulging in a thought experiment. Imagine, they would say, that a man uses a time machine to go back and kill his grandfather as a little boy. Then the boy wouldn't grow up to have any

The measure of all things

children, or grandchildren, and the killer would never come into existence. So he couldn't kill his grandfather, could he? A world that allowed such a contradiction would be a world where the laws of physics were incoherent, and the one thing we know about the laws of physics is that they're coherent. Therefore time travel is impossible."

"Then came a big embarassment," said Lewis, "Professor Adamenko and his team used the gravitational properties of cosmic strings to build a time machine. It worked. Which raised the interesting question: where does that leave the famous grandfather paradox? So we conducted an experiment."

"And the results are fascinating," said Adamenko. "In all nine cases, the subject failed to go through with the killing. They all report a sudden, overwhelming, feeling of compassion. If it was just one or two of them, it might have been a change of heart. But all nine? We believe it was something different. We believe that the universe intervened to protect itself from incoherence. It did so by overruling their free-will."

"Psychologists argue about free-will," said Lewis. "Whether it exists at all, or whether it is simply an illusion. But I think they'd have to allow that, in the end, free-will, or the semblance of free-will, is governed by the laws of physics, like any other process in the human body. It seems that those laws can sometimes direct it quite explicitly."

"Oh," said Joe. He couldn't think of anything else to say.

They that take the sword

* * * * *

Adamenko and Lewis are quite convinced that the story they've just told Joe is the exact truth. What neither of them realises is that in fact they enrolled *eighteen* subjects in their little experiment. Nine of them found out that they couldn't go through with the killing. Not so the other nine.

The universe has more than one way to protect itself from incoherence. The hate-filled grandson fires at the child who was his grandfather. The child dies. His children, and grandchildren, wink out of existence. The child, no longer dead, wonders at the strange shuddering feeling that came over him momentarily – almost as though someone had walked over his grave. But the miscreant grandchild, deleted from existence, stays deleted. The coherence of the universe is preserved.

Sing a dirge for nine of your fellow human beings – flawed human beings, it's true, but humans nevertheless – whose names are not recorded in any book, or anyone's memory, and of whose passing there will never be any record.

Or, if you prefer, don't. They never existed, after all.

Last man standing

Thursday 1st February, 2035

The professor wants me to keep a diary. Fine, I don't mind doing that. But I told him that it doesn't give him the right to read it. Also, I don't intend to write it every day. Once every six months should be enough.

What does one write in a diary? I don't really know. Perhaps I should start by describing myself, and my life.

My name's Ural. After the Ural Mountains.

I was born in the Hublin Institute, here, fourteen years ago. My mother was a surrogate, and I never met her. I was brought up by a succession of children's nurses. They were always pleasant, always professional. Just occasionally, one of them would show me some real warmth. I remember Nurse Sarah, who would read me a bedtime story, and give me a hug and a kiss before she turned the lights out. I cried a lot when she left.

Wednesday 1st August, 2035

Re-reading what I wrote, I realise I missed out a couple of things. If I were an ordinary kid, I would tell you about my father. The truth is, I didn't have one. I was constructed out of DNA scraped out of old relics. Very, very old relics.

Last man standing

And I didn't say what was happening in the world. Wars in Africa, financial crisis in Latin America, the European Union in danger of splitting in two, China flexing its muscles as the new top superpower. Exciting times, they tell me.

Friday 1st February, 2036

It's been a turbulent year. I got fed up with my teachers. Once or twice, I lost my temper and hit one of them. They restrained me, and I shouted at them. It happened three – no, four – times. It always ended with them fetching the Professor, so he could soothe me. And, yeah, he does always manage to calm me down. A quiet chat, where he tells me he understands how hard it is for me. "You're strong," he'll say, "And you've got a big brain. In fact, you've got stronger muscles and a bigger brain than your teachers. But I want you to realise that you don't have to prove it. You should respect each other. You should respect them because they know more than you do – they should respect you because you're unique. There's no one else like you, in the whole world." Which is all very well, but I know they don't respect me. Sometimes I eavesdrop outside the staff-room door – I've got sharper hearing than they realise. "Those arms, and those fists," they'll say. "Don't you feel threatened?" And "He's so self-centred. And so ugly." They're talking about me, of course. Well, I'm sorry, guys; *you* may think I'm ugly, but that's your distorted perception. I'm actually the handsomest guy in my entire race. Which means that I've got a right to be self-centred.

What's happening in the world? Latin America looks to be getting over its financial crisis. The European

The measure of all things

Union decided it couldn't afford to split in two. China hasn't colonised the rest of East Asia yet, though everyone expects them to. One of those wars in Africa – the one between the Congo and Greater Nigeria – has turned particularly nasty: they've started to use germ warfare. A lot of people killed, and still no sign of an end to the war.

That last made me think of the Neanderthals, of course. They died out about 24,000 years ago. There's a long running debate as to whether they went extinct through natural causes – a pandemic infection, say – or whether the human beings exterminated them. The evidence for the "extermination" theory is looking a bit thin, but, based on what I read in the press every day, I wouldn't put it past the humans.

Friday 1st August, 2036

The feuding between me and the teaching team got worse. I went on the Internet, and found some other kids who couldn't stand their teachers. What do you do? I asked. Play hookey, they said, or put on a concealed pair of earphones and listen to music through the class. Yeah, right. I'm the only one in the class, and I'm locked in this place. They'd notice if I wasn't there, and they'd notice if I were listening to 21st century rock music.

Then, last June, I had an almighty great bust-up with them. Rather to my surprise, the whole team then resigned, and the Institute brought in a new one. I like the new lot much more. They let me follow my own ideas. If I spend the whole day on the Internet, that's just fine with them.

And events out there in the world? Might be a good time to invest your money in Latin America – I'd say they're at the bottom of the slump. The European Union changed its mind and did split up. The world was generally pleased when the Chinese invaded North Korea and made it a colony. They weren't so pleased when they did the same to South Korea.

Sunday 1st February, 2037

In December, I came close to busting up with the Professor. I got it into my head that he'd promised me a companion. One of my kind. Oh, let's be honest about this. I'm talking about a mate. A bed-mate. I watched some Internet porn, and I thought, that's what humans do – I'd like to find out what I can do.

Anyway, it was preying on my mind, and in the end I demanded a meeting, and demanded to know what he was doing about it. He sighed, and looked at me with those sad, blue eyes.

"Ural," he said, "I have to tell you it's never going to happen." He paused, and then he said, "You know what you are, and where you came from?"

I said yes, of course. "I'm a Neanderthal. You found some Neanderthal DNA, and cloned it."

He nodded. "In the Byzovaya cave, in the Polar Urals. We found part of a frozen corpse. Forty-one thousand years old, and the DNA had hardly degraded at all. All the same, it was technically very difficult to turn the DNA into a living being. You, that is. It cost more than a million euros, plus the cost of bringing you up. There wasn't enough money to make two of you."

The measure of all things

"But ... you've made more money since then, haven't you?"

"Some money, yes. By selling the knowledge we got from studying you. Your body chemistry, mostly; it's quite distinctive. The big pharmaceutical companies were very interested. But that's in the past now. We've become something of a backwater. No one wants to invest in us."

"There *must* be something you can do. Just repeat what you did when you made me. Make a woman. Skimp on the education – I'll teach her what she needs to know."

"They've changed the law since then. It's now illegal to make anything that is even close to a human being. Anyway, she'd be much too young for you, and she'd be your sister." He sighed again. "I'm afraid you're one of a kind, and destined to remain so. Can you forgive me?"

I did forgive him, of course. He's the nearest thing to a father I've got.

Saturday 1st August, 2037

Out there in the world: the Latin American slump got worse. Chinese leaders are making speeches that sound like nineteenth-century European colonialists. Some of the European states are, too, but they're too small and puny for anyone to take any notice. That war between the Congo and Greater Nigeria ended when the germ-warfare attack turned into a full-blown plague, and practically everyone in Central and West Africa died. No doubt the germ warfare specialists thought they had a serum to protect their own people, but it didn't work. Exciting times indeed.

Last man standing

Monday 1ˢᵗ February, 2038

Something in me says that I should write another entry in this diary. Stupid, of course. But a psychologist I spoke to, a few years ago, said that we Neanderthals have habits that are stronger and have longer time-spans than humans. Something to do with our temporal lobes having stronger links to the limbic system. So, here's my annual report.

The Professor retired last summer, but they made him an emeritus, so he still came by every now and then. I was there when he died, in October – I held his hand and murmured comforting words. And then I cried.

But I didn't have long to grieve, because everyone else was dying too. Pretty soon, I was the only one left alive in the Institute. I let myself out of the front entrance. There was no one there to stop me.

You see, those African germ warfare scientists had done their job pretty well. No one could find a cure for Nigerian-Congolese Plague. 100% infection rate, 100% death rate – much more impressive than anything Mother Nature could produce. And, with modern air travel, it spread everywhere like wildfire. No need to worry about Chinese colonialism anymore, or the Latin American economy, or the fate of Europe. No one left on any of the seven continents.

Why didn't I catch it? Because I was the only person in the whole world who didn't have human body chemistry. So much for the big muscles and the big brain: in the end, they didn't count for anything.

So it falls to me to say farewell to the human race.

The measure of all things

Goodbye and God bless. I forgive you for what you did to my people, if you did it.

I shall miss you.

A masque

Halfway between their landing site and the city of Sikkerhavn, they met a minstrel. He was a small, elegant figure, dressed in a silky costume in magenta and violet, with a black velvet cap, and carried a lute. The Colonel had the driver stop the half-track, and leaned out.

"Do you mind if I ask who the hell you are?" she asked.

The figure bowed, a courtly bow that wouldn't have looked out of place in 16th century Italy, and said, "My name is Dainius, and I am a minstrel. I see from your uniform that you are a military personage – a colonel. May I assume that you command the rescue party? And may I ask your name?"

"My name's Colonel Bryony Ellis, and yes, you're right about the rescue party. Now what in the name of blazes is a minstrel doing on this planet?"

Dainius shrugged disarmingly. "A newly-colonised planet can be a soulless place. The Colonisation Authority thought it would add a little colour, a little character, if the colonists were greeted by a minstrel-robot, who …"

"Right. You're a robot. Lachlan, is this plausible? A minstrel-robot?"

The Colonel had half turned to Major Lachlan, sitting in the back of the half-track.

The measure of all things

"I'd say so, Colonel," he replied. "I've had some dealings with the Colonisation Authority Cultural Division. They've got some pretty weird people working for them – poets, artists ..."

The Colonel turned back to Dainius. "You're a robot. That explains why you're still around. Tell me, are any of the colonists still alive? If so, where?"

"Sadly, no. I have long searched for anyone who could be my audience. The last time I met a living human was 32 days ago, and he only lived for 71 minutes. He asked me to compose a song, and sing it to you."

"Later, maybe, Dainius. First things first. Are you armed?"

Dainius contrived to look slightly shocked. The subtle shift in his facial features was really quite impressive. "No colonel, I do not carry arms. There are no wild animals on this planet. And, of course, I would not wish to do harm to a human being."

"Right. You won't object if we check, will you?"

"Colonel, I am your obedient servant."

The Colonel issued a curt order to Corporal Vester, the driver, who climbed out onto the road, lugging a portable scanner. Dainius leaned his lute against the vehicle's track, and stood with his arms stretched out on either side, as Vester pointed the beam at him. After a few moments, the machine beeped, and displayed a screen-full of data.

"Nothing dangerous, sir," reported Vester. "No projectile weapons. No blades. No explosives. And no radio transmitters."

A masque

"OK," said the Colonel. "Climb aboard, minstrel. You're going to guide us round the city. Budge up, Lachlan, Reto."

Majors Lachlan and Reto made room, as best they could, and the robot seated himself nimbly on the back seat, with his lute on his lap. Lachlan gave him a prolonged sidelong stare. Close up, there was no doubt that he was an android: his face was too smooth and evenly coloured to be flesh, his limbs were too slender to be human. His hands had been carefully crafted with long fingers and thumbs, presumably so that he could play old-fashioned stringed instruments. Lachlan half expected him to smell of machine oil. But he didn't: there was a faint odour of orange blossom instead.

"What happened?" said Lachlan.

The robot knew he was referring to the disaster. "There was a heatwave. The humans couldn't cope with the temperatures, and they died. They sent out a distress call, as you know. It has got cooler since then, as you also know."

"Any evidence of enemy action?"

"I beg your pardon, sir?"

"Oh, come on. The Federacy has enemies – the Vegans, the Damarians – and it's not unknown for them to attack our colonies."

"Forgive me sir. I have been programmed with dance, musical and poetic skills, and with language, but I know little of politics."

"Colonisable planets are a rare commodity – a precious commodity," interjected the Colonel. "We humans fight over them like dogs over a bone.

The measure of all things

Everyone died here on Alpha Mensae 4. *Of course* there's the question of whether our enemies did it."

"I don't think they did, madam. I think your meteorologists just got it wrong about the climate. It was quite pleasant when the colony was set up – warm during the days, cool in the evenings. Then it started to get hotter and hotter. Not that I notice these things, on a personal level …"

* * * * *

For a while, the road was in good condition. They drove past great bluffs of brown sandstone. Reto seemed to be enjoying the scenery: he had grown up in a desert region of his home planet, and it stirred childhood memories. For Lachlan it was all too austere and desolate. He liked his hills to be clothed with vegetation, preferably green. A few trees would have been welcome, too.

They drove over a low hill into the basin that had Sikkerhavn at its centre. The quality of the road deteriorated. The road was concrete, and in places it appeared to have disintegrated into enormous chunks.

"High explosive?" asked the Colonel.

"I don't think so," replied Reto. "Concrete breaks up like that, if you heat it up enough."

Alpha Mensae 4 had an ocean, its surface thick with blue-green algae, which explained its oxygen-rich atmosphere. But it had no vegetation, or even microbial life, of its own on its landmasses. However, the region around Sikkerhavn was supposed to be bedded with Earth-type soil and planted with Earth-type crops. They passed what had been a field, but

A masque

which was now just black stubble. They all got out and examined it. It smelt like an abandoned furnace.

"SuperWheat-sixteen," said Reto, as he took samples. "I'd say the temperature was between 70 and 75 Celsius. Didn't stand a chance."

"Dainius, sing us that song" said Lachlan.

In reply, Dainius put his lute to his shoulder and sang a sad little air:

Oh, we must linger, we must wait –
Hot sun, hot wind, hot earth, hot sky.
If you don't come we know we'll die,
Our death is sure, and black our fate.

Release us from this dreadful state
We plead – for God's sake hear our cry
Oh, we must linger, we must wait –
Hot sun, hot wind, hot earth, hot sky.

We stand before a hellish gate
Oh, rescue ships: be quick, draw nigh
But if our world you should pass by
You know our path to death is straight

For we must linger, we must wait –
Hot sun, hot wind, hot earth, hot sky.

It was a melancholy tune, with a lot of C-minor chords. Dainius' voice was plangent, and his fingerwork was excellent. Tears welled up in Vester's eyes.

"Control yourself, corporal," said the Colonel.

"It's a *rondel*," said Dainius. "But then I expect you knew that."

The measure of all things

"No, we didn't," said the Colonel, shortly.

"It's not my best work," said Dainius, apologetically. "I would have preferred more thematic variety. But the man I was with – he was called Jeffrey Macquarrie, by the way – he was quite insistent about the message I should convey."

"I'll bet he was," murmured the Colonel.

"I could compose a song for you, if you liked" said Dainius.

* * * * *

Sikkerhavn hardly deserved to be labelled a city: twenty-five streets of undistinguished one or two storey buildings. In the extreme heat, almost all the paint had flaked off, and the windows had fallen out. There was no railway or bus station or airport, since there was nowhere else on the planet worth visiting.

They scanned every street for signs of a living body, and found none. There were plenty of corpses, mostly in their own homes. There were quite a few dead pets: cats, dogs, and the six-legged guinea pigs that had been fashionable a few years back. None of the bodies had rotted: the prolonged dry heat had mummified them, and sterilised the whole area of any spoilage organisms.

Reto located the office of the Planetary Meteorologist, Dr Hunter, and read his daily log. The last entry said: "72.6°C. The mayor shot himself today. May God forgive me. I didn't understand this planet at all."

Lachlan located the city's water supply system. The pumps were in perfect working order, but there wasn't any electricity to power them.

A masque

The Colonel radioed the rescue ship. "My compliments to the Captain. Don't bother to unstow the hospital: no survivors. We will need a large burial detail – break out a big excavator, and some trucks. Send a message back to Beta Hydri 3: 'Sikkerhavn no survivors natural causes'". The Federacy insisted that all interstellar messages should be extremely short.

All the dead had personal communicators, but very few of them were still working. One or two *were*, and they contained harrowing last messages from the colonists.

"The heat is unbearable! Everyone is dying! The power station has failed, and we haven't any way to keep cool! We've drunk all our water. We were never told this would happen. *Why won't you come and rescue us?*"

The rescue party stood around, angry, impotent. Dainius looked deeply sympathetic. "You'll want to hold a mass funeral. I shall compose and perform a threnody, if you think that that's appropriate."

* * * * *

The Regimental Sergeant Major briefed the burial squad.

"You're to search every building in the town, and find every body. When you find one, you'll carry it out and load it onto the truck in the street outside. It won't weigh much – they're all dried out. You'll detach the ID tag, and hand it to your section leader. Now, this is a tough job, but I know you're up to it. You're professionals."

They worked through the twenty-five streets one by one, from one end of the town to the other. Dainius

The measure of all things

stood and watched them; his clothes had changed to a subdued grey. No one asked him to help. Somehow, he seemed too slight, too delicate, to be a corpse-carrier.

Once in a while, a soldier – male or female – would sit down by the roadside and quietly sob. When it happened, Dainius always seemed to be nearby. He would kneel down, put his arm around them, and murmur comforting words. After a while, the soldier would get up and go back to their work.

* * * * *

Lachlan, with Dainius in tow, found Reto in the office they'd set up for him, as Chief Scientific Officer – a tent in the town square. He was gazing at half a dozen charts, laid out on a trestle table. Behind him, on a computer screen, was his half-written report.

"Bearing up?" asked Lachlan.

"Yeah," said Reto, with a sad smile. "But this is the grimmest mission I was ever on."

"For me too." Lachlan tried to make sense of the charts, and gave up. "Have you found out what caused it, yet? The hear-wave?"

"Nope. The meteorological model we were using when we planned the colony obviously doesn't work. But I haven't got enough data to build a new one. Ideally, I'd like to stay here until it happens again. But the Captain and the Colonel aren't going to allow that."

"Can't say I'm sorry. We might not be able to take off under those conditions. Then *we'd* go the same way as the colonists. Some of us, anyway." Lachlan sat down

A masque

on a camp chair. "So what will you say in your report?"

"I can describe what happened on a day-to-day basis. I've got all the data that Hunter recorded. Plus what I've been able to gather since we got here. Dainius, can you read?"

"Yes, sir, I can."

"You lived through it. Have a look at what I've got on screen, here, will you? See if I've missed anything? See if anything's wrong?"

Dainius read through the report, a good deal faster than a human could have done. "No sir, it all seems entirely reasonable. I'm afraid I have nothing useful to add."

"Fair enough. I'll treat the report as finished. It can all go back to the boys on Beta Hydri 3: they can work over the raw data. They've got better computers than I've got here."

* * * * *

They buried all the colonists in a mass grave. The whole ship's company, and the regiment, stood to attention and bowed their heads as the Colonel read a short prayer, the ship's Captain standing beside her. Lachlan delivered an oration, dwelling on the lofty mission that the colonists had tried to fulfill, so cruelly cut short. Dainius, dressed this time in black silk, performed his threnody – his voice strong, and enormously comforting, his lute chords somehow exactly capturing the tragedy of the moment. The ship's engineers erected a granite obelisk, made the previous day, and inscribed with the names of all the

The measure of all things

colonists, next to the newly covered grave. The ship's photographer took pictures.

And then it was time to prepare for take-off. Colonel Ellis had Reto's report on her desk. In the absence of any survivors, there was nothing more they could do. No one suggested a period of rest and recreation. Too many ghosts. Too much fear that the terrible heat would return.

Dainius asked to speak to the Colonel.

"Colonel Ellis, I have a request to make that may seem rather strange."

"Go on."

"I would like to remain on this planet, when you leave."

"Well, that *is* unexpected. Why, Dainius?"

"I was first activated on this planet. It's the only one I've known. I regard it as my home."

"Dainius, are you telling me that a robot can feel affection for a place? That he can feel homesick if he leaves it?"

"Well, I can't speak for robots in general. But a machine such as I – a machine attuned to human sensibilities, human emotions – yes, I can certainly feel affection for a world. And I do. I really do."

The Colonel looked thoughtful. "Well, you're not a soldier under my command, or a spaceman under the Captain's command. So I suppose ..." She drummed her fingers on the desk. "It's for the High Command to decide whether we re-colonise this world. But I imagine we will. Just as soon as we've mastered the climatology." She came to a decision. "Request

A masque

granted. You can stay here. And when the new colonists arrive, you can repeat your original mission."

Dainius' facial expression showed a deep gratitude. He bowed, and left the Colonel's cabin.

The last they saw of him, as they blasted off, was seated with his back to an outcrop, playing his lute and singing to himself of who knew what.

* * * * *

Dainius finished his song, and sat for a while, musing on the tenuousness of human existence. All the colonists had been in the prime of life. So had their funny little pets. The grim reaper had claimed them all, before a single one had had the chance to grow old. Tragic.

Then he composed and transmitted a report, using the transmitter concealed in his lute, and the communications satellite that had just risen over the horizon. It read: "To Damarian 23rd Army Commander. Alpha Mensae 4 is ours. The Federacy Government aren't suspicious. They have no knowledge of our climate-wrecker, and didn't suspect me of sabotaging the power station. We have plenty of time to colonise and fortify before they return."

Then he resumed his song writing. The new, Damarian, colonists deserved an anthem of welcome. For a moment he looked puzzled. Not for the first time, he was trying to think of an elegant rhyme for 'Alpha Mensae 4'.

Made in the USA
Charleston, SC
05 October 2014